ROSIE'S REBELLION

Book #3 in Home At Last Series

Jenny Wheeler

Published by Happy Families Ltd
Copyright © 2023 Jenny Wheeler

ISBN 978-1-99-118256-2 (Paperback)
ISBN 978-1-99-118255-5 (EBook)
ISBN 978-1-99-118254-8 (Kindle)

OF GOLD & BLOOD SERIES

Poisoned Legacy #1

Brother Betrayed #2

Double Jeopardy #3

Tangled Destiny–A Christmas Novella and Prequel #4

Unbridled Vengeance #5

Hope Redeemed–A Spanish Novella #6

Tainted Fortune #7

Captive Heart–A Hawaiian Christmas Novella #8

Ancient Deception #9

Dangerous Desires #10

Book Bundle Of Gold & Blood Series One, Books 1–3.

Book Bundle Of Gold & Blood, Series Two Books 1 & 4–Elanora's Story.

Book Bundle Of Gold & Blood, Three Holiday Novellas (Books 4, 6 & 8)

Book Bundle Of Gold & Blood Series Three, Books 5 & 6

Book Bundle Of Gold & Blood Series Four, Books 7 & 8

Home At Last Trilogy

Sadie's Vow #1

Susannah's Secret #2

Rosie's Rebellion #3

What's next? Rosie's Rebellion is the third and final book in the Home At Last trilogy. But if you enjoy Jenny Wheeler's historical mysteries, look out for the next series, Sisters of Barclay Square, set in 1860s Sydney, Australia, featuring Nathan Russell's three half sisters.

The first book in the series is Polly's Dilemma. Details at the end of Rosie's Rebellion, with a Preview link.

(We first met Nathan in Poisoned Legacy, Book #1 Of Gold & Blood series)

ROSIE'S REBELLION

By Jenny Wheeler

When the rain washes you clean, you'll know
You'll know.

Dreams–Fleetwood Mac's only No1 hit -written by Stevie
Nicks.

One

Alex de Vile waved his twin sister Isabella off in a hired hack back to her place and lingered on the front doorstep of his Montgomery Street villa. He savored the lively night scene spread out before him, breathing in the cosmopolitan vibe of one of San Francisco's main north-south through fares.

How he'd love to capture a daguerreotype of the vibrant street life that pulsed right outside his sunflower-yellow front door.

He was seeing a typical Friday night in his downtown neighborhood, a few blocks up from the wharves where travelers came and went from China and Oakland. The air was ripe with yeasty beer and the saline nip of the ocean.

His eyes roved to the bar across the way, to the church on the corner, to the throngs of partying pedestrians, all intent on celebrating being alive for one more day.

Sadly, though, recording this scene for history wasn't yet possible.

One day.

The daguerreotype process his father and other early photographers used relied on posed studies. How could he capture what he saw before him on the silver-dipped copper plates filed away in his studio?

That Spanish señorita, leaning out of the bar window opposite, with her ruffled bright pink neckline and the flower behind her ear?

Would she consent to come into my studio and sit for me? And if she did, would that image capture the vibrant atmosphere out here?

Stored heat from the earlier August scorcher of a day seeped up through the pavement. The humidity turned hair limp and armpits sweaty, but the evening crowds didn't notice. They thronged the sidewalks. Laughing girls paraded arm-in-arm in ankle-length walking dresses in a rainbow of colors. They traded jibes with hefty sailors who called and cat-whistled from bar windows that opened on the street.

As he waited for Isabella's cab to slip from view, taking her to the house in a neighboring suburb she shared with her husband Sebastian, he bit into his lower lip. He didn't like Isabella leaving alone. Seb was away for a few days on business, and Alex would have preferred her to stay the night with him. He ran up the front steps of his fresh-painted villa and closed the front door quickly behind him.

She'd insisted that Sam and Betty Butler, the couple's live-in cook and house manager, were expecting her and would look after her.

"Besides, my friend Rose is arriving tomorrow," she'd said, laughing and waving her hands in excitement.

"Remember her? The gorgeous Irish girl I met when I ran away with Lotta Crabtree's troupe?"

She'd giggled at the memory.

Alex shrugged, recalling only the vaguest memories of Isabella's theater friends.

He hadn't even known Isabella back then. They'd been eighteen when his twin had defied her adoptive mother Huldah and "run away" with a traveling musical show. It had been a short-lived rebellion that resulted in a bosom pals friendship with a fellow performer.

"Can't say I do," he said, already thinking about how he'd pose Isabella for the portrait she'd promised he could shoot of her in the next few days.

Photography was his passion, and Isabella's news tonight had jabbed deep into his heart. He had to capture this moment. Their lives were flashing by, and any minute now, everything was going to change.

He slipped behind the desk in the back room he'd converted into a studio and relaxed into his studded, leather-backed captain's chair.

He'd spent many happy hours here, breathing in the sharp, familiar smell of iodine and mercury, chemicals used in the photographic process.

Behind him, the dark room took up the back half of the space. In front of him hung some of the historic daguerreotypes he'd rescued from a tragic fire, including one particularly special to him.

He reached over and pored himself a small brandy nightcap from a decanter on a tray at his elbow, then stretched his long legs out under his desk and gazed at the historic frame. He'd stared at the family portrait many times before.

For several long minutes, hands clasped behind his head, he meditated on the image of a beautiful woman surrounded by three young children.

And then he turned to his brandy and lit a cigar.

He was savoring the throat burn of the liquor, the cigar's answering soothing balm, basking in the room's relative coolness after the swelter and noise of the street, when he heard a faint squeak of the front door.

The air in the hallway stirred faintly, and he caught a whiff of horse dung on it. He went on high alert.

Silently, he drew his legs back, reached into his smooth-running desk drawer. He drew out the revolver he'd kept close ever since the day of the fire.

He rested it in his lap and waited. If he'd not been on edge, listening intently, he'd have missed the muted creak of a floorboard in the hall.

But as it was, he was ready, gun raised, when two men slid into the room, one stationed at each door pillar.

One was dark-headed, one ginger, and both carried revolvers. Alex shot to his feet and ranged the snout of his Colt between them, waiting for them to speak. A deathly silence hung like a cloud.

Then a glittering flicker in Ginger Head's eye told Alex he was about to pull the trigger. He dove for the floor and rolled on one shoulder while firing upwards through the open front of his broad desk.

He lay panting, gun still at the ready, his shoulder stinging from the impact of the hard floor, as the room echoed with a short, chilling scream. A moment of silence. And then there was a scuffling noise, like rats in the ceiling, and the thump of running footsteps.

Alex edged around the corner of his desk, still at floor level, with his gun out in front.

Ginger Head lay sprawled before him, his guts spilling out like a raccoon hit by a Wells Fargo coach, and no weapon of any description in sight.

Alex stared, numbed at the sight.

Then two thoughts came to him.

Thank the heavens Isabella wasn't here.

And Hector's mordant bass sounded in his head.

"Nice work, son. It was you or him. He'll be the one put to bed with a shovel."

And then all hell broke loose.

Two

Alex threw his twin sister a look of mute appeal and buried his head in his hands.

"They just burst in on me, Izzy. They never said one word."

He sucked in great gulps of air through his fingers, his breath erratic and rasping.

Isabella moved to stand behind his chair and gently massaged the back of his neck.

"I know. I know. You couldn't do anything else…"

She cooed like a dove, her voice soft and sweet.

Across the room, her friend Rosie sat in embarrassed silence.

He raised his head from his hands and cast an anguished glance back at his sister.

"But he's dead, Izzy. He's dead. And I don't know why he was there or what he wanted."

The police had removed the body and told him not to leave town. And now Alexander de Vile was dissolving into a messy puddle of shock and remorse before Isabella's eyes.

He'd hammered at her front door until a sleepy-eyed Sam Butler had let him in and woken Isabella.

They stood together, with Izzy stroking the back of his neck.

For several minutes, the only sound in the room was the steady tick of the gilt-rimmed, enamel-faced clock on Isabella's mantel.

Her consoling lavender fragrance wrapped around him.

Then she slipped from the back of the couch and nestled in beside him on the couch, draping her arm around the back of his neck as she snuggled close.

"You've had an awful shock, Alex. You've got to give yourself time. Everything will work itself out."

He raised frantic gray eyes and glanced in Rosie's direction, but he wasn't seeing her.

"It doesn't make sense," he said, suddenly jerking to his feet and shrugging off Isabella's consoling arm.

"He was a rich boy. Bram Gordon's son. Not some common thief."

He whirled on Isabella, whose body had stiffened like she'd received a body blow at mention of the name.

Her azure eyes widened and her eyebrows raised to meet her blonde fringe as she gazed up at him.

"You know who it was? How?"

"The cop said."

"And it was Alistair Gordon?"

Bram Gordon was one of the richest men in California, a famed rancher and real estate king. And Alistair was his only heir.

Her voice was hoarse, but the words seemed to pass Alex by. His face wore a dazed, blank look.

"Why did he do it, Isabella? Why?" he whispered.

"You're sure it was him?"

He stared at her, his eyes still dulled in confusion. Then he shook his head, as if clearing his mind of the horror.

"I don't know him. But that's who the sergeant said it was. The one who took him away. He recognized him."

Alex lifted trembling hands to his face and ran them down both cheeks.

"I can't believe it, Izzy. I just can't believe it. I killed Alistair Gordon."

The last statement was deliberate, emphatic, as if he was convincing himself of something unbelievable.

She jumped in, her voice in shrill denial.

"But he fired first. You said he did. And he wasn't alone. There were two of them. You were lucky to get out of there alive…"

She stepped close again and placed her hand on his shoulder.

When she spoke next, her voice had dropped in pitch and was back to its careful, comforting tone.

"They broke into your house with guns drawn, Alex. You had no choice."

Another long, empty silence rested between them, and then Alex muttered in a thin, faint voice, "Maybe I overreacted. What if his father comes after me?"

Three

"Have you heard from Alex this morning?"

Rosie picked up her hot coffee and gazed at Isabella over the top of her cup.

Isabella detected straight away that Rosie deeply cared about the answer, though she tossed it off like a throwaway line with about the same level of gravity as "Did you hear the rain overnight?" or "What are you planning to do with yourself today?"

Despite her somber mood, she gulped back a spontaneous laugh, letting the question hang in the air.

Fine actress she might be on the stage, but Rosie failed miserably in concealing the anxious edge in her voice. The parallel worry lines that dipped between her eyebrows gave her away.

"What?" Her friend was all wide-eyed innocence, though Isabella detected an insolent smirk at the corner of her mouth. So typical of Rosie's Irish rebel personality.

"Nothing," Isabella said airily, swallowing down a small bite of dry toast and smiling on secret knowledge.

"And no, I haven't seen Alex yet today. It is only eight

o'clock in the morning, Rosie, but I suppose it's a fair enough question.

"I got no sleep last night and I'm betting he didn't either. Even though he was planning to get extra security for his house."

"A sensible idea," Rosie said. "You never know what that Bram Gordon might do. From the way people talk, he's a law unto himself."

The dry toast Isabella had just swallowed lodged in her throat, and she erupted into a paroxysm of coughing.

When she regained her composure and could sip the cold water Rosie had rushed to her, she lifted an inquiring brow.

"You know Bram Gordon? Have you met him?"

Rosie shook her head. "I've seen him at a distance, that's all. He wouldn't waste time on the likes of me. I'm far too down the ladder for the likes of him.

"But a few months back, he hung about offering his arm to Lotta, but she wasn't seriously interested."

"Really? Doesn't he have a wife of his own?"

Rosie shook her head. "She died recently, as I recall."

"And the son? The one that died?"

"An unholy terror. Very good-looking, like his father. But all the showgirls gave him a wide berth, even though he carried oodles of money and handed it out to all and sundry."

"Why did they do that? Avoid him, I mean."

"Because he was hot-headed and unpredictable. And he seemed to enjoy humiliating people. A barman refused him a drink once—said he was drunk enough—and he put a gun to his head and forced him to guzzle whiskey until he passed out.

That's the sort of guy he was."

Rosie shuddered at the memory, and Isabella felt a sympathetic ripple of nausea low down in her gut.

"Sounds like it's as well someone stopped him in his tracks," she said with a sniff. "I'm just sorry it was my brother."

"Alex will need to be careful." Rosie nodded. "Starting with the extra security."

"Seriously?" Isabella pushed away her plate. She'd barely eaten, but the conversation was killing her appetite.

Rosie dipped her head in confirmation and her copper curls bobbed.

"Seriously."

***

Alex arrived at Isabella's late in the afternoon carrying a package under one arm wrapped in a soft suede cloth. He greeted her with a kiss on each cheek and stepped back to hand her the parcel.

"This is for you. I want you to take care of it for me, and if anything happens to me, I want you to have it."

Tears sprang into Isabella's eyes.

"Oh Alex, no. Nothing is going to happen to you. What are you talking about?"

She led him into the lounge on the sunny side of the house and gestured to a chair in the middle of the room.

He glanced across to where Rosie sat in one corner with a jigsaw puzzle spread out in front of her on a coffee table. She rose as they came in and dipped her head in his direction.

A cool cloud crossed his face when he saw her.

"I'm happy to leave you to your conversation," she blurted. "I could do with a rest."

She waved a wrist that was bandaged and hung in a sling from her shoulder. It was the first time he'd noticed the injury, and a hollow sense of shame grabbed at him.

"No. no. Please," he said. "I'm sorry. I didn't realize you'd hurt yourself. I know you and Isabella keep no secrets. You're welcome to stay."

Rosie flicked a quick inquiry to Isabella, who nodded. "Stay, Rosie."

She turned to Alex.

"Rosie's seen both Bram and Alistair Gordon in action," she said. "And it isn't pretty."

Alex's finely chiseled face sparked with interest.

"Now that I would like to hear. But first, I want to tell Isabella about this gift I brought over."

"Which I don't want," Isabella said quickly. "All this talk about 'if anything happens to me' is unnerving. I don't want you thinking that way."

Alex glanced at Rosie, this time with piercing intelligence in his eyes.

"You know what the Gordon code is, don't you, Rosie? Tell her."

"It's rumored it's the Latin phrase '*Aut neca, aut necare*,'" she said.

"They have it carved over the entryway of their mansion at the ranch. And I bet you don't know what it means," she taunted Isabella with a playful grin.

"I bet I don't too." She laughed. "Tell me."

Rosie's face turned serious. "Kill or be killed. That's what it means. Kill or be killed. A nice motto to live by, isn't it?"

Isabella's face drained of color, and she reached out and took the parcel from Alex.

"They sound like awful people. I'm glad you got him first."

She smiled and then sat with the parcel on her knee.

"When I think about it now, I'm glad too."

He paused and glanced at Rosie again.

"Thing is, I had a flash in my mind's eye. I can't explain it, really. Like a moment of certainty when I knew in my soul that he was about to pull the trigger.

"It was as if I could read his mind. And I got in a fraction of a second ahead of him. I suppose technically I opened fire first. But I knew somewhere deep inside me he was going to do it."

Isabella pulled at the rough, string-tied bundle and drew the object he'd wrapped out of brown paper and held it up to the light.

"Oh Alex, it's your most precious possession. The image you found in Charles's studio of our mother and us together. I can't take this…"

She gazed at the daguerreotype glass with rapt affection.

"You can, and you will," Alex said.

"I wouldn't put it past them to fire my house, like those other hooligans did Charles Durant's studio. And I want to make sure it isn't in there if they do. Most of what I've got is replaceable, but not that."

He gave her a sly, warm smile. "Besides, in your present state, I'd imagine you might be asking more questions about our roots? About where we came from? This is one small place to start."

Rosie's head snapped up from her jigsaw puzzle.

"Your 'present state'?" she interrupted. "Does that mean what I suspect it means?"

Alex shot Isabella an apologetic stare.

"Oh dear. Have I let the cat out of the bag?"

"Not really," laughed Isabella. "Yes, Rosie, there will be another little person joining us soon. And I'm glad you heard about it with Alex here, because I'd like both of you to be godparents."

Alex's mouth turned down and his jaw clenched. "I don't know if that's such a good idea," he said. "What if I…?"

He stared into Isabella's pale face, stopped, and shrugged. "Fine," he said. He switched his attention to Rosie.

"Rosie, if anything happens to me, you'll have to step up to double duties. I hope you understand that. And she's a perfectionist as an overseer. Just so you know."

Isabella punched him playfully on the arm.

"Oh, shut up." She gazed down into the picture. "To think our father took this picture of us and our mother, and neither of us remembers anything about him. We know even less of his family."

She pitched a grin across the room to Rosie, who was pretending to do the puzzle jigsaw while she listened avidly to every word.

"You're always complaining about being swamped by your big Irish family, Rosie. Try to imagine what it's like to know absolutely nothing about one side of the family. In our case, the Spanish side.

"All we have is this picture and a few memories from

Graysie, who lived with our father until she was about twelve. When he died, she ran away. That's what she says."

Rosie pushed up from the jigsaw table with her undamaged hand and crossed the room to sit next to Isabella. She drew her right hand from the embrace of her sling and clasped Isabella's.

"Congratulations, dearest friend. I couldn't be happier for you. You'll make a wonderful mother."

She drew Isabella into her shoulder gently.

When she emerged from the neck ruffles of Rosie's dress, Isabella said with mock solemnity, "Don't count your chickens. We haven't got there yet."

Momentarily, she looked like a lost child.

"I agree with Alex on one thing. Having your first child makes you think about your own parents and wonder about all sorts of things."

"Like what?" asked Alex.

"Ohhh… Like, what was our father's childhood like? Did he get on with his parents? Did he have any brothers and sisters?

"You never know, we might have cousins and uncles and aunties out there somewhere. I've never really thought about that before. I was so glad to find you and Graysie."

Alex's eye moved to Rosie, speculation glinting in his clear gaze.

"So, what sort of childhood did you have, Rosie? Where did you grow up? And did you have lots of brothers and sisters?"

Her shoulders tightened under the twins' questioning eyes. It occurred to Alex this was one spotlight the would-be stage performer didn't welcome.

"Rather too many of them." She trilled with laughter, as if to turn her statement into a humorous quip, and for the second time that day, her statement rang hollow.

The downturn of her voice at the end of the sentence, the slight edge of bitterness, spoke volumes.

There was an awkward silence.

She took a deep breath. "Nothing like yours or Izzy's childhood. We were Irish poor in New York. With eight mouths to feed, my folks rarely knew where the next meal was coming from.

"Like little sparrows in the nest, we were. All with our beaks open, chirping. Pa died from booze and any day now overwork is going to have Ma Ma pushing up daisies."

It was as if someone had sucked all the air out of the room. Neither Izzy nor Alex knew where to rest their gaze, so they all stared at the Turkish rug at their feet. The colorful fruit and flower abundance of the design somehow mocked every word that had come from Rosie's mouth.

"What will happen if your mam dies?" Isabella finally asked, raising her head to confront Rosie's challenging eyes.

"I suppose it will all fall on me," said Rosie. "Not much different from now, if the truth be known."

Isabella started, "Rosie, I'm sorry… You never said…"

Rosie gave a sad smile.

"I never said because I want sometimes to forget it. Pretend it isn't what it is. But folks like you and Alex…" She glanced at the man who sat opposite them, his elbows scrunched on his knees, his face twisted with concern.

Rosie began again with a big gulp.

"I know you had a pretty rum start, with your mother being killed and all. But look what the good Lord rained down on you, Alex.

"A rich senator adopted you. And Huldah was a loving stand-in mother for you, Isabella. You both had homes where people cared for you and protected you.

"Honestly? Worrying about people you've never met?

"Seems to me you're damned fortunate if that's all you've got to be concerned about. Try growing up in Five Points. The stink hole of New York."

They sat like mute statues, stunned by her outburst, and then Alex stood.

"Whew," he said. "Good to know what you really think of us, Rosie."

He braced his shoulders and flicked his eyes to Isabella, who remained beside Rosie, her hand resting on Rosie's knee as if to comfort her.

"I'd better get back home to my comfortable house and the killers who are probably lying in wait for me.

"But, hey. At least I had a rich daddy. Even though he's a dead daddy now. But never mind that. What's to worry?"

He turned his eyes on Rosie, the gray irises darkening to slate as he gazed down at her.

"I'm sorry you feel that way, Rosie, I really am. I hope your friendship with Izzy survives this dumping, because I know my sister really loves you."

And with that, he turned and fled.

***

As soon as the thump of Alex's footsteps had faded from the front path, Isabella rounded on her friend.

"What's gotten into you, Rosie? That was plain mean."

Her normally calm blue eyes were sapphires, darting with indignation.

"As if he hasn't got enough to cope with, without you letting loose on him."

Rosie shrugged. "Someone had to say it."

"Say what exactly? I've never known you to take your bad mood out on other people."

She gazed at Rosie reflectively. "I've never known you to have a bad mood, come to think of it."

"Well now, you know I do." Rosie's voice was sullen. "Nobody's perfect."

"So, what's the poor guy done that's annoyed you so much?"

Rosie shrugged. "Just being him, I guess."

"But I thought you liked him." Isabella stared at her friend in confusion. "You know. Like really liked him."

A pink flush rose on her friend's neck and into her cheeks.

"Oh Izzy. Wherever did you get that idea? The girl from the poorhouse and the prince? That kind of thing only happens in fairy stories. Not in real life."

Isabella made to interject, but Rosie talked over the top of her.

"Besides…"

Isabella swallowed her tongue and let her friend continue.

"Besides, my family comes first. I can't put anything before them. We live in different worlds and it's good for me to remember that."

<change of speaker, Isabella talking>

"And do you really think of me like that, too? Like some precious little princess protected from real life?"

Isabella's voice was soft and tinged with embarrassment.

Rosie shook her head. "You've faced up to a lot of trouble, I know. What with Alycia's murder and all."

Alycia had been a treasured intimate, a replacement grandmother, related to Isabella by marriage through her mother. She'd died in a gun attack nearly three years ago.

Rosie darted Isabella an apologetic smile.

"I'm sorry. I don't know what got into me just now. I'm an ungrateful cow. And you're a wonderful friend."

She fell silent, and then a wicked grin spread across her face. "Except when you eat all the ice cream, of course."

Isabella pounced and tickled her ribs until they were both rolling around on the sofa, giggling.

Four

My dearest Eilish,

I broke my wrist when I fell from a pony while we were travelling between shows in the middle of the night. I'm off work for a few weeks with my arm in a sling.

I'm not able to work for that time, so I'm glad I put a little extra away to keep you all going.

I'm staying with my good friend Isabella in San Francisco. Remember I told you about the girl who ran away from home to join Lotta's troupe? She only stayed a short time because this crooked cop was accusing her of stealing some valuable jewels? Sorry, it's a complicated story. I'll tell you the full version sometime. That's Isabella.

She's married now and living in a nice place here in San Francisco.

How are you and the boys?

I hope everything is okay and that Mum's health is better than it was the last time I was home.

Are you still helping as a teacher's assistant when you can, and are you enjoying it?

You can write to me at the address on the top of this page because I am going to be here for a while. If I've gone back to Lotta by the time it gets here, Izzy will forward it on.

I enclose the usual to help with food and other essentials. Take care, my darling.

Sis, you know I love you all very much. Kisses to the sky.

Rosie signed off with a flourish and pushed the notepaper and two five-dollar bills into an envelope and addressed it.

And then she lay back on the plumped-up pillows that cosseted her on every side in the deep, soft bed and gave a painful sigh.

He'll hate me now, but that's all to the good.

A whiny little voice answered from deep inside her.

Really? Is this what you truly wanted? For him to hate you?

You keep believing that, girl, the whiny voice said.

It would never have worked out, so it's best to save myself the trouble.

Keep telling yourself that, too. It's certainly safest that way.

She closed her eyes and allowed her imagination to roam. She pictured Alex bending over her and drawing her to her feet.

"I claim the next dance, madam," he said, gazing into her eyes with a cheeky grin. He took her in his arms and twirled her around, her skirt billowing around her.

A delightful warmth started at her navel and spread right up through her chest.

I'm in heaven.

She reared up from the pillows, her cheeks blazing hot.

What sort of nonsense am I wallowing in? Get a grip, Rosalie.

That's what her mother would say.

She bounced off the bed and crossed to the door.

Find yourself something to do that fits your station, she told herself, reaching for on the bedroom door handle with a determined grip.

Like help Betty peel potatoes.

Five

Unlike his son, Bram Gordon was a man who never took rash actions. He calculated his every move, because more than anything else, he planned to win.

Aut neca, aut necare. Kill or be killed.

His father had drummed those words into him, and his father before that.

What a tragedy that Alistair took that family motto literally.

There's never been any subtlety about that boy.

Gordon sighed and raised a ham-sized fist to his forehead, pushing back his abundant salt-and-pepper hair.

At fifty-six, he was a man still in his prime; a six foot four towering column of muscle which he worked hard to preserve with strenuous ranching activities and equestrian events.

Roping in a young heifer? He could give the youngest and fittest of his vaqueros a run for their money.

As one of the most powerful pastoralists in the state of California, he controlled thousands of acres of choice grazing land. In addition, he owned dozens of urban and commercial properties. He'd no need to engage in physical work.

He paid squads of vaqueros to do it for him, but he liked to show the world that he was still one of the best handlers around.

That was another subtlety Alistair never grasped.

You must show competence for others to want to follow you.

Bram sprawled back in his big leather chair, tree-trunk thighs spread in front of him, and brooded, one hand clutching his to his chest, and his tombstone heart.

The minutes ticked by, marked by the steady clack of the grandfather clock in the hall, its mechanism loud enough to reach him in his study.

Outside his adobe farmhouse, the lowing of cattle drifted on the night breeze. The home was a legacy from his wife and her Californio family, one of the original Spanish land grants, a sloping, scrub-dotted grassland that ran down to the marshy coast.

His men would be out there on night patrol, although there were no more bears, no deer, elk, or beavers anymore.

Only the occasional cry of a coyote and the keening of sea birds, feasting on the teeming fish life on the shoreline.

Bram Gordon flexed his paws, with their scarred, supersize cigar fingers, squeezing them in and out, in and out, as if he was a prize boxer warming up for his next round.

Far-sightedness, he mused.

He'd failed to teach Alistair about that, as well. From childhood, the boy's attitude had always been "I want it and I want it now."

He should have done more to teach him restraint. To rein in that overweening pride.

Because now he lay in a coffin at the undertakers, ready for delivery to St John's Presbyterian church in the morning.

Two funerals in little more than a year. First his wife Maria's, at Easter, and now his firstborn and only son's.

Alistair could never grasp the thrill of the long game, which is why he'd barged in on the de Vile boy with a brash, scattergun approach.

He'd probably been drinking, and wild companions, their bellies full of liquor, easily led him astray.

Now he, Bram, was an entirely different animal, a logroller who would devise any devious machination, join any unsavory alliance, to get what he wanted.

How else had he originally gained the 2000-acre Gordon Ranch?

He reached for the consoling brandy balloon glass filled to the brim at his elbow, and savored both the burn of the booze, and thinking of himself in the third person.

Bram Gordon, the church-mouse-poor Scottish bairn, risen to real estate magnate, California run holder, and hidden powerbroker.

The Gordon Ranch was his home, but he could buy and sell men, any number of them.

His mouth tightened at the memory of a couple of upstarts who'd defied him, but he wouldn't waste precious brain power on them. They'd got their just desserts.

He snuggled further into his big rocking chair.

If she was here, Maria would point out that balloon glasses weren't meant to be filled to the brim. But he'd good reason for drinking to excess.

And he was glad she wasn't here to bury their boy tomorrow. She'd have been distraught, and he didn't need the distraction.

If he was going to win this long game, he'd need to be deliberate in his revenge.

There'd be no rushing in, no "give it to with both barrels" for him.

His revenge would be calculated and sweet, and that de Vile pup would have no inkling he'd been robbed of a fortune.

***

Bram Gordon had drunk enough brandy to raise red veins in his granite-dark eyes. The burning liquid had broken the tombstone in his chest into pebbles, still painful and hard, but the burden he carried was no longer monumental.

The booze might have contributed to his fuzzy hearing and his blurred sight, but his mind was still razor sharp.

So when the lawman in a dark blue suit with a gold star on his lapel stepped into the study without knocking, he stared down the barrel of his Springfield rifle.

"Jumping Jehoshaphat, put that thing down, old man," the newcomer growled, his voice harsh from the smoke of a thousand cigars.

"You don't want another corpse to bury tomorrow, do you?"

Gordon's eyes flashed with anger. He laid the gun across his knees and his red eyes glared.

"Don't call my boy a corpse," he snarled. "Have some respect."

His companion dropped into a seat at his side, his voice softening. "Sorry, Bram. You gave me a fright, that's all. I came as fast as I could."

He glanced around him. The Gordon estate lay outside the

legal boundaries of San Francisco town, accessed by a long ride around coastal inlets with no direct road.

Night had fallen hours ago, but Bram sat in darkness, the ornate brass lamp on the side table unlit, the wall sconces doused.

"Can we order some coffee and put a light or two on in here?" the visitor asked.

"It would help if I could see what's going on."

Bram roared his instructions, and a buxom black woman in a white apron appeared, turned on the lights and returned with coffee in short order.

Once they'd settled with the steaming brew in hand, the caller spoke again.

"I came to see what you wanted to do. Just give the orders, and I'll take care of it.

"With old man de Vile out of the picture, it'd be no problem to pick off the youngster. I presume you want to get even."

Bram Gordon's coffee cup rattled in its saucer.

"Of course, I want to bloody get even. More than even. I want to grind that de Vile brat into the clay. I've got business to settle with him. And to do that, I have to play my cards with finesse. There'll be no shotgun massacre."

"He's got no idea he's Angel's grandson?"

"Apparently not. And that's the way it needs to stay."

"What about that kid lawyer that's sniffing around?"

"Ewan Campbell? O'Leary's second? He's got no clue Alex is Angel's grandson, either. Why should he? The boy carries the de Vile name and is proud of it. He's never wanted for any other."

"So, what do we do next?"

"Next? We make sure you arrest him and hang him from a highest oak tree for my son's death.

"He shot him down in cold blood. You can testify to that. My boy didn't even have a weapon on him when they found him.

"You saw that yourself, I'm told. No gun on him."

Bram's caller wondered how he knew that, when he'd not been anywhere near the scene himself, but he wasn't asking.

Gordon's full lips twisted in a predatory grin.

"No weapon. An innocent man, shot in cold blood. So get out there and do your job, Police Superintendent. Arrest the murderer and hang him. What are you waiting for?"

Alex saw the two men lounging on his Montgomery Street veranda from half a block away and knew immediately they weren't his security detail.

He stopped in his tracks so abruptly at the sight that the fellow striding on his heels cannonaded into him. The tray of hot pies he carried, ready to sell to hungry passers-by who'd missed supper, tumbled onto the sidewalk.

Had Bram Gordon sent men to deal with him so soon? Were they going to gun him down on his own doorstep, in view of the passing crowds?

By the time he'd apologized to the vendor, helped the fellow clean up the smashed pies, fed them to the dogs that appeared from nowhere, and compensated him for his loss, the "intruders" were alongside him, helping with the cleanup.

"Jack! Kaleo!" He hugged and pounded each of them on the back. "I thought I was going to die in a hail of bullets as soon as I put a foot on my bottom step," he laughingly acknowledged as they retraced the path to his house.

Jack Cabot was a trusted friend, an East Coast trust fund heir who'd recently pulled himself out of despair and dissolute living to care for his young niece.

And Kaleo Manolo was the natural son of Hector de Vile, Alex's adopted father. They shared in running the de Vile empire now Hector was dead, but so much more, as well.

Alex, the adopted son, had benefited from Hector's parental care and affection from early childhood. Kaleo had only become aware that Hector was his father in the last months of the patriarch's life, and hardly had any time to get to know him before his dramatic death.

Nudging six feet in height as Alex did, there were few men he looked up to, but around these two Alex always had the sensation of being pint-sized.

Jack and Kaleo converged, one on either side of Alex, each placing an arm around his back to propel him the last few feet home.

And as soon as their arms made contact, their strength surged into him and Alex realized he'd been on the verge of collapse.

"Man, am I glad to see you two?"

Alex couldn't suppress a light-headed gasp of relief.

"It's been one heck of a day."

"That's what we thought," said Kaleo in his rumbling church-choir bass. "We've come to the rescue."

Alex laughed once again, the heavy cloud of despair and self-doubt that had descended already lifting.

"I surely need one." He turned to Jack. "Where do I begin?"

They rushed him up the stairs, where stood the sturdy security men he'd left guarding the place while he went to Isabella's blocked entry.

"Friends, not foe," Alex said in a singsong voice. "Let them through."

The wall of muscled chests parted like the Red Sea and they pitched through the gap into the front hall.

"Am I glad to see you?" said Alex. "Never was I in more need of sound worldly advice. It's times like these you realize just what a capstone and shield Hector was."

"We'll be doing well if we can measure up to Hector's record," said Jack. Alex could hear the ring of respect in Jack's voice.

"But we'll sure as heck give it our best shot. Now show us where this mess happened and we'll take it from there."

Alex led them into the study, where rusty blotches stained the green carpet.

"I'm going to have to ditch this carpet," said Alex in an aside. "I can't understand why the police department hasn't returned and inspected the scene already."

Jack made a wry smooching gesture with his mouth.

"I'm afraid you'll find our collecting evidence isn't a top priority with our Bay police. They rely more on innuendo and who's paying."

He shot Alex a wry grin, and Alex wasn't sure if he was joking or serious.

"Who's paying? What do you mean?" asked Alex. "Aren't they all paid by ratepayers and the City fathers?"

"Some of their pay, yes, comes from legitimate sources. A big whack of it, though, comes from 'contributions' from the wealthy in return for favors."

Jack gestured to the wall. "You look like you've been in a

real street battle here," he said. "Look at how much firepower they used."

Alex gazed at the wall and tried to recall the exact sequence of events.

"You know, I can barely remember when they fired those. I was too busy diving for cover."

"Just as well you did," said Kaleo. "You'd be dead if you hadn't."

Jack wandered over and ran his finger over the studded holes in the scrim-covered matchwood that lay beneath the wallpaper.

His forefinger lingered on one in particular, and he wandered over to the desk and picked up a paper knife and returned.

"One bullet has stuck—and I bet we'd find more if we searched for them," he said. He gently pried the casing out and held in up triumphantly between his thumb and index finger.

"This looks to me like a bullet from the new Smith and Wesson revolver," he said.

"That doesn't come from the usual two-bit store. This is a sophisticated piece of firepower. I think it gives us a clue that these certainly were not your average hustlers."

Alex grimaced. "We already know that, Jack, if there's any truth to the police report that the guy I killed was Bram Gordon's son, Alistair. What I don't understand is why he'd come here after me.

"Our company has no connections that I know of with the Gordon outfit. We're not in direct competition with them anywhere that I know of. Isn't that right, Kaleo?"

His taciturn half-brother nodded but didn't comment further.

"I don't understand why he'd turn up here wielding a high-powered piece of artillery and fire on me. Because believe me, he had a gun in his hands.

"He was about to fire on me. His mate must have picked it up and run off with it when he saw he was dead."

Kaleo leaned against the desk and gazed around him with that far-sighted stare he had about him. The look Alex imagined he used when he was assessing the wave break and deciding whether the surf was good for board riding.

The Hawaiian loved the sea and back home was a king of ocean sport.

Then, in his typical unhurried, droll way, Kaleo asked, "What do you know about your father's family?"

"My father? Well. You know about as much as I do…"

"Not Hector. Your blood father. Rafael, the photographer. What do you know about them?"

"Forgive me for asking Kaleo, but how is this relevant? I know practically nothing at all about my Spanish family. But why are you asking?"

Kaleo slipped his hand into the inside pocket of his jacket and displayed a piece of gold braid in his open palm.

"I picked this up on your doorstep while we were waiting for you to return. And if I'm not mistaken, there's another piece of it just there."

He pointed to the carpet at Alex's feet. Alex bent over, scooped it up and examined it, turning it over delicately in his fingers.

"Braid sewn with sequins…" he said, a questioning wonder in his voice.

Kaleo's dark eyes never left his face.

"And who wears jackets with sequins on them?" he asked.

"The old-style Spanish administrators. And their sons," he added quickly.

"From families who are desperately hanging on to their past importance."

Alex fingered the remnant and then took the few steps to Kaleo and laid the piece he had found alongside the one that Kaleo held in his open palm.

"They match," he said.

"Which leads me to conclude that Alistair Gordon came here with one of his Spanish cousins. You know his mother was Spanish? She was Maria de Rameros. That's partly how Bram got his hands on the old Rameros ranch."

"How on earth do you know that? I didn't know that and I'm part Spanish."

Kaleo shrugged. "I read it in the newspaper, partner. She died a while back and there was quite an obituary. She comes from one of the old *alciade* families."

"Fancy you remembering that," Alex said, his voice still laced with surprise.

"It's our business to know this stuff," said Kaleo, slightly reprovingly.

"Why do you think Hector was successful at business? He knew who was who and what they were up to."

Alex gave him a warm grin.

"You're a chip off the old block, no doubt about it. And am I glad you are?"

Jack had come and stood close by as they'd been handling the fragment, and he raised his hand in warning.

"Don't get too excited about this, Alex. Firstly. I'd counsel you not to let on to the deputy when he arrives that you've found it. You'll be handing them evidence they will immediately destroy, if it suits them."

Alex's throat choked with indignation.

"What do you mean?"

"I mean, I know the way Bram Gordon and men like him work. I'm sorry to have to tell you, but Hector operated the same way. Most rich men do."

Alex's mouth took on a mutinous line.

Jack pulled at a lock of hair that had fallen over Alex's eyes and continued.

"There are a few good men left. But most of them, if they've got the loot, have cops and justices and other high officials on their payroll.

"They can buy any solution they want. And right now, Bram Gordon is setting you up to face a charge of cold-blooded murder. That's why whoever was with his son removed his weapon. They're not stupid."

Alex felt the breath whoosh out of his lungs. A gaping vacuum opened up deep inside, and he had to battle to get air back into his chest.

"So… so what can I do?" he stuttered.

A long silence rang between them. Then Kaleo pocketed the two pieces of braid.

"We find out more about this Spanish connection. Why are they suddenly interested in you? There must be something to do with your father's family to set this off. We have to find out what that is."

Seven

Alex shifted uncomfortably on his chair at Izzy's breakfast table and desperately searched his mind for small talk.

He'd lit out as soon as he felt it was socially acceptable to call on his pregnant sister. But when he'd arrived, the kitchen maid standing in for Betty informed him that Isabella was ill and wouldn't be able to speak to him for a while. No one knew exactly how long.

He was boiling over with his news, wanting to tell her about Kaleo's discovery of the braid. And she might recall having heard about their Spanish family from their half-sister Graysie, from anyone. He was desperate for new information.

Instead, he found himself stuck in the breakfast room with Rosie, battling to find something to say. The last thing he wanted was to provoke another tirade.

He stood suddenly, propelled by an urge to announce he'd call later in the day, when Isabella hopefully felt better. He then sat again abruptly, intent on talking to her as soon as he could.

She might have some vital detail stored away in her memory that he'd completely missed.

If Alex was honest with himself, he'd treasured his father's occupation as a gifted photographer. But he'd had no curiosity about the rest of his story. His father died when he was a toddler, and he'd no personal recollection of him. He was happy to leave it at that.

But now that Isabella was pregnant, he was going to be an uncle. Apart from the mystery over the attack on his house, he'd suddenly become overwhelmingly curious about his forefathers.

When had they come to California? Where did Rafael grow up? What did his grandfather do?

He couldn't remember if he'd ever asked those questions, and what Graysie might have replied.

"Did you sleep at all last night?" Rosie suddenly interjected, peering at him. The morning sun was behind her, lighting up her red-gold hair like the halo on a Botticelli beauty, and for a moment, his words caught in his throat.

She was a beautiful maiden, all right. Beautiful and extremely bad tempered.

"Sleep? Not really. Some friends came around and spent time with me, helped me to think things through a bit… But I got little sleep."

His eyes flicked to the door.

For goodness' sakes, Izzy, come down and rescue me. I've got nothing to say to this girl.

"I think Isabella has got morning sickness," she volunteered. "It's hard to know how long she's going to be."

He stood again, suddenly unable to bear the torture any longer.

"I'll be going," he said. "You made it very clear yesterday

you can't stand me. It's just plain awkward to hang around. I'll come back later."

She jumped up in an answering impulse. "No please, don't… I mean, I'm sorry. I don't know what came over me yesterday. I apologize. I was completely out of line."

He shrugged. "You were honest. Nothing to apologize for about that." He smiled, suddenly overcome with an awareness of the humor of the situation.

"I know most people don't come out and say it, that's all. But I guess I can admire your forthrightness."

He laughed as the absurdity of it all rolled over him in waves.

He'd just missed being shot to death by a couple of gangsters. He was under threat of being arrested for murder by a crooked cop.

He'd no other strings to pull, no police superintendents up the line he could buy off, as undoubtedly Hector would have done.

And this girl was apologizing to him for telling him a few home truths?

"You're probably quite right. I deserved it. The events of the last twenty-four hours have made me see I have no idea how the real world works.

"I've been in a protected pocket, with my stepfather looking after me. I do not know how I'll get out of this jam with him gone."

She opened her mouth to speak, and a hammering on the front door interrupted her.

The blood drained from his cheeks.

"Speaking of crooked cops… which we weren't," he said

with a pathetic attempt at a game smile.

She stared at him, her mouth open, and then slid across the room and grabbed him by the shoulders.

"Go out through the back door of the kitchen—where the tradesmen make their deliveries," she said. "I'll stall them till you've had time to get away."

His jaw dropped. "I was joking," he protested.

She fixed him with a stern glare and then propelled him to the side door that adjoined the kitchen.

"I'm not. Get out of here," she whispered in a harsh tone. "If it's just a delivery man, you can always come back later."

As he scampered through the kitchen, he heard the housekeeper, Betty Butler, come into the breakfast room.

"Miss Rosie, there's a police officer here to see—" Her eyes roamed the room, empty apart from Rosie, and quick as a flash she said, "Miss Isabella."

Alex didn't dawdle to hear any more. He shot out of the trades entrance, fought his way through the overgrown back garden, leaped over the fence and was gone.

***

Rosie stepped forward with her most winning smile and extended her hand to the policeman who stood, scanning the room with suspicious piggy eyes.

He looked like all the crooked Irish cops she'd dealt with in her short life as the daughter of a man who lived half of his time on the wrong side of the law.

Surely, that was in New York, and this was San Francisco. But she doubted they'd be too different.

Like his New York counterpart, he was ginger haired, freckled, with a full, pouty mouth he held in a peeved scowl, and fuzzy sideburns that crawled from his ears to his chin. He did not respond to her welcoming hand, instead punching the air in frustration and stating, "I'm police superintendent Seamus O'Halloran. And who exactly are you?"

"Rosie Kelly. From west Munster. You're a Paddy too? And where are you from?"

He scowled. "None of your business. I believe you're harboring a dangerous felon. Where is he?"

Rosie gasped and brought her hand to her mouth in what she had to pray was a convincing display of horror.

"A felon? Why Superintendent O'Halloran, I don't know what you're talking about! I'm staying with my best friend Isabella Russell, wife of Deputy Sebastian Russell, and I'm enjoying a quiet morning coffee."

Her eyes grazed the cold cup sitting half drunk on the other side of the table.

"Isabella was just here with me, but unfortunately, she took a turn of sickness and went back up to bed. So, I'm here alone." She gestured around her.

"Tell me, would you like a coffee while we talk?"

"And where is Mrs. Russell now?"

"Why, as I say, she returned to bed." She moved closer, much closer, to the policeman and leaned in to him with a confidential air.

"She's in the family way, and she's got the morning horrors."

She watched with satisfaction as his cheeks reddened at the disclosure.

"If you truly don't believe me, I could take you up to her bedroom, but I'm not sure her husband, or her patron, Basil Stockton, would be very pleased.

"Mr. Stockton owns the house, you see. Isabella and Sebastian occupy it because Sebastian handles all his business here in California."

O'Halloran jerked away from her, as if she'd slapped him across the face with a dead fish.

"Basil Stockton? He owns this place?"

"That's right. We're expecting him back in town any day now. And he's very particular about his privacy not being interrupted. Of course, I quite understand you have to do your job.

"If there was any evidence—who is this felon you're chasing? We've not noticed anyone threatening, but I could see if Isabella has noticed anyone hiding in the garden?"

O'Halloran made another long, suspicious scan of the breakfast room, his face a picture of hardened frustration.

Her brainless amazement hadn't taken him in for one moment. She could see that. His apple pip eyes glittered with conjecture.

And there wasn't a thing he could do about it.

He whirled for the door, hesitated, and then pivoted back to confront her.

"You've won this round, Miss Kelly. But don't pour the champagne just yet. I'll be back with a warrant to search the place. And next time, your 'best friend' won't get off so easy."

Eight

Alex slipped through the Lick House foyer and glided up the wide marble staircase to the hotel's third floor like a wraith. He'd pulled his hat down over his face like a disappearing man, avoiding eye contact with any of the other guests.

He paused in front of his half-sister Graysie's hotel room door and knocked softly. A wave of relief washed over him as he heard sounds of movement from within. She hadn't gone out. She was still here.

The door opened as he stepped back, reluctant to be caught eavesdropping. One of the Russell brothers, Graysie's Australian husband Nathan, greeted him with a wide grin.

"Alex! Great to see you! What brings you by so early?"

He ushered Alex in and gave him a brotherly clap on the back as he closed the door behind them.

Alex hesitated. What to say?

Someone's tried to kill me, and I wonder if Graysie knows why?

I'm on the run and I need somewhere to hide?

"It's complicated," he said, his voice jerky and breathless. "Is Graysie here?"

Nathan's brow settled into a confused line. His hazel eyes

bored into Alex with an interrogatory glare.

"You look upset," he mumbled. "Sure, she's here. We're just finishing getting the kids' breakfast. Come on through."

Graysie sat with a relaxed air at the dining-room table, surrounded by two youngsters. Closest sat a pretty, dark-headed girl with a rosy round face and dancing eyes, who Alex knew to be Minette, Graysie's eight-year-old ward.

Next to his father's empty seat was three-year-old George, perched up at the table on a cushion.

At the sight of Alex, George slipped off his chair and gave a squeal of delight.

"Uncle Alex," he crooned. "Can we go play?"

Alex bent down and tousled his hair, and then kissed the top of his head.

"Maybe later, Georgie. Mummy will want you to finish breakfast first, and I've got some things I need to talk to Mummy about, too. We'll have to leave it for another time. I'm sorry."

George gave a soft pout and Alex picked him up under his armpits and settled him back on his cushion, which had slipped off the chair.

"I see you've got oatcakes there. They look yum."

His eyes went to Graysie, who was rising from her seat with a worried frown on her finely featured face. A curtain of abundant sunshine-yellow hair framed her eloquent emerald eyes.

She darted a nervous hint to him with her eyes, but avoided admitting in words she'd sensed something serious was amiss.

Don't upset the children, she warned.

Alex let out a long breath and slipped into the seat beside her.

"I've just been at Isabella's," he said.

The furrows in Graysie's brow deepened.

"Izzy? She's all right, isn't she?"

Alex glanced at the kids and attempted to lighten the anxiety he guessed was showing on his face.

"She's fine. She was still in bed, actually. Too early for her to be up in her present condition."

Graysie raised her eyebrows in surprised delight.

"Does that mean what I think it means? We only arrived late last night. I haven't caught up with her yet."

Alex grinned, despite the churning nausea in his gut.

"It does. I shouldn't have said anything. You'll have to pretend you don't know when you see her."

They both laughed, and Graysie gestured to the chair next to her.

"Sit down, Alex, and I'll order more hot coffee. Have you had breakfast yet?"

"No. No, I haven't." The recollection of his near miss with the cops that caused him to forget breakfast brought the scowl back to his face.

"Izzy's got that friend of hers staying from the Lotta Crabtree show—you remember that Irish girl, Rosie? I talked briefly with her and then had to leave."

Graysie again communicated silent warning with her eyes and then turned to her husband.

"Nat, if the children are finished with breakfast, could you get their Nanny Blamchett to get them dressed for the park?

Give us a chance to catch up over coffee?"

Nathan gave her a knowing smile. "Sure," he said.

***

As soon as the door was safely closed behind the departing children, Graysie took Alex's face in her hands and gazed into his eyes.

"What's going on?" she said. "Alex, you look terrible. Like you've seen a ghost. Tell me everything."

Nathan had resumed his seat opposite them. "You *are* looking a bit rum, mate."

Alex shot them a relieved grin.

"Thanks for that, guys. You'll understand why when I tell you what's been happening."

For the next few minutes, he regaled them with his tale of woe. The men who broke into his house, his lucky shot defending himself, which had unfortunately killed someone else.

"And not just any man. Alistair Gordon."

"Alistair Gordon?" Nathan's eyebrows rose in amazement. "That big shot Bram Gordon's son?"

Alex nodded. "The very same."

"But what's he doing in your house, coming gunning for you?" Disbelief edged Graysie's normally melodic voice.

"Exactly what I'm asking," Alex said. "And now we get to the part that I wondered if you might help with." He looked from one to the other.

"Jack and Kaleo came round last night. I was so glad to see them. I didn't realize how much I needed someone like them at my side. They're both so wise about the world.

"And while I was muddling along in shock, not really wanting to believe what's happened, they got right to the point."

He pulled the metallic decoration Kaleo had picked up out of his breast pocket and laid it on the dining table.

"Kaleo found this piece of braid on my studio floor—it looks like it's come off a man's jacket."

"He says—and I'm pretty certain he's right—that it most probably comes off a Spanish jacket like they all used to wear in the old days. Not so much today, I know, but someone who wants to emphasize their Spanish connections still wears them."

He hesitated, thinking that he couldn't recall now if the second man wore a fancy jacket. He'd barely had time to lay eyes on him before he was under his desk.

"He thinks this could mean those two villains were at my house last night because of some Spanish connection. The most obvious thing would be something to do with my father ..."

His voice trailed off, and he twisted his mouth in an apologetic grimace.

"Thing is, Graysie, it made me realize I know little about my father except that he was a brilliant photographer. I've never asked myself about his family. Or his early life.

"So, I'm left wondering. What could there possibly be in our background that could lead to an attack like this?"

He went quiet and then stood and stretched. "Have you got any idea?" He stepped over to the window and surveyed the street.

"Man, this has got me all riled up. Even as I sit here telling you all this, it occurs to me—you might be in danger as well. If he's after me, then maybe he could come after you, too?"

Graysie had gone pale as he'd been speaking, but she now shook her head vehemently.

"No, you forget, I'm not Rafael's daughter. He was my stepfather."

Alex let out a long breath.

"Yes, but does whoever is behind this know that? I mean, you lived with him as his daughter. And it's never become public knowledge that your father was actually Eugene Mountfort."

He sat with a resigned thump and turned his gray eyes on Nathan.

"We need to make sure your whole family is safe until we understand more of what it going on here, Nat."

They sat in an appalled silence for several minutes, trying to digest what this new threat might entail.

Then Graysie spoke up again.

"You know, I remember little about Dad's family, either. Mother said his father attended their wedding in New York, and then they went to stay with them.

"I'm not sure if that was in New Orleans or Mexico. Probably New Orleans, because things in Mexico were politically unstable. It was soon after the war with the US."

"I think Mother said that Rafael's mother was Scottish, and her name was Fanny. But they never came to visit that I remember when we were in California. I've got the idea they might have gone back to Spain.

"And then Mother died. As I've said many times, Dad was never the same again. Really, her death destroyed him."

Alex edged toward the front of his seat. "So, you've got no idea what might be behind this attack?"

She shook her head. "Sorry, Alex. We never heard from his family again. I wouldn't even know if they're still alive."

Nathan had picked up the golden braid, with its black sequins, and was fingering it thoughtfully.

"Why have you got this here with you? Surely, this is evidence the police should have?"

"Ah. Well. That's the other thing."

"The other thing?" Graysie echoed. "There's more?"

"Afraid so. Jack says Bram Gordon is one of those guys who has the top officials in his pocket.

"There're all sorts of rumors about how he got his hands on so many of the ranches that belonged to the old Spanish land grants, for example. The commission usually finds in his favor when these disputed cases come up."

Alex fiddled with the fringe on the armchair upholstery.

"Jack says I should lie low for a while, to let things cool down. Without someone like Hector here to protect me, the cops might charge me and convict me overnight.

"I'd be dead before we dispute the evidence if Bram Gordon had his way."

He licked his lips nervously.

"And one of the weirdest things I haven't mentioned yet. When they charged in, Alistair Gordon definitely had a gun in his hand, aimed right at me. I know little about weaponry, but if I had to guess, I'd say it was a Colt revolver.

"He was about to pull the trigger on me—I could see it in his eye. But we never found a gun on his body. His mate must have picked it up and run off with it.

"The cops will say I shot an unarmed man in cold blood. How good does that look?"

He glanced from Nathan to Graysie and bit his lip.

"And you know how these things can blow up? Bram Gordon could have a lynch mob outside my house tonight calling for justice.

"I can't even go home. Or go to Isabella's. The police came looking for me there this morning."

Graysie's mouth dropped wide. "No! Not really?"

"Really. It was only thanks to the quick thinking of her friend Rosie that I got away," he said. "She practically pushed me out the back door and kept him busy while I ran out through the garden."

Graysie uttered a cry of distress.

"Oh Alex. What are you going to do? Where are you going to go?"

"I've no clue," he said. "Except it can't be anywhere near to any of my family. Bram Gordon is probably not going to give up until I'm dead."

Nine

"You're not getting it, Alex—you really aren't. This guy is dangerous."

Ewan Campbell was tall, a slim reed of a man with a pale, freckled face. His piercing hazel eyes glowed with a fierce inner force.

Alex recoiled, unprepared for the passion in Campbell's delivery. The California-born son of a Scots father and a Mexican mother, he identified more with his Spanish heritage than his Americano blood.

His melodic baritone accent still carried the faintest hint of a Scottish burr on his tongue—a rolling of his "r's" that softened his fervor.

"Guys like Bram Gordon are in a straight line from the criminals who shot my great uncles in cold blood at Bear Flag," said Ewan.

"They arrived out here, married daughters of the original rancheros, and took over the farm. Lock stock and barrel."

His eyes shone with indignation.

"If there's some historic land issue behind this, then be warned. Bram Gordon stops at nothing to get what he wants.

And he's got the police and the judiciary in his pocket—enough of them to ensure he always gets his own way."

Alex squeezed his eyes shut and wished for the umpteenth time that he'd never got mixed up with anything to do with the Gordon family.

He wanted back his old tranquil life. Going to the office, chewing things over with Kaleo, and then escaping into his photography as soon as he could justify leaving Kaleo to it.

For the last 48 hours, he hadn't been able to live in his own home or visit his sister.

Jack and Kaleo had cautioned him about letting O'Halloran or one of his sidekicks "find" him, advising him to hide out until the storm had passed over.

"Give yourself time to dig around and see what's behind it," Jack advised. "You're fighting in the dark right now."

Alex glanced around the tight circle of four men seated at a table in the cozy library in Kate Buchanan's Morton Street boarding house.

Kate's establishment, close to Chinatown, was famous as an upper-class fancy house, offering fifteen upstairs bedrooms as private rendezvous.

He currently occupied one of those rooms as a paying guest, thanks again to Jack's remarkable network of contacts.

"Kate's a good friend, and she runs an impeccable house. You'll be safe there. Even the cops respect her space," Jack had said, and Alex found he was right.

He'd kept a low profile, and no one had bothered him, though the police kept a regular watch further down the street for "known criminals."

I suppose that includes me. A "wanted" man.

The thought came out of nowhere and disrupted his attention to Ewan's speech.

That's the problem with lawyers. They love the sound of their own voice.

They'd gathered to ask Ewan about connections between Gordon's private affairs and the de Vile family. Or more specifically, Alex de Vile.

They'd placed a security detail at Isabella's, but so far, unwanted attention hadn't bothered her. It seemed Alex was Alistair Gordon's particular focus. But why?

Ewan Campbell was an expert on early Californio society, recognized as an up-and-coming lawyer in land issues. However, Gordon had swallowed up the last vestiges of his family's original thousand-acre land grant just last year. The case had gone all the way to the Supreme Court.

And because the one clue Kaleo picked up—the sequined braid—seemed to indicate a Spanish connection, they'd asked Ewan to come and give them his views on what could be behind the attack.

"You seem to know very little about your father's family," Campbell commented.

He peered at Alex questioningly over round, gold-rimmed glasses, his nose wrinkled in concentration.

Alex lifted his long fingers and flexed them, a moony distraction in his eyes.

"I'm afraid you're right. I know practically nothing about them, except that my father was a gifted photographer who died young."

He ran both hands down the sides of his face to the line of his jaw.

"Hector was such a big personality, always on the move, and into some new venture. He filled my life. And gave me everything I could want or need.

"I'm embarrassed to admit it now, but apart from being thrilled at discovering my father's historic daguerreotypes, I haven't given him much thought.

"I know the general outline—that he never recovered from our mother Elanora's death. I've given little thought to what might have gone on before."

He shrugged. "From what Graysie told us, Elanora's family was quite wealthy, but when she married Rafael, they cut her off.

"They considered him 'unsuitable.' I suppose that left me with the impression he was a step or two below her on the social ladder."

He glanced at Jack, appealing for understanding.

"You know. A poor, itinerant photographer. Graysie met no one from his side of the family. Maybe they're all dead."

Ewan steepled his fingers under his chin in thought.

"If it's not got anything to do with Hector's business—and at this stage we don't have enough information to know one way or another—then I'd suggest you need to look at two areas: his photographic work, and your family tree.

"Who were his father and mother and what did they do? Has he got any family still alive? That would be the best place to start."

Jack clapped his hands and half rose from his seat, as if

signalling he was going to get started right away.

"Sounds like a great idea to me."

Alex got up too.

"Where do you think you're <space> going?" Ewan asked.

"With Jack, of course. I'm not leaving him to do all the work."

Ewan shook his head. "It's still too dangerous for you to be walking the streets. Gordon has probably got a lynch mob looking for you.

"If they find you, they'll have you strung up before you can say 'Lawyer.'"

"No!" Alex cried. "I can't just sit around here waiting."

"You won't be 'just waiting,'" said Ewan.

"I've got a mass of old land grant documents you can go through. And some old ladies who go back to the early days might tell us what went on. You could write to them?"

"Write to them?" Alex snorted in disgust.

"I suppose you want me writing to old photographers, too?"

Ewan shot him a sympathetic smile. "Not a bad idea at all," he said. "We can start a dossier. Who was where at what time and what they learned?"

Alex glared in frustration. "You're not joking, are you?"

Ewan shook his head cordially. "I'm not joking."

Alex opened his mouth to protest when there was a commotion at the library door and a small, dark-haired boy slipped into the room, closing the door behind him.

He recognized Jack and grinned broadly.

"Mista Jack. I got a message for you."

He glanced nervously around the other faces.

"It's OK, Shark. You can talk in front of them. They're with us."

The dirty-faced urchin gave Jack a smile that lit up his entire face and made his violet-blue eyes dance in delight.

"The Countess sent me," Shark said. "She told me to tell you the coppers have got busy, like. They've got the papers."

Alex watched Jack's face for a clue what the boy was talking about. It was all garble to him.

"Papers? What papers?" He directed the question at his friend.

Jack waved away his question with a lazy hand, his full attention focused on the kid.

Alex noticed the boys' clothes needed a wash, but looked relatively new and in good repair.

"You know, Guv. The ones they need to put a fella in gaol. Or string him up. Those papers."

"An arrest warrant? Is that what the Countess said?"

"I told you," the boy said, his voice wearing ragged with frustration.

"They cum to the Countess's place, and to some other ones as well, I fink. Waved the papers around and said she'd be for it if she 'harbored a fugitive.' That's what they called it."

A quiet bubble seemed to expand in their midst. No one said anything. They didn't even look at each other. They stared at the table or the floor, keeping their thoughts to themselves.

And then Ewan brought his slender hands down on the table's edge with a confronting thump.

"I think that settles the question about you going out and about, Alex. Bram is getting impatient. He's setting the bloodhounds on you. It's even more important than before that you lie low."

He flashed him a sympathetic grin.

"I wasn't joking about the land grant records. Of course, it would help immensely if we knew for sure what your grandfather's name was. But in the meantime, how's your Spanish?"

"My Spanish? Pretty well nonexistent," said Alex.

He recalled the game they'd played when he was very young and they went to the beach. Dig a hole and you'd get to China. That's what the kids said.

I've dug that hole without realizing it. And I'm not in China.

I'm deep down in a place I don't recognize and might never climb out of.

Ten

Sacramento, November, 1852

Graysie Castellanos was a big girl now. She'd be six years old on her next birthday, but she'd never seen a letter like the one the stagecoach driver delivered minutes ago right to their door.

The eye-watering smell of bleach told her that her stepmother was doing the laundry at the back of the house.

Graysie hated wash days, with the odor that caught in her throat like a knife. It scared her.

If I breathe in, my throat might bleed, and I might never sing again.

She loved singing, so she made herself especially scarce on washing days.

She usually stayed as far away from Mrs. T. as she could anyway, because nothing she did ever seemed to be the right thing, and she was so tired of being scolded.

She was on the pavement outside her daddy's studio, playing hopscotch with the Israel boys and stroking a tortoiseshell kitten that always visited when Mrs. T. wasn't around. The daily stagecoach drew up outside her father's studio.

It was easy to find their place, because a giant painted sign hung across the front window: "Castellanos Studios; Finest Portraits Guaranteed."

She was reading now, and she'd asked her Papa to read the sign to her a hundred times. She teased him she couldn't remember it, but of course she could.

It was just that she loved to hear him read it, because for that short time, he was all hers.

He was away so often, and she only had the nasty Mrs. T. for company. When he read the sign to her, his deep voice rounded with pride, and his handsome face softened as he gazed down at her.

"Bella Graysie," he'd whisper, tracing his finger down her cheek. "You're so like your beautiful mama."

Then his attention would wander off into his memories, and his face would grow sad again. She didn't like it when that happened.

The coach that brought Papa's important letter bore crates of chickens and mail. The hens pecking through the bamboo bars distracted her until a man stood in front of her and said, "A letter for Castellanos…"

He gazed down at her kindly and said, "A mighty fine letter too."

She reached up her hand to take it and the man shook his head and said, "No sweetheart, I need to give this to your mummy. Or your daddy."

And her heart pinged inside, like someone had flicked her face with a raw rope and made it sting.

She took a big swallow and said bravely, "My mummy's

dead and my daddy is away taking pictures."

The coachman leaned down and patted her on the head. "You're the photographer's little girl, are you?"

He looked like he knew who she was, but that didn't surprise Graysie, because it seemed most people knew who she was.

She was her daddy's only child. The others had all died.

For a moment the familiar rock rose in her throat, stopping her from swallowing or breathing, and she bent over double and coughed to make it go away.

Then she thrust out her hand and said, "I can take the letter to our housekeeper, Mrs. T. She's looking after me, but she'd doing the washing right now. She won't want to stop it to come outside."

The driver scrunched up his face like he didn't like the idea.

"She won't want you coming inside either, and I'm going to be six soon. I can take Mrs. T. a letter…"

The driver smiled, reached into his pocket and pulled out a candy wrapped in paper and handed her both the sweet and the letter.

"Run along then," he said. "And make sure you give Mrs. T. the letter."

***

Graysie's hand trembled as she clutched the thick white envelope to her chest and tiptoed up the stairs to her father's studio.

She loved hiding away up here, especially when her father was at home working and she could nestle in a corner and watch him. As long as she kept quiet, he was happy to let her stay and watch him.

He wasn't home much these days, though. He said it was because he had to work hard to keep them all fed.

That was true, he did. But she also knew he had lots or arguments with Mrs. T and they upset him.

The kitten had followed her upstairs, and it snuggled up against her in a basket chair lined with sheepskin as she fingered the envelope.

It was thick, not the thin paper like most envelopes. And it had a lovely smell, like the lavender bushes in the garden in San Francisco, where her mother took her to jump with her skipping rope and they'd smell the orange trees.

She ran her fingers across the paper, remembering the velvety purple flowers in the garden that were very like it. Somehow it made her think of Mummy.

She hugged it to her chest and traced the edges of the red waxy seal on the back, like a shield.

The kitten purred, and she smiled.

It must be a very important letter.

It was hot, and she was tired, and just for a moment she could daydream that her mother was still here, or that she'd come back one day.

Graysie wasn't a baby, so she knew dead people never came back, but just for a minute she let herself dream it could happen.

And then she fell asleep.

***

When she woke up, the kitten had gone. She fluttered her eyes, remembering where she was.

In Daddy's studio with his important letter.

She turned it over and stared at the writing on the front. Big round writing in black ink, grown-up handwriting.

And she knew enough, she remembered her lessons with Mummy well enough, to know what it said.

Whoever was writing it had addressed the envelope to her father: *Señor Rafael Castellanos y Ordonez.*

And underneath it said, in the same round writing:
From Marquésa Fanny de Castellanos y Ordonez,
Palacio Real de Madrid
(The Royal Palace of Madrid).
Spain.

An enormous hole opened up inside of her, like someone had blown up a balloon and shoved it into her tummy.

The Royal Palace?

That was what those words said, wasn't it? She remembered those words from the fairy stories Mummy used to read, *Cinderella* and *Rapunzel* and oh… So many others. No one read her stories like those any more.

But the feeling in her tummy frightened her. This was an important letter, and she was supposed to give it to Mrs. T.

She slid off the basket chair, the sheepskin rug falling to her feet as she clambered down.

She was clutching the letter with one hand and trying to put the sheepskin back on the chair with the other when she heard the thump of feet up the stairs. Mrs. T. was at the studio door.

"What are you doing in here, you wicked girl? You know

you're not allowed in here. Especially when your father is away."

Mrs. T. had that spiteful look on her face, the one that was there all the time when she wasn't pretending to be nice to her when Daddy was there.

Graysie dropped the sheepskin, clutched the letter to her chest with both hands and backed away further into the big room. Further and further, until she was in the dark room in the corner, with its strange smell of chemicals.

Mrs. T. followed her, and her legs were a lot longer than Graysie's.

She grabbed her by the hair and dragged her out of the darkroom corner.

Graysie yowled and lifted her hands to her head. The letter dropped to the floor.

"What is that you've got there, you awful child?"

The old woman swooped down on it. The smell of bleach combined with the red carbolic soap Mrs. T. used filled Graysie's nose. Mrs T. washed in carbolic once a week, and the stink of it was always there on her skin and clothes like a horrible medicine.

She gagged.

Mrs. T. turned the letter over and saw the red seal on the back.

Her eyebrows rose to meet her dark brown hair.

"What are you doing with this, you wicked girl?"

She mouthed the address softly to herself, stumbling over the foreign words.

Marquésa Fanny de Castellanos y Ordonez…Royal Palace of Madrid.

She fixed Graysie with the dark brown eyes, which always looked angry when they were together alone.

Then she reached out and grabbed Graysie's earlobe between her thumb and forefinger.

She pinched so hard, Graysie yowled like a cat. Then she marched her back into the dark room and slammed the door shut.

"If you say one word about this, your father will send you to the nuns," she shouted.

"You'll stay in there until I'm ready to let you out! And I warn you, not one word to your father, or it's off to the nuns for you!"

Eleven

Temptation Thompson didn't bother to steam open the photographer's letter. She'd already decided Rafael would not see it, because she wasn't passing it on.

A royal palace?

Some fancy Fanny Marquésa?

Her heart thundered with indignation at what he'd kept hidden from her.

Here she was, stinking of bleach and carbolic, her hands red and wrinkled with endless work, looking more like an old hag every day. And he'd never mentioned he had a royal connection?

If that was so, why were they crowded into a few stuffy rooms in Sacramento's rowdy Main Street, where drunks banged on the doors most nights? Why was the house all taken up with his infernal studio and camera gear?

And why was she lumbered with his kid for weeks on end while he swanned off taking pictures of rich folks she never met?

Years of being overlooked and mistreated erupted into a volcano of bitterness that roared through twenty-nine-year-old

Temptation, who'd never been married despite adopting the title of Mrs.

She couldn't bear the shame of being a spinster at twenty-nine, of never having found a man to marry her.

She brought her hand to her throat, which was burning all the way down her gullet.

She'd come out West as a mail-order bride, but the surly bastard who'd paid for her fare treated her like a kitchen skivvy.

He'd never tied the knot before his unmourned death under the wheels of a runaway cart.

When she'd spied Rafael Castellanos, punch-drunk with grief at the loss of his wife and two babies, she'd seen her opportunity.

Hitch her wagon to his star, offer to keep house and look after the child, and she'd slither her way between his sheets and get a ring on her finger in no time.

He's too stunned to notice, and everyone says I'm a good-looking piece.

That's what she'd thought.

Except she hadn't wormed her way into his bed. Consumed by his blackness, Rafael hadn't noticed her at all. It was like competing with a ghost.

If she heard the name Elanora one more time…. And that kid of his…

Shining like a sunbeam, just like her mother, always reminding him of his dead-and-gone gorgeous wife.

Temptation slumped down on the sheepskin and ripped open the letter. She read:

My darling son,

It is with a heavy heart I write, seeking word of you and your darling family. It's so long since we had any news from you, and I am consumed with a deep fear that something terrible has happened to you. More terrible than Elanora's death, I mean.

We'd only been back in Madrid a few months when we heard of the coach accident and Elanora's terrible accident.

Since then, we have heard nothing, and every day the ominous silence from California tugs at my soul.

In the first year after the birth of your precious twins, Elanora wrote regularly, sharing news of their growth and of your growing success in your work.

The last news she sent was to say you were setting up business in Sacramento and that she and the children were traveling to join you there soon. That is the last I heard of you, and I am so fearful some fresh, awful event has befallen you.

Have the children come down with smallpox? Have you succumbed to your grief?

Anxious imaginings grab at my mind, and I have had no rest for months now.

Your father's time is fully taken up with the complicated goings-on at court here in Madrid, where the affairs of state are in an awful mess.

Young Queen Isabella daily needs the counsel and guidance of a wise man like Angel if she is to hold on to her throne, so we can't come to look for you.

I am fearful that the stress of so much responsibility is having a deleterious effect on his health.

And we have another growing concern. Your sister Clara has married one of the palace guards, Andrés de la Fuente, an ambitious young man who grows impatient with the slow pace of change in the court.

There is a lot of grumbling following the revolution in France—you will appreciate absolute monarchies are in disfavor with the rabble.

Angel and I are fearful that Andrés will take matters into his own hands and join the anti-monarchist forces.

Even the son-in-law of a Marquésa who is a royal councillor is not protected from the harshest punishment if he steps over the boundaries, as I'm sure you will understand.

You always had such a gracious spirit, my Rafael, my oldest and wisest child.

We are deeply embedded here, and it is impossible for us to make a journey to California to satisfy ourselves that all is well.

Perhaps a letter from you has gone astray. A ship gone down, or something similar, one carrying your letters to us.

We know the children have lost their mother, but we don't know anything more. I pray they are all safe. If there is anything we can do to support you, please tell us what it is. You know you can appeal to us for help at any time.

We would move heaven and earth to ensure you are all well and loved and cared for.

Indeed, I would come myself to see you home, if that was the best option for you all.

I pray this missive finds you, my darling son, and that you know you are remembered and loved and that we want you home with us.

Your ever-loving mother,

Fanny

Temptation Thompson rolled the pages between her fingers and lifted the letter up and breathed in its fragrance. The smell of money, of blue blood, of fine food and wine… All the things she didn't have and never would have.

Oh, my goodness. If he got this…

If he got this letter, he would join his rich mummy and daddy in Spain. He spoke the lingo. They'd have no problem sending him the fare.

And where would that leave me?

Back in the pastry shop where she'd first caught Rafael's eye, that's where. If she was lucky. Coming up to thirty years, an old maid, with no one and nothing going for her except her waning beauty and her wits.

She stuffed the letter into its envelope and concealed it between her breasts. One place she could guarantee he'd never look.

She'd keep a keen lookout from now on. The dead wife wasn't the biggest threat to her continuing comfortable life, she saw now.

The relations back in Spain were far more dangerous.

Twelve

Isabella slammed the door on O'Halloran's back for the third time in as many days and stomped back to the drawing room where she'd been sharing afternoon tea with Rosie.

She'd discovered that in her "delicate condition" she couldn't face food early in the day. But by mid to late afternoon she was ravenous, so they'd developed a new ritual of "playing ladies" with the Stockton's silver tea service.

They were drinking Betty's Iced Tea, a potent mix of green and black tea with lots of sugar and half a pint of rich sweet cream.

In a lot of households, they would transform this into Iced Tea Punch, with the addition of a bottle of claret or champagne slowly stirred into the mix. But the girls agreed that was a step too far at four o'clock in the afternoon and with Izzy pregnant as well.

"We want to keep ourselves on an even keel," Isabella said. "I'd hate for Sebastian to come home and find us sozzled!"

Betty Butler relished the opportunity to prepare them little snacks of cucumber and gherkin club sandwiches, tiny lemon honey tarts, and yeasty little buns with cream and jam. All of it was the latest rage from England.

O'Halloran was like a bloodhound on scent, popping up at different times of the day in the hope of "catching them out" with Alex here.

As if the recurring morning sickness wasn't enough to deal with. She wondered how much longer it would go on for? On top of that, her head and bones ached with anxiety about the brother she'd begun referring to as "Alejandro."

After all, it seemed the Spanish connection had caused this upheaval.

She savored his birth name, rolling it on her tongue, dredging up faint memories of the time before their abrupt separation after their mother's death.

They'd been caught up in a coach accident in a wilderness stretch to Sacramento, with Graysie the family's only survivor.

Their mother died instantly, and when rescuers arrived hours after the toddler twins, she and Alejandro, were gone, presumed taken by wild animals.

The idea of that had given Graysie nightmares all her childhood, she'd told them.

Isabella recalled very little of that time, but her whole body flushed now with a warmth from glimpses coming back to her.

Maybe I'm remembering because I've got a baby of my own coming soon?

She felt Alejandro's clammy little hand stuck to hers, wet with heat and tacky with candy that had melted on their tongues.

Sugar matted his hair, and the perfume of him as he bumped along with wobbly toddler steps was as sweet as violets and as sharp as horse pee.

Their parents had named them Alejandro and Gabriela—she realized now to mark them as the children of their Spanish father.

Rafael was laying his claim to them because he knew Elanora's secret. Their half-sister, Graysie, was not his daughter.

They'd been christened into that Hispanic identity. But they'd never been raised in it because of their mother's death and their disappearance.

They were stolen children, placed into families of privilege, but abducted from their rightful heritage.

Neither of them spoke their father's language, nor had they ever been curious about his origins.

As she settled back onto the drawing-room sofa and picked up the ladies' fashion magazine she'd been leafing through before O'Halloran disturbed them, she held her hand protectively over her stomach.

She'd never been as aware of the loss as she was today, anticipating the arrival of her first child.

Her little son or daughter was already safely lodged inside her, and a surge of mingled gratitude and love overwhelmed her.

Our mother was only my age when she died.

How had she managed with two babies at once, out here in California, far away from her family? It must have been tough for her.

Her eyes filled with tears. She wiped them with the back of her hand and glanced self-consciously across to where Rosie sat with her back to her, gazing out on the street. Her silhouette appeared hunched over against the bright light from the window.

Isabella fought to maintain a bright demeanor around her, so as not to spoil her friend's stay, and clenched her jaw tight. She didn't want Rosie to see her crying.

She rested in her chair, soaking in the silence, stroking her tummy in self-consolation for a few more minutes before glancing up again.

That's when she noticed Rosie collapsed forward in a deep slump, her shoulders heaving. Her muffled sobbing broke the silence of the room.

Isabella shot to her feet, the magazine on her lap tumbling to the carpet, and then brought herself up short.

It was so unusual for Rosie to be upset. Misgiving shot through her. Was she reading the signs correctly? Rosie was always the sunshine girl.

She called softly.

"Rosie! Are you all right?"

Her only reply was another wave of sobbing. Her friend's shoulders shook harder.

Isabella picked her way across the room and laid a hand on the back of Rosie's neck.

"Rosie! What's wrong?"

More gasping sobs greeted her inquiry.

The mantel clock ticking seemed louder than before, as if determined to make itself heard above this emergency.

"Oh Rosie. What's upset you so? You can tell me."

Rosie swung in the chair to face her, slashing angrily at her cheeks with her hand as she did.

"You've got enough worries, Izzy, without hearing about mine."

She attempted to smile through her tears.

"I'm just being an idiot. Don't worry. I'll be right in a tick."

Isabella leaned over her. "Don't be silly. Come and sit with me over there and tell me all about it. If it's got you this upset, it's definitely something."

Rosie allowed herself to be led to the sofa, and they settled side by side as Rosie wiped her eyes with a damp handkerchief and the sobbing gradually died away.

She drew in a stuttering breath and gave Isabella a wry smile.

"You have enough to worry about without my woes," she said, her green eyes capturing Izzy's concerned marine-blue ones.

"I can't belief that awful policeman. Pestering us! Coming here with a warrant! I'm glad we got Alex away in plenty of time."

"Never mind Alex," Isabella said. "I want to hear about you."

Rosie shrugged in resignation.

"I've had a letter from my brother, and my mam's not well. That's not so unusual. I'm afraid she's never going to be well again. But what's upset me is my sister's ill too, and Liam says she needs a doctor."

Isabella nodded. "Ohh. I'm sorry to hear that."

She took one of Rosie's hands in hers.

"You've never told me much about your family. This sister. How old is she?"

"She's a year younger than me. She got sick when she was a

baby. We never had money for doctors and she lost the movement in one leg. She's crippled."

Tears flooded down Rosie's cheeks. Isabella had never seen her friend cry before, and realized with a start she knew very little about her life back in New York.

"What's her name?" she asked, her voice soft and halting with emotion. She could feel the tears welling up in the back of her eyes again.

This baby is turning me into a goo-ball. What's wrong with me?

I'm immediately imagining what it would be like if that happened to my child.

Rosie dabbed her eyes once more and sniffed.

"Eilish. It's the Gaelic form of Elizabeth. It means pledged to God and she's pretty much a saint, what she puts up with and how much she helps our ma ma."

"And why does she need a doctor?"

"Liam says her foot is swelled up and sore and she's real down in the dumps. Not her usual cheery self at all. He's scared there's something is seriously wrong with her."

"Well, he'll have to make sure she gets to a doctor then, won't he?" Isabella spoke with determined certainty.

Rosie shook her head. "You don't understand. We don't have enough money for doctors. Even with the money from my work, we are barely making enough to take care of everyone. Ma Ma can't work anymore. She's too ill.

"And now I'm off work from Lotta's with this darned arm," she waved her sling in the air grumpily, "we're struggling even more. I need to get back to work as fast as I can."

Isabella's heart rose in her chest.

"Rosie, you know you can't go riding horses in the middle of the night with your arm like that. You'll fall off a mountain bridge next time, and never be seen again. Don't be daft."

Lotta Crabtree's troupe was famous for covering perilous miles at night. They visited gold mining towns all over the state, travelling in all weathers on overloaded packhorses.

Rosie had fallen asleep on her horse and slipped off, bashing her wrist as she landed. She was lucky they were on flat ground.

"They won't have me back until it's healed," she said. "I'm frightened they might never have me back. I don't know what we'll do then."

"Oh Rosie. You're one of Lotta's star turns! They won't let you go!"

"The longer I'm away, the more likely they'll find a new girl to take my place."

"Now that's just the glooms talking," said Isabella. "Stop that right now."

A long silence settled between them, and then Rosie said in a quiet voice:

"My dream was to earn enough to set my family up, but I guess it won't happen. Someday soon I'm going to lose both my mam and Eilish."

"Rosie! Stop." She patted her friend's arm and rose to her feet.

"I'm going to see to getting some more tea and cookies from the kitchen, and then we're going to work out a plan."

Rosie clutched at her wrist to halt her departure.

"I feel bad about the things I said to Alex the other day.

Especially now he's in so much trouble. I was mean.

"It's just when I know how tough my folks have things, sometimes it's hard not to feel envious."

Isabella gazed at Rosie's red-rimmed green eyes, her own blue ones wide in shock

"You knew about this then? You've been keeping this secret all this time?"

Rosie's face reddened, and she sucked in her breath sharply through her teeth.

"You've already been so kind to me. I don't know where I'd have gone if you hadn't had let me stay here. I haven't got the money for a hotel."

"Oh, Rosie!" Isabella leaned down and gave her friend a light hug.

"Haven't you heard the expression 'That's what friends are for?' I'd have felt terrible if you'd kept this a secret and something awful happened. What is that other saying, 'A problem shared is a problem halved?'"

She brought her hand to her mouth and giggled. "Corny, I know. I'm quite the fount of folksy wisdom today, aren't I? Don't get mad at me…"

She stared into Rosie's sad eyes, noting her downturned mouth. It was the most depressed she had ever seen her normally bubbly friend.

"We're going to work this out," she said, her voice taut with forced brightness. "You saved my brother from that awful policeman. It's my chance to return the favor."

Thirteen

"Rosie!" After an awkward pause, Alex stepped aside and trailed behind her as she followed one of Kate Buchanan's girls into a room she'd described as the "library," although at first glance, she couldn't see any books.

Alex planted himself in front of her as soon as she paused by a chair, hesitating to sit down. The library was a calm haven, away from the buzzing activity in the entryway outside.

A wonderful ethereal light streamed in from double-hung windows that opened onto the back garden. It lit up the shelves which Rosie saw held a few leather-bound books she doubted anyone read.

"What are you doing here?" Alex demanded. "I thought you couldn't stand me."

She swallowed down her shock at his bluntness, and then registered that his voice held no resentment, only curiosity.

She gazed up into glittering gray eyes above an aquiline nose, and her insides melted.

Why does he have this effect on me?

"I didn't mean… It wasn't …" She took a deep breath.

"When I let loose on you… I was having a bad day," she

spluttered, and then stiffened, as she noticed they weren't alone.

A snowy-haired Spanish señorita, clad in a shiny red and gold dress, sat in the room's central sofa in front of a low coffee table littered with paper. Her hair was caught up in a topknot secured in a mother-of-pearl clasp.

Piercing light brown eyes met her own and roamed up and down, calculating.

"Oh. I'm so sorry. I'm interrupting. I didn't realize you had a visitor."

She was on stage again, a gringo under examination.

The eyes remained fixed on her.

Hadn't anyone told her it's impolite to stare at people you don't know?

Alex stepped up and said quickly, "Rosie Kelly, meet Countess Christiana de Sánchez-Navarro."

Countess? What am I supposed to call a Countess?

"Countess," faltered Rosie, unable to hide the surprise in her voice.

"I do apologize. I didn't know Alex had another visitor. I don't mean to interrupt."

Christiana's eyes crackled with mischievous humor.

"He's stuck here, isn't he, so he had to find something useful to do with his time?"

Her bold directness reassured Rosie; she wasn't one to easily take offense.

She felt instantly at ease, caught up in the other woman's challenging presence.

"Oh? And how is he managing that? To make himself useful, I mean."

Rosie tilted one brow and allowed the faintest quirk in her red lips.

Christiana gurgled with laughter, and the polished blue stone necklace that hung around her neck rattled with the movement.

"Alejandro is learning about his ancestors. Not his bloodline, you understand—we don't know what rock he sprang up from under." She flashed a teasing smile. "You've heard of the Treaty of Guadalupe Hidalgo, have you, my dear?"

Rosie shook her head in confusion. "Guadal what? No, sorry. I haven't."

"Ah well, then you'll have heard of the Great Irish Famine? By the sound of your voice, I'd guess so."

Rosie's cheeks were hot. "I've heard my papa speak of it, yes."

"Same idea. People come into your village, and they don't ask, they tell. They make promises they don't keep. And they take the land, so the original folks starve. Much the same story."

Rosie shot a desperate glance at Alex—or should she call him Alejandro now?—hoping he'd rescue her.

What was she supposed to say to that? She knew about as much about Irish history as she did about Mexican, or Spanish, or whatever it was this grand old lady was all about.

Alex sensed her embarrassment and took this as his cue to direct her to a seat and offer her coffee.

"We've got Mexican coffee, that's plain black, made a couple of different ways, or *Cajeta de leche y piña*—milk and pineapple caramel—one of the Countess's favorites from childhood."

"That sounds delicious," said Rosie with a conspiratorial smile at Christiana.

"Coming up!" Alex responded, turning to a silver jug on a tray.

He glanced over his shoulder as he picked it up to pour.

"Getting Christiana in was all Jack's idea," he said. "Or not so much Jack, but a chap Jack has brought in to help me, a lawyer named Ewan Campbell.

"Ewan knows a lot about Spanish Mexicans in California, and he's arranged for Countess Christiana to help me learn more about our history."

"And are you enjoying it?" Rose asked, when Christiana remained silent.

Alex's eyes brightened. "Immensely. I'm ashamed to admit I knew nothing about it. And now, thanks to Christiana, I know a lot more."

He poured a caramel drink for her and Christiana, then a plain black for himself, and brought them all to the side table. As he passed them each a cup, Rosie felt her brow crinkle into worried lines.

"I've missed some essential detail here, Alex," she said. "I'm sure it's all very interesting, but how is learning about the old Spanish Californio history going to help with getting you out of this mess you're in?

"You know O'Halloran has issued a warrant now? He's been to Isabella's three times in the past two days, hoping to catch you out."

Alex sat heavily, slopping some of his beverage into the saucer.

"Nooo. Just what I was trying to avoid!"

"And he made it clear she'd be arrested too if she 'harbored a fugitive.' She'd dearly love to come and see you, but she's worried he might have someone tailing her."

He blew out a frustrated breath. "I don't want her under any extra stress. She's got nothing to do with this."

He stood abruptly, his body taut with a pent-up energy he couldn't contain. He blew into his clasped fingers.

Rosie took a sip of her caramel drink and raised her brows appreciatively.

"This is absolutely delicious, Countess. I can see why it was a memorable part of your childhood."

The Countess beamed but remained silent. Rosie turned to Alex and continued with her line of thought.

"O'Halloran went to Elizabeth Westerhoven's as well. Why on earth he has to bother her, I don't know. She sent one of her men over to warn us."

"Bram Gordon is obviously applying the heat," said Alex.

"He is indeed. But you still haven't explained about the history lessons."

Countess Christiana cleared her throat. "Perhaps I can explain that for you, Alejandro?"

She set her head at an imperious angle which discouraged disagreement.

"Sure," said Alex with a wry grin. "Be my guest."

"Once upon a time before the gringos arrived, the Spanish Mexican rancheros worked magnificent spreads of land under grants from either the Spanish king in the early days, or the Mexican administrators later. My uncles were among them.

"When the Americans arrived, everything changed. They justified any behavior to get their hands on our land. They bought, stole, murdered, cheated—and when that didn't work, used the finer points of the law—to take it from us."

Christiana's proud mouth twisted at the memories and Rose was a child back in Ireland, cringing behind her mother's skirts, watching a British soldier prodding her weeping aunt Bridget in the chest, ordering her out of her home.

Close to starvation, she hugged her dead baby boy to her chest.

That's why I'm in America, not in Ireland.

"They murdered my brother and his fine twin sons, and Gordon finally got the land he wanted from them last year through the courts."

Christiana dabbed the corner of one eye with the back of her hand and stared into space, remembering the unspeakable.

The light from the windows had dimmed, the air in the room cooled, as the ghosts of past outrages took up their vigil.

After long moments, her eyes flickered and her drawn-out stare drifted from Rosie to Alex. Prickles ran up and down Rosie's arms.

The Countess stood and wandered toward the windows. Her burnt orange shawl drifted from one shoulder over the gold-embossed dress like a declaration of forlorn hope.

Perched on a window seat overlooking the purple and pink hydrangeas below, she resumed her story.

"Outrageous dealings have gone on ever since Guadalupe—when the Yanks promised we'd keep ownership of the lands we held and then broke their word time and time again. For forty years now, we've had to 'prove' our rights repeatedly with paper records.

"This lawyer Alejandro is using, Ewan Campbell, is an expert on the finer points of the law. He's up to Bram Gordon's tricks, and he knows the various family records in minute detail.

"But even he couldn't save his family's lands. Last year, Bram Gordon got their last few acres."

She flicked her eyes to Rosie in explanation. "Ewan's great-grandfather was a Scotsman who married Catalina Lopez, whose family had a big land grant near Sonoma.

"They've had to justify that claim for twenty years, and finally the system cheated them. Legal challenge after challenge, from shyster greedy lawyers.

"What they didn't have to sell to pay lawyer bills, the courts took away from them."

Her dark eyes were pools of sadness.

"When it suits them, the judges decide the records are faulty, or forged, or the original grant was never made—any excuse to take the land away from us.

"This farce has been crawling through the courts for decades, and they've pretty well taken everything they can now. And Bram Gordon is one of the worst."

Rosie's head was spinning.

"That may be, but neither Alex nor his father had any dealings with Bram, did they? Why should that matter?"

Christiana hunched her shoulder in semi-defeat.

"We don't know why it matters yet, but I bet it does. Somewhere in the murky past, Alejandro's family's fortunes entwined with Bram Gordon's somehow. We're working on putting it all together now."

Fourteen

Alex didn't want Rosie to go, but he couldn't think of any excuse to have her stay.

Countess Christiana said her farewells, promising to visit again in a few days. She reminded Alejandro he was to search through the records Ewan gave him.

"They might give you clues to what links the Gordon and the Castellanos families," she reminded him as she departed.

Without her mediating presence, an awkward silence fell over them. Rosie was aware of the lingering fragrance of Christiana's strident perfume, an Oriental blend of vanilla, amber and musk.

She glanced up, steeling herself to meet Alejandro's eye, and when she spoke, her voice was strained.

"Isabella wanted to come but—"

Her penetrating green eyes wavered from his to the far windows. She suddenly seemed unsure of how to continue.

Alex jumped in to fill an uncomfortable gap.

"You're thinking Kate Buchanan's isn't exactly a suitable place for a young married woman of excellent reputation to visit, aren't you?

"And you're right, it isn't, even apart from the problem of leading O'Halloran here," Alex said.

He edged closer to her, gazing across the gap between them that had shrunk so that their knees were close to touching.

"Rosie, I don't want her to come, and you shouldn't either. I'm dangerous to know. And Kate's isn't exactly the place to be seen for either of you."

He gave her a wry smile.

"I'm grateful you came to give me news. She's okay, right, but next time, send Sam. I don't want her upset. She is all right, isn't she? I mean, with the baby coming and all."

Alex shifted his feet on the spot uneasily.

Rosie smiled reassuringly. "She's fine," she said, in a drawn-out Irish brogue, twitching at his seriousness.

She was aiming for a touch of stage burlesque to defuse the tension between them. He could see that, and he smiled.

"She's a little off her food first thing in the morning, that's all. I gather that's normal."

She returned him a wry smile. "But she makes up for it later in the day. We've developed this crazy routine of playing at ladies' afternoon tea. Betty loves the excuse to cook up a storm, and she gets to eat dainty sandwiches and yeasty cream buns."

Alex grinned.

"If you can keep her company and lift her spirits, that's the most important thing," he said. "I can't think of a better companion for her with Seb away. You're always so full of sunshine..."

Rosie's cheeks flushed, but the smile faded. "Not always..." she murmured.

And then her hand flew to her mouth. "Oh, I almost forgot. Isabella gave me a letter for you too… To make up for not being able to come herself."

Alex took the note and tore open the envelope hungrily. Then he stopped himself.

"I'm sorry. Here I am being rude again. Why don't you stay and have another coffee while I read this?" he said." I might want to send a reply. If that's all right?"

He poured her a fresh caramel drink, and she settled back and opened a fashion magazine from a nearby table.

"I'm sure the coves who visit here find this fascinating reading," she said with a dimpled smile. "Do the girls leave it lying around hoping they'll buy them a dress like one of these?"

Her words had an ironic edge that made it clear she understood the menfolk came to Kate's for one thing.

He'd buried his head in his letter and glanced up, distracted.

"You didn't tell me about your sister," he said.

"Is that what she's on about?" Rosie's face flushed red. "I'll kill her."

"Don't do that," he said with a crooked smile. "But why didn't you mention anything about your troubles at home?"

She stood abruptly and the fashion magazine slipped unnoticed to the floor.

"We're not exactly best friends, Alex, and I don't hang my family's dirty washing out for all to see."

Her husky voice was hot and urgent.

"There's nothing to be ashamed of in being poor," he said, his face coloring to match her embarrassment. He stood up and moved closer, drawn by the desire for her to understand.

"Do you think because I've had the good fortune to be raised by Hector, I haven't figured out others aren't as lucky? No wonder you thought me a spoiled daffy down dilly."

She shook her head in denial, but he moved even closer and continued

"Your quick thinking saved me from arrest in that kitchen this week," he said. "That's good enough for me. I'm indebted to you. It's a matter of what can I do in return?"

She attempted to increase the space between them, and the back of her knees bumped up against the sofa. She fell back into her seat.

"Nothing… You don't need to do anything. Really. As soon as my wrist mends…" She looked despairingly at her right wrist, which hung in a sling from her neck.

Serious-faced, he sat down beside her and bore into her with his slate-gray eyes.

"Uh? I'm not belittling your efforts, Rosie, but is that going to be enough to cover doctor's bills?"

Her eyes dropped to her hands, knotted in her lap, fingers entwined as if she held her sister's future in them.

Alex leaned back, giving her more room to breathe.

But he didn't let up on the emotional pressure.

"What would you ideally like to do for them? Your family? Your sister and mother especially?"

"Ideally?" She let out a long sigh, her intensity draining away.

Her head dropped, as if she was suddenly exhausted.

"Ideally, I'd like to bring them all out here to live with me."

Alex stared at her, his dark eyes glittering.

"Then why don't we do that?"

Her mouth dropped open. "There's no way… I couldn't… No Alex, it's not right."

"Why not? What's wrong with the idea? It would make up for me being such a selfish oaf, thinking the world revolved around me. I wouldn't like me either, if I were you."

"Oh, that's unfair. You aren't an oaf. I was plain rude, too consumed by my own problems, that's all.

"I'm scared Mum's going to die and then Eilish will work herself into the ground trying to take care of the rest of them. I'll lose them both."

Her voice broke on the last sentence. "It's stupid, I know, but I can't help it. I send them money every month, but I don't have the grinding life they do, in a flimsy fourth-floor tenement with no running water.

"I can't go back to that. But I couldn't stand it if they died on me."

They gazed at each other for a long moment.

Rosie's white teeth bit at her bottom lip. Her green eyes were wide open and glittering with pain.

Alex let out a despairing sigh.

"I don't know how this business with O'Halloran is going to end, Rosie. But I want to ensure whatever happens, that Isabella isn't endangered, especially now."

His eyes, faraway, flicked to the windows.

"If this Gordon business is tied up with our family somehow, Izzy may also be at risk, and I can't stand that thought.

"What if they get rid of me and then go after her? I can't let that happen."

He stood abruptly and turned on his heel to face the door.

"Knowing so little about everything makes it hard to predict. So how about this? We'll do a trade.

"You act as the go-between for me and Isabella, and I'll see what I can do about helping your family. It's only fair to repay you for being so kind to Izzy and me."

Rosie's rounded cheeks flushed a deeper pink.

"There's no need! It's what friends do, and Izzy's my best friend. We both want to see you out of the mess. No repayment needed."

She stood and gathered her reticule to her side. "I've been gone quite a long time. Isabella will start worrying soon. I must get back."

Alex held up his hand like a maître d' delaying departing hotel guests.

His stomach tightened uncomfortably.

Suddenly, he wanted her to stay longer, not go.

"Hold on. Give me a few minutes to reply to Izzy's letter," he said.

"Can you take it back with you? Please?"

She flopped back down on the sofa.

"Be quick then."

"What? You're tired of my company already?" he joked. "Can't stand me any longer?"

He stared into her green eyes, and wishing he could make the moment last.

"Oh Alejandro Castellanos, what a shameless tease you are! Your sister should have warned me."

Laughter bubbled up from a deep spring within him, and

the pounding ache in his head that had been there ever since he'd shot Alistair Gordon vanished. He dashed his right hand up and swept stray locks from his eyes.

This woman brings sweet fortune.

"Agree to be my go-between and we're quits," he said, flashing her an unrepentant smile.

Then he sat down to write something else altogether in his letter to Isabella.

Fifteen

"There's a gentleman here to see Mrs. Isabella, Miss Kelly. I've explained the lady of the house is indisposed."

The Russell's Man Friday, Samson Butler, stood at the top of Isabella's front door steps, facing off to a man who cut an imposing figure from behind.

The caller had on a tailored dark blue wool jacket that stretched across broad shoulders and fitted around them in all the right places.

His hair, probably shoulder length when loose, rested at the back of his neck in a ponytail tied with a flat bow of black velvet ribbon.

Rosie, fizzing with news of Alex she was eager to share with Isabella, stared up at Sam. She caught the concerned appeal in dark eyes that usually twinkled with good humor.

The responsibilities he'd assumed during Sebastian's absence were wearing their house manager down.

"Oh dear," Rosie said. "I'm sorry to hear Mrs. Russell is unwell."

At the sound of her voice, the newcomer wheeled around and gazed down at her from his vantage point a step or two above her.

She saw immediately that the antiquated, romantic hairstyle was well-matched by a tanned, handsome face. The stranger had a broad brow set over direct hazel eyes and a striking classical profile. He flashed her a smile through strong white teeth.

Like an old-time troubadour, this one.

It instantly reminded her of Jason Carver, Lotta's "main man" in the traveling theater from which she was taking leave.

Every drama needed one of these, the potent masculine presence that dominated the stage and made other men look colorless by comparison.

A leading man. I know the type well.

His strong thighs were snugly wrapped in thin leather trousers he wore over tooled leather boots, the leggings slashed from knee to ankle. A bright red wool serape that swung from one shoulder completed the ranchero style.

It was a garb that suggested its wearer had slipped easily off a horse after a dash across open ground. And it would have been high fashion two decades ago.

On most men, it came across as antiquated and mildly eccentric, but on this fellow, it was overwhelmingly glamorous.

He swept his scarlet cape back and bowed. "Dionisio Garcia, at your service, madam."

She scanned his clean-cut features and realized he was younger than she'd first assumed.

Not much older than me, she thought. He probably hasn't yet reached thirty.

Rosie dipped her head, startled but not overawed by his unexpected arrival.

"Well, Señor Garcia, as our house man Samson Butler here has advised, Mrs. Russell is not receiving visitors. I suggest you make an appointment for a more suitable time."

"And would that appointment be with you, charming miss?"

His eyes brimmed with undisguised masculine appreciation as he left the space open for her to volunteer her name.

She shook her head with a cheeky grin in reply.

"Leave your calling card with Samson, and Mrs. Russell will get back to you if she wishes," she said.

He stepped closer and placed his right hand under her elbow, a gesture which was commanding but not domineering. Warmth radiated upwards and her throat tightened.

I hope I'm not blushing.

He lent over her and murmured in her ear, "Allow me to escort you in for coffee and I will share information of benefit to Mrs. Russell and perhaps even to you, lovely lady."

She wanted to appear unmoved by his mysterious whispering, but she couldn't suppress a frown as her eyes met Sam's.

She stepped around Garcia and closer to the houseman.

"Sam, show Senor Garcia into the library, and bring us some coffee," she said.

"I'll see our guest on Mrs. Russell's behalf and pass on any information he might have for her."

***

"I believe I've seen you somewhere before, Miss Kelly." Over the coffee Sam served, Garcia eyed her like a wolf sizing up a kid goat.

She smiled primly. "Oh, I doubt that very much, señor," she replied.

He lifted a knowing, dark brow. "The Crabtree troupe, if I'm not mistaken? "

Despite her guardedness, her heart seesawed, and the pleasure of recognition heated her veins.

This fellow is adept at tickling a woman's vanity, no question.

He allowed a pregnant silence to fall as his eyes roamed from the hem of her dress to the top of her head.

"But I see you have suffered some misfortune, yes?"

He gestured to her arm, hooked in a sling across her chest.

"A nuisance tumble," she demurred. "No long-term damage. A mere inconvenience."

She sipped her coffee. "Remarkable of you to recall Lotta's show. Thank you."

What's his game?

He's done some homework. This isn't some random visit.

"I am passionate about the theater," he said. "I go to see divas like Magdalena da Silva whenever I can."

Her eyes widened in surprise. His flushed complexion hinted he spent his life on horseback. But apparently, she was mistaken.

"Oh yes. She's a magnificent performer," she said primly. "You've good taste."

The wariness she'd experienced from the moment she laid eyes on Senor Garcia buried itself deeper within.

"And what is your connection with Mrs. Russell?" she asked, swallowing down on her racing heartbeat. "Are you a friend of the family?"

The flare of amusement in his eyes told her he found the inquiry funny, but he quickly quenched it.

"In a manner of speaking," he said, with studied solemnity.

"I'm probably more concerned about her association with Alex de Vile. He's her brother, I believe?"

She was certain that if he'd asked around about her and Lotta, he knew very well Alex and Isabella were twins, so why the pretense?

"It's well known that they're twins? It's no surprise to anyone who knows them."

Garcia made a display of carefully setting down his coffee cup on the table and fidgeting uneasily.

All playacting.

"And may I be so bold as to ask what he is to you?"

"That is out of line, señor."

Her cheeks burned fiery red.

"But for your information, he is the brother of my good friend. Nothing more, nor less."

She loaded her voice with indignation, but he didn't bother to acknowledge it.

"That's good, because I'm here to warn her—and you—from people who have your best interests at heart."

"Warn us? About what?" She battled to keep an amused note from her voice.

We're descending into farce now.

"About her brother. Alex de Vile. Give him a wide berth. He's dangerous to know."

She glanced up in startled surprise and her first inclination was to laugh in his face.

But as she studied his midnight-blue eyes, she gleaned an icy glitter she hadn't noticed before.

A shard of threat and malice.

His jaw tightened and a tense nerve pulsed under the delicate, faintly blue skin beneath his right eye.

The man is serious.

"Whatever do you mean?"

"It's not complicated. Stay away from Alex. The rich boy has got a warrant out for his arrest, and anyone who gets close to him is asking for trouble. I'd hate to see a beautiful woman harmed needlessly."

A stunned silence opened up between them. Rosie fought the urge to make fun of Garcia's ridiculous warning.

What is this about?

She swallowed hard.

"You understand that the unfortunate death the other night occurred in self-defense? Two men broke into his house and attacked him? He's lucky to be alive."

Garcia sat back in his chair and regarded her as if seeing her from a long distance.

"And he's unlikely to remain so for much longer. That's what I'm saying. Take notice or you may live to regret it."

The debonair cavalier who'd presented himself to the "lovely lady" on the front doorstep twenty minutes ago had vanished.

A man of icy menace stared across the room at her, his jaw set, his eyes intense, his arms folded lazily under the red cape.

She saw a man who killed for sport.

Is he hiding a gun in the fold of that cape?

What might have seemed like a joke ten minutes ago now appeared frighteningly likely.

"Who sent you, Señor Garcia?"

"I'm not at liberty to say."

"If it was Bram Gordon, you can tell him he's got it all wrong."

He eyeballed her in an ominous silence.

"Alex acted in self-defense," she repeated.

"It doesn't matter. He's dead meat. Him and anyone who stands up for him."

Rosie's hands trembled. She stood abruptly.

"Is that it? You'd better be going, señor. And don't expect to hear from Isabella."

Before she'd joined Garcia, she'd instructed Sam to stay close in case she needed him. She guessed he was probably outside the library, his ear pressed hard to the door panels.

"Please leave. Go now."

The door opened, and the house manager loomed in the gap. Alongside Garcia's leonine threat he was a pussycat, but at the sight of him her insides flooded with a freeing relief. Her hands stopped trembling.

Garcia lobbed one more threat, like a Ketchum hand grenade, across the calm silence of the book-lined room.

"I've warned you. Don't blame me if you get hurt. And tell his sister if she wants to live long enough to be a mama, don't go near him."

Long enough to be a mama?

How much did this man know about them? Izzy's pregnancy was a closely guarded secret. Even Sebastian didn't know about it yet. So how could this man be in on it?

That thought was followed hard by another, equally troubling.

I'm not telling Izzy a word about this. She'd be terrified. But I am going to find out how this man knows what he knows.

Sixteen

The Marquésa Fanny de Castellanos y Ordonez leaned against the frigid ship's rail and gazed out onto San Francisco Bay in the pearly dawn light.

The steel of the railing was damp through her fine kid gloves and she gripped it with ferocity as she gazed out on the glassy surface.

The water's as calm as a millpond, and yet you're holding on for dear life.

The air danced with sparkling droplets of mist that dampened sound and gave the scene an ethereal, timeless quality.

I've never been here before, but this place has haunted my dreams for so long, it's familiar.

She lifted her hand from the numbing rail and ran her index finger down her cheek.

The instant chill reminded her that Fanny McLeod, Scottish merchant's daughter and the widow of a former Spanish ambassador to Mexico, was about to step off onto India Dock and embark on the final grand adventure of her life.

She drew her cream cashmere shawl tightly around her neck

and prayed she wasn't too late.

She glanced down at her full skirt in an old Macdonald tartan, the design of which that was at least a hundred years old. The rectangles of green and blue overlaid with red checks glowed in the early light. The trimmings of white lace at collar and cuffs gave the outfit a pleasant sense of authority.

She'd created a sensible, almost military appearance. She knew the task ahead of her was going to draw on every ounce of command and determination she had at her disposal.

I'm sorry, my darling Angel.

She should have come here a year ago, but she couldn't avoid the delay.

You know what Queen Isabella's court is like. I couldn't leave until I got Clara and the children safely back in Scotland.

She hoped her husband, eighteen months dead now, heard her and understood.

"Now it's time to find our boy," she whispered. "Our oldest son."

"I beg your pardon, Marquésa?

A round-faced, dimpled young woman appeared on her shoulder, fair locks hanging in damp strips around a face lit up by bright blue eyes.

"Did you want something?"

Fanny's quietly musing heart leapt in her chest.

"Oh, by Bonnie Prince Charlie, Juliana! You gave me a fright!"

Juliana Dunbar's rosy cheeks creased in merry laughter.

"Oh fie, Lady Fanny," she protested. "You've never been one to panic."

She regarded her employer with warm familiarity. "Even when Andrés went rogue and threatened revolt against the Crown, you were ice cool and talked sense into him. Being a tourist in San Francisco doesn't come close."

If sightseeing was my only purpose for being here, she'd be right, Fanny mused. She turned back to gaze toward the staunch timbers of India Dock, looming out of the foggy whiteout.

She smiled as she stared over the water.

"I'm very much looking forward to being a simple tourist," she said. "You realize I spent a lot of time in New Orleans when Angel was a diplomat during the War, but I never made it this far west, much to my disappointment."

"The War?" Juliana asked. "That was the war between Mexico and America? When they took over California?"

Fanny turned her back on the water. "That's right, Juliana. I'm old enough to recall those days. Isn't that dreadful?"

She smiled dreamily, her thoughts going back nearly three decades.

As a young man, her husband had known this coast when it was Yerba Buena, and Mexican, administered by Spanish Mexican appointees, the *alciades*, as the administrators were called. He'd had close friendships here.

The young woman at her side smiled indulgently.

"Not dreadful at all," she said. "Your ladyship still turns heads."

Fanny raised her finger in admonishment, but her smile showed she was not offended.

"Now that's cheeky, Juliana! But I suppose that's my fault

for bringing my niece along as my traveling companion."

Juliana's mood turned somber.

"How long is it since you had news of Rafael and his family?"

A sharp pain knifed between Fanny's ribs. She stiffened and then stilled herself to mask the deep jab of grief.

"Nearly as long as it is since I've been in America," Fanny said. "Angel was called back to the Spanish court in 1851. We'd only been in Madrid a few months when we got news that Elanora had died in a coaching accident.

"Rafael had a studio in Sacramento, and I wrote to him again and again seeking news, but he never replied."

She leaned back against the ship's rail and clasped her hands against her chest.

"If I can find some photographers who were working in those years and talk to them, I'm hoping to find out what happened. "

She slowly turned back to the water. Gold rimmed the horizon as the morning sun penetrated the mist.

"I gave up hope long ago that he's still alive. But I can't stop believing maybe his children are here. Adults now, of course, but still my grandchildren."

Juliana tucked her lithe form close and slipped her arm around her waist.

"I'm happy to do all I can to help you find answers, Aunt," she whispered.

"That's very sweet of you, dear," Fanny said. "Most of my generation has passed on. It will be helpful to have a young one to help."

She cast a sidelong glance at the eager-faced girl, her eyes brimming with enthusiasm.

"These old chaps might be happier to talk to a pretty young thing like you than an old dowager like me. Rafael was your uncle, after all."

As far as Juliana was concerned, they were here to see the Mathew Brady show and hunt out and talk to some of the old daguerreotype operators.

No need to mention my secret mission. The most arduous task I'll ever undertake.

Seventeen

The words slid sideways out of Bram Gordon's mouth, uttered in a barely audible whisper, but they carried a fierce bite.

"After this, Dionisio. I want a word."

They paced shoulder-to-shoulder down the main aisle of San Francisco's Roman Catholic Cathedral, trailing Alistair Gordon's coffin out to the open grave awaiting him in the grounds outside.

The deep groan of the church organ vibrated in his chest, and Dionisio fancied for a moment the doleful music was warning him of danger.

The old man's face had slumped overnight, like a water-logged hillside that could no longer carry its weight and had fallen ruinously away.

Loose skin that just days ago was firm, hung under from a jaw. He looked ten years older.

Dionisio sneaked another quick sideways scan and noted his cheeks, which before Alistair's death had been plump and ruddy with good health, were caved in and turning a sickly yellow.

The creeping decay was clear in his sloping shoulders, which had taken on the dangerous lean of a collapsing building.

But the glitter in his red-rimmed eyes was ferociously aware, and the statement he'd just spat out was a command, not a request.

Dionisio's stomach tightened, an involuntary response to its accusing edge.

Am I imagining it, or has he got his dander up?

Dionisio waited until they reached the main doors, and cold, fresh air blasted them before responding.

"Is something wrong, Bram?"

"Something more than my boy being dead, you mean?" Gordon glowered. He paused, staring into Garcia's face.

"And what hand did you have in that?"

"Bram!" Dionisio's response was instant, denying. He urgently glanced around, checking to see if anyone was noticing the exchange. The last thing either of them needed was a public scene on the steps of St Mary's.

He moved in closer and spoke into the old man's ear slowly and clearly.

"Whatever's biting you, old fella, leave scratching it till we've finished here, will you? Or you'll have the whole town talking."

***

Later, much later, after Bram Gordon had fulfilled his role of grieving father to the satisfaction of the curious onlookers gathered to watch one of the city's richest men bury his son and heir, they stood toe-to-toe in Gordon's Lick Hotel suite. This was his home away from home.

The ranch was too far out of town to serve as a full-time base, and Bram had split his life between town and country for most of his investing career.

The hotel staff, aware this was a landmark occasion for their valuable guest, had already prepared the suite. They turned the occasional lamps on tables on. They'd set out liquor and fresh cigars in the living area.

Dionisio knew that next door in the sleeping quarters, they'd already be turning down the bedcovers and setting out Bram's night attire.

"What were you getting at, back there?" he asked.

Dionisio figured he'd best go straight on the offensive as soon as they were alone. He wanted to have his say before Bram reached for the whiskey.

"I'm sure waiting to hear it."

Bram squared up to him like a boxer entering the ring.

"When were you going to tell me you were with Alistair that night?"

Dionisio stayed silent.

"The night he died. You were there. Don't deny it."

He's certain of his sources. There's no point in lying.

"Alistair and I went to most places together. Why should that night have been any different?" he countered.

Bram sloshed liquor into a glass, fixing him with a piercing stare as he poured.

"You were an eyewitness to his death, and it never occurred to you to mention it?"

Dionisio shrugged. "I figured it was too painful to talk about right now. But yes, we went there together."

"And why did you do that? Why, as the older and supposedly more mature one, didn't you calm him down and rein him in?"

Dionisio held his ground, maintaining his eyeballing stance.

"Why should I? It was all a bit of fun. We both wanted to do it. I still do. Ridding the world of Alex de Vile? What do you object to about that? Don't you want revenge?"

"That's the thing about you, isn't it, Dino? All brawn and no brain."

Dionisio's blood roared in his ears, but he held himself in tight check.

He's insulting me. But at least he's back to using my nickname.

"No need to be insulting, Bram," he said evenly. "It was all Alistair's idea. I just went along to keep him company."

Bram stepped back and his eyes turned from raging fire to cold ice.

"How convenient. He's not here to contradict you, so you can say anything you like about it, can't you?"

Dionisio followed the big man's lead and widened the gap between them further.

"Now, don't be like that, Bram. We were like brothers, you know that. I'd have been happy to take that bullet for him. It didn't work out that way, that's all."

Bram scoffed. "You'd have been happy to take that bullet? It's not much of a trade in my eyes, as I'm sure you realize. Now who's being insulting?"

"Who told you about it, anyway?"

He knew he was on tricky ground, but he couldn't resist asking the question. He'd make sure they'd suffer for telling tales.

Bram fixed him with alerted suspicion.

"What? So you can take it out on them too?"

He shook his head and dropped his gaze to the chestnut-colored liquid in his glass.

"I want you to keep right out of my business, Garcia. From now on. Ten thousand acres of Los Putos ranch is quietly passing into my ownership in the next few weeks, and I don't want your big maws on it.

"You'll stir up trouble and people will sit up and take notice. Leave it—and the de Vile honcho—alone."

Keep out of my business... Leave it alone... Not much of a trade...

The words flared inside Dionisio Garcia like fiery Comanche arrows.

If you had any idea how wrong you are, buster...

He wanted to lash out, put him right, give it to him with both barrels.

Instead, he swallowed down hard on his rebellion, and the image of that juicy peach, de Vile's "friend," the one he'd fronted today. What was her name? Rosie? Irish red hair, a creamy complexion, laughing eyes, flashed into his mind.

He coughed to subsume a smile that threatened to surface. Bram Gordon would get right chewed up if he knew about his house call today.

Suddenly, he knew what his next move would be.

He'd track that doxy down and see if she led him to Alex de Vile. And then, despite what Bram Gordon said, he'd get his revenge for Alistair. And no one would be any the wiser.

Eighteen

Alex took a firm grasp of Ewan Campbell's hand and shook it vigorously.

"Well, am I pleased to see you? I'm going crazy with cabin fever!"

The minute he heard he had a visitor, he'd headed out to greet Ewan in Kate Buchanan's entryway. The stained-glass cupola overhead threw pretty geometric patterns onto the mosaic tiles under his feet.

"I'm grateful for the temporary refuge, Ewan. But what's the latest news? And when can I go home?"

Ewan stepped back and arched a doubting eyebrow.

"Being a man of leisure surrounded by pretty, available women? Not too many men would consider that a hardship."

Alex threw back his head and laughed. He gestured toward the library. "Come in. I think we can talk in private in here."

He led the way across the rotunda.

"The excellent Christiana was here yesterday, so we're unlikely to be disturbed this time of day."

When they stepped into the silence of the library and checked they had the space to themselves, Ewan asked: "And how have the lessons with the countess been progressing?

"Have you come any closer to digging up why Alistair Gordon came after you?"

Alex slumped down in the armchair closest to the door.

"Not one hint. She appears as flummoxed as I am."

Ewan sank more sedately into the chair opposite him.

"Pity," he said. "Though I admit it's like looking for a needle in a haystack. There have been so many transactions over the last thirty years, many of them murky. And we don't know where to start."

"My time with her hasn't been entirely wasted, though," Alex said quickly.

"I've got a much better idea of Spanish-Mexican history in California. And of what it must have been like for my father to come here.

"I don't know much about his history back East, but I presume he left a photographic studio somewhere like New York to venture overland here."

Ewan's face flushed pink, and he flashed a pleased smile.

"That's what I want to talk about. Why I came to visit today," he clarified.

"There's a photographic exhibition setting up here you'd be interested in. And more importantly, it will probably attract a lot of old guys who know a lot about the beginnings of the business here. Some of them might have even known your father."

"What's the exhibition?" Alex's chest inflated with hope.

Ewan leaned forward, his hands clasped under his chin, elbows on his thighs.

"It's showcasing the work of one of the Civil War photographers. A chap called Mathew Brady. He got himself up to the neck in debt chasing war photos and now he's trying to raise money to stop from going bankrupt. "

"Civil War?" said Alex. "My father was out in California by the time the war started. He had nothing to do with it."

"I know. But he might have known Brady before he came out here. This show isn't the war pictures. People are sick and tired of the war. They don't want to see those anymore."

Alex tapped his fingers impatiently on the arm of the chair.

"What are these pictures, then?"

Ewan grimaced and fixed him straight in the eye.

"They're portraits of society folk. Important people who allowed Brady to take their pictures over twenty years ago. A lot of American presidents, and some of their wives. Dolley Madison for example—James Madison's First Lady."

He ran his hand through his blond hair distractedly. "It's the sort of show that all the old-time boys will want to go to. And one of them might remember your father. It's certainly worth checking out."

Alex gave a dissatisfied growl and screwed up his mouth in frustration.

"How am I going to do that? Stuck in here?"

"That's exactly what I wanted to discuss with you."

Alex stood and prowled the room, stretching his hands over his head as he did.

He went back and stood behind the chair he'd previously sat in and glared down at Ewan.

"What exactly are you suggesting? That I go in disguise or what?"

Ewan chuckled indulgently. "That's one option. But no. Your brother-in-law Sebastian Russell is back in town.

"I've talked to him. We're suggesting he see Seamus O'Halloran and offer to put up a substantial guarantee that you'll stay in town and answer any questions they have.

"You're more or less giving yourself up, but Seb will talk him down on the idea of arresting you immediately. He'll pay enough money to convince him to hold off until he's got more evidence."

Ewan rushed on, as if expecting Alex's objections. "Before you get on your high horse, it's not a bribe. He won't get to keep the money—which you'll have to put up for Seb, I might add.

"But it buys us some breathing room to find out what's going on and discover who was there with Alistair Gordon that night."

"Sounds great," said Alex. "There's only one problem I can see. Apart from Seb convincing O'Halloran to take the bait. What about one of Alistair's friends trying to take me out? Have you thought of that possibility?"

"We have," said Ewan, his expression grave. "And we figure in the meantime you'll need extra security."

"Where will you find that?"

"We're working on it. If you approve, I'll ask Seb to see O'Halloran this afternoon. In the meantime, you stay here. If O'Halloran goes for it, we'll move on to the next stage. You never know, Seb and Jack might like the idea of linking up and working together."

Alex leapt to his feet.

"I don't want Seb put in danger on my behalf. He's going to be a father soon, and I want him alive and well to see that day."

Ewan shrugged. "Jack and Kaleo then. Maybe they'd step in. First, though, Seb's got to get O'Halloran to agree."

Nineteen

A gorgeous bunch of congratulatory after-show flowers in reds and golds lay across Rosie's knee as she waited in Magdalena da Silva's waiting room. Through the thin dressing room walls, she could hear the thunderous applause and appreciative catcalls the star of the show was receiving.

She knew the theater staff, so it was a simple mission to gain access to Magdalena's private quarters. The fact that they'd also performed together in the distant past before Magdalena's meteoric rise was a useful coincidence.

What better place to find out more about Senor Garcia than here?

She might even be the recipient of "between the sheets" confidences. She'd no idea how close Garcia and the smouldering grand dame of the stage were. But gathering salacious gossip wasn't beneath her if it helped keep Isabella safe.

She shivered again as she thought of Garcia's blatant threat. Supposedly made "for their protection," but really a tactic to divide the family and isolate Alex from their support.

What's he done to earn such venom? she asked herself for the umpteenth time. Cavalier, carefree Alex. He wouldn't hurt a fly.

She realized with a start that the cheering was dying away. The final curtain fell with a creak and a thump. She rose expectantly, the flowers outstretched, as Magdalena sailed into her dressing room, perspiring and radiant in an imperial purple gown that gave every appearance of making her an Empress.

Taller and ten years older than Rosie, Magdalena commanded any room she entered. Her dark hair, creamy complexion and flashing black eyes intimidated the staunchest gentleman, and Rosie knew she'd enjoyed the attentions of several wealthy patrons.

Sensing someone in her private sanctum, the star of the show halted abruptly. Then at the sight of Rosie, her majestic pose melted, and her face wreathed in broad smiles.

"Rosanna!" Her pet name for Rosie. She liked that it sounded more Latin.

She flowed across the room and enfolded Rosie in her arms, crushing the flowers in one affectionate movement.

Rosie giggled into her hair and pulled back in mock indignation.

"Careful! I've spent the last of my injury money of these flowers!"

They stared into one another's faces in open pleasure.

"Sure, and you always were a canny lass! Ye must be wanting something, though I dinna ken what."

The broad Irish brogue she'd wittily pulled off within a flash of their meeting sent them both into giggles.

Magdalena flopped into a straight-backed chair in front of

her mirror and gestured for Rosie to perch on another alongside her. She took out a ball of cotton wool and dabbed at her hairline and down her cheeks, touching up her makeup as she went.

"What? Are you expecting a gentleman caller?"

Rosie's voice was alert with alarm.

What if Garcia's coming calling tonight? That would be rum luck.

Magdalena gazed at her from under long, false eyelashes.

"What if I am, *preciosa*?"

Rosie tapped her upper arm playfully.

Another favorite endearment.

"You're amazing. You remember everything. Not just your lines. Everything."

Magdalena's laughter tinkled, and she turned and held her friend by the shoulders, regarding her with affection.

"Still as fresh as an English rose, I see. And yes, I know you object to being called English. But why aren't you still with Lotta? And what have you done to your arm?"

Rosie glanced around the dressing room with a dizzy sense of urgency. "I'll tell you that long, boring story another night," she said. "But you're right. Tonight I want a favor, and I think you're the only one who can help."

Magdalena's merriment sobered. "Anything, *preciosa*. If I can help you, I will."

Quickly, Rosie outlined her tale of woe. Staying with Isabella. Izzy's brother Alex shooting a man in self-defence. And this fellow Dionisio Garcia coming around and threatening her and Isabella.

"He said he was one of your admirers," Rosie said. "And I wondered if you could tell me anything about him. Anything that might help us work out who he's working for and why he's involved?"

Magdalena's bold eyes flickered to the dressing room door and then back to her.

Rosie understood instantly.

"He's the one you're expecting? He mustn't find me here…"

She jumped up.

"Honestly. I think he means us harm. I can't risk him seeing me here."

She bent her ear to the corridor and imagined she could already hear the tramp of heavy leather boots.

Magdalena grabbed the top of her healthy arm and led her across the room to a back door.

"This goes straight out onto a landing at the back of the theater and then down the back stairs. If the door to the street is locked, you'll have to find the usher with the key.

"Meet me tomorrow at Brandy's for a late breakfast. Or an early lunch. Say at 11:30? Us old girls need our beauty sleep like never before."

She pecked Rosie on the cheek, pushed her out the door and closed it decisively behind her, before whirling back into the dressing room to receive her guest.

"More flowers?" Rosie could hear Magdalena's voice, pealing in delight, as she scampered away. "You nearly missed out to one of your competitors."

Her giggles trailed Rosie as she tiptoed downstairs, nervous that at any moment Garcia might barge out after her.

Twenty

Rosie Kelly stared aghast, her emerald eyes flashing daggers at him, her creamy skin flushed with indignation.

"You what?"

The library was as silent as a church, but a companionable hum leaked in from Kate's entry rotunda. The air buzzed with visitors arriving and girls departing for carriage rides and afternoon shopping.

Alex was vaguely aware of the tap of young women's feet on the mosaic tiles, and the occasional cry of delighted recognition as friends met. But in the library, a tense silence stretched between him and his surprise visitor.

"Rosie, don't get upset," Alex soothed, scanning her flawless peach complexion with a warming sense of gratification. "There's nothing to worry about."

She cares. That can't be a bad thing.

"Nothing to worry about? Haven't you heard a word I've said? I've just spent the last twenty minutes telling you about this arch rogue, an associate of Bram Gordon's? And you say there's nothing to worry about? Magdalena says he and Alistair were best friends."

Like a rising wind, the pitch of her voice spiraled upward as she spoke.

He let a long pause ride in the air between them, and then took a deep, pacifying breath.

"It's not that I don't take you seriously, Rosie."

He gestured to the tray of hot coffee one of Kate's staff had deposited on the occasional table between them.

"Please. Sit down and let me pour you a coffee while we talk this over."

Rosie remained upright, glaring in silence for a long minute, and then sat with a resigned bump and a frustrated huff.

"I can't see what there is to discuss," she said.

"It comes down to the simple question of whether you want to live or not."

"Oh Rosie, stop being overdramatic," he protested, pausing mid-pour and smiling at her across the small table.

She continued to bore into him with stormy eyes.

"You're dismissing Magdalena's information. Why? Because she's an actress and so obviously 'over-dramatic'?"

She curdled the word on her tongue, letting the sarcasm leak out of it.

"It's not that," he protested. "Nothing like that. I'm as desperate to find out more about what's going on as you are. I can't prove my innocence stuck in here. All my researching of old records and the Countess's stories, it's getting me nowhere. I'm wasting time. I can't stand it any longer."

Rosie's curvy mouth set itself in a mutinous line.

"You'll have no time left to waste if this Dionisio character gets you. I'm telling you. He's dangerous. Even Magdalena thinks so, and he's always on his best behavior around her. She's seen enough of men like him to know his type."

Alex gave a light shrug, and her eyes flashed angrily in response.

"Rosie…" he said in a wheedling tone. "I'm leaving this place. I have to. I'll go crazy if I don't.

"Now Sebastian's back, he's setting it up with O'Halloran. They're doing a deal. Ewan describes it as like getting bail with no charges laid."

She opened her mouth to object.

"And they're organizing extra security for me as well, 'just in case.' That should make anyone who wants to come after me think twice."

"Why aren't you taking anything I say seriously?" she objected. "He turned up at Isabella's. He made threats against us about what would happen if we helped you.

"Magdalena says he's some kind of 'fix it' man for geezers like Bram. He likes to rub shoulders with them and pretend he's in their class.

"If he thought he could win favor with Gordon by killing you, he'd do it in a wink. Can't you see that?"

Alex sighed.

"I take you seriously, Rosie. I do." He knew he was protesting too much, weakening his argument.

"I'll make absolutely sure I have extra security wherever I go. And I'll organize extra security for you and Izzy, too."

"We won't need it if you're dead," she cried. "You said there were two men who broke into your house that night Bram's son died. What if this Dionisio guy was the other one with Alistair that night?

"Maybe he's scared you could identify him. Did you have time to see that man at all?"

For a second, Alex's heart turned over at the thought, and then he instantly dismissed it.

"You're letting your imagination run away with you," he said. "I didn't see him, because I was under the desk. He was gone by the time I got up to look. He didn't hang around, that's for sure."

"He didn't care about his pal? He didn't stay to check whether he was still alive?"

Once again, Rosie's questioning brought him up short.

She's right. Why didn't he back up his companion?

A long silence hung between them as Alex gazed at her, frowning.

He let out a long breath he wasn't aware he'd been holding. Rosie's voice penetrated his foggy thinking.

"If he was a paid hit man, I wonder why he didn't stay and take a second shot at you?"

Alex shook his head, unable to take his eyes off Rosie's grave face.

Where is she going with this?

"I guess he wasn't a paid hit man," he said. "And that makes it less likely it was this Dionisio guy, doesn't it? From what you say, he's a killer, so he would have stayed to finish the job."

***

I guess he wasn't a paid hit man.

Rosie bit her lip, lost in deep concentration.

He's destroying my line of argument by agreeing with me.

Magdalena said Dionisio and Alistair were like brothers. They were always out carousing together. So, Alex is right, isn't he?

A good friend wouldn't run out on a mortally wounded companion, would they? And a hit man would stay to finish the job.

Maybe it wasn't the Garcia fellow after all.

Rosie stared across the yawning gap between her and Alex and wondered what it was about him that got under her skin.

She stared at his sparkling slate-colored eyes, always alive with mischievous humor.

His finely tuned mouth, which crinkled at the edges when life's ironies displayed themselves, which was often. He always looked on the bright side.

The guy is an irrepressible fountain of optimism. That's it.

And why did she find that alluring and irritating all at the same time?

She shivered.

He'd just had life so easy he didn't have a clue how tough it could be. Was that it? How unfairly good fortune was shelled out?

He bounced along, expecting everything to work out fine. And so far, for him anyway, it had. Even his adoption by Senator Hector de Vile had turned tragedy into opportunity.

She wanted to shake him by the shoulders until his teeth rattled and scream at him that life wasn't like that. Not for most people.

But his cavalier remark had brought her up short. She'd given no thought to the minute-by-minute events of the fatal night when

Alistair Gordon died. Now she ran through it again in her mind.

Why did the second man vanish so quickly after Alistair went down? And was Alex on the right track, frivolous though his remark might appear?

If they had been intent on killing Alex, wouldn't the second man have stayed and finished the job? Alex was on the floor under the desk, an easy target.

She brought her hands to her cheeks and clasped them. She was grasping to hold on to good sense amidst the whirling contradictions that threatened to overwhelm her.

She sank back into the back cushions of the chair she'd been teetering in, and let out another deep breath.

"Did you notice anything at all that night?" she asked. "Any smells? Beer? Brandy? Cologne? Anything at all? Did you hear their voices? Did they exchange any words?"

Alex averted his eyes to the Oriental rug. He screwed his eyes shut in intense focus.

"Smells…" he said, sounding almost as if he was in a trance.

"Probably at least one of them wore cologne… and yes, their breath smelt of beer."

He opened his eyes wide.

"The only hard evidence we found was bullets lodged in the back wall of the studio and two small pieces of sequined braid Kaleo picked up. One at the front door and one in the studio where they'd been standing.

"He's got eagle eyes, that guy. It was lying there like it might have got ripped off by a sudden movement."

"Sequined braid?" Rosie's heart leaped to her throat. "Like the old conquistadors wore?"

Alex frowned. "I suppose." He shrugged. "I don't really know."

There was a tap on the door, and Ewan Campbell poked his head into the opening frame.

"Oh. Sorry to interrupt, Alex. But it's all set. O'Halloran's agreed."

Alex jumped up, suddenly energized.

"You mean I can leave? Right now?"

He threw an apologetic glance in Rosie's direction.

"My sister's friend Rosie Kelly has been trying to talk me out of leaving," he said to Ewan.

"Rosie, this is Ewan Campbell, who's helping me get to the bottom of all this."

Rosie tipped her head in Ewan's direction.

"And how is that going, Mr. Campbell? Any major breakthroughs on the horizon?"

Ewan flicked his eyes to Alex, as if to say, "who is this forthright young woman?", and then shot her a sheepish grin.

"Nothing imminent, I'm afraid," he admitted. "We've come up against a lot of dead ends so far."

"And what's your theory for why the second man didn't stay longer?"

"The second man?" Campbell's face crumpled in confusion.

"The second gunman. Why did he scarper so quickly? He could have stood his ground and taken another potshot at Alex. He could have gone to the aid of the Gordon boy. Why didn't he do either of those things?"

Ewan stared at her, his mouth pulled into a perplexed scowl.

"Do you know, until this moment I had given little thought?

I can't scramble together a satisfactory answer at this moment."

"So, you're willing to put us all at risk—Alex, Isabella and even insignificant little me—just so Alex can go to a photographic show? You know there's a dangerous man making threats against us?"

Ewan's head swung from Rosie to Alex and back again.

"What is she talking about, Alex? Let me in on the secret, will you?"

Twenty-one

Former California governor Carlos Montoya Alvarado shot the Marquésa Fanny de Castellanos y Ordonez a wintry smile over his balloon glass of brandy.

"You know, I bowed out of California politics when the Americanos took over."

It was a rhetorical question. Of course, she knew. Carlos was one of Angel's closest friends when she first met her husband, and she'd heard all about his doings from Angel.

But it had been many years since they'd met in person, and the debonair ladies' man of her memory had thickened up and slowed down.

Another reminder our time is running short, she thought, as she fingered the icy glass.

Carlos bowed over his brandy as if protecting it from predation.

Still rather over fond of his drink, she silently observed. That would partly explain the sense that his once acute mind had also clouded with the years.

She was sipping mint julep with peach brandy rather than bourbon. In the quiet room she sat, questioning whether the pain of recalling what the passing of the years had stolen was worth the gentle pleasure of a nostalgic reunion.

Their subdued meeting took place in the Society of California Pioneers club rooms on the corner of Montgomery and Gold Streets. Carlos was a halting ghost of the man she once knew, but Fanny fiercely nursed the secret hope he would have some good news about her son Rafael.

Any kind of news would be welcome. That he was still alive would be a miracle. She'd had no replies to her letters over many years, but there could be an explanation for that, couldn't there?

I won't ask about him just yet. Leave it to the end.

Carlos—born in California in the early 1800s—had lived under three flags—Spanish, Mexican and American—and was a certified founding member of the "Pioneers." He was frequently found there reminiscing about old times.

When they'd last met, he was an ambitious upstart, soon to become—at twenty-seven—the youngest governor the state had ever seen.

"We had a few golden years in the fifties when the Gold Rush settlers flooded in, wanting our ranch meat to eat. But those days are long gone.

"I've been a struggling ranchero landowner for the last fifteen years, Fanny. And for the last decade I've had to spend money I don't have defending my rights to live on the place.

"My wife Maria's father willed the property to her. But now she has to prove ownership all over again to the Land Claims Court."

He fell into a deep coughing fit at the injustice of it all.

"The land we've lived on for the last forty years…"

Fanny made a sympathetic tut-tutting sound with her tongue against her teeth.

"After the Hidalgo Treaty supposedly guaranteed original settler rights, too."

Alvarado snorted.

"Don't we know it? Like many other old Californios, we'll probably have to sell what we've left with to pay the bills. I doubt if there will be anything left for our children once the lawyers and land sharks have taken their bites."

He took another belt of sustaining liquor.

"How about you? I was sorry to hear of Angel's death."

"Yes. It's coming for us all, isn't it?" She gave him a resigned smile.

"Memento mori." Her voice cracked, refusing to sustain her bravado.

"It's really why I'm here, Carlos. To settle any loose ends Angel left in our affairs before I join him."

Alvarado's jowly face creased into a grimace, his black brows dipping under a white fringe.

Her friend had always been a ladies' man, and besides his legitimate family, it was widely known he kept a lifelong mistress and had recognized several "natural" daughters.

"I seem to recall Angel had a share in a ranch at one point—before he got called back to Madrid?"

"Your memory serves you well. It was before I knew him, but his mind was consumed with it in his last days. I promised him I'd come back and discover what's happened to it. One of our children might still be interested in moving here."

Alvarado laughed in her face, his full lips widening to show straight white teeth that flashed with good humor.

"Que Dios te oiga."

I hope God hears you.

Fanny chuckled. "You think I'm going to need the Almighty's help?"

"Who of your family do you think might want to take it up?"

The pain that permanently lodged under her ribs like a sleeping lion reared up and roared. She gasped and clutched her side.

"Marquésa. Fanny. Are you all right?"

Alvarez rose in alarm and reached toward her.

She took in a few deep breaths.

"I'll recover soon," she panted, still holding her side. "It's Rafael. Whenever I think of him, my heart breaks."

Alvarado waited in silence, shaking his head sadly.

After a long minute, he said quietly, "Losing any child is terrible. But losing a first son? And a fine lad like Rafael? That's tragic."

Fanny stared, her face a ghostly white.

"You know for sure? He's dead? We've never... no one ever..."

She buried her face in her hands.

Alvarado got up. She heard him ordering brandy for the Marquésa.

He returned and resumed his place at her side, sitting quietly, giving her a private moment to grieve.

After a few more minutes, she lowered her hands and gazed at him through wet lashes.

He thrust the brandy toward her.

"Drink," he said. "You need this. You truly didn't know?"

She shook her head and took the glass in both hands to steady her trembling. She gulped several mouthfuls of burning liquid, feeling an immediate sense of fortification in her veins.

Tears leaked from her dark eyes.

"We heard about the coach accident. About Elanora's death. We got official notification of that from the Sacramento sheriff's office. We heard the rumor that the twins were missing, but never anything confirmed.

"Our letters went unanswered. We never heard another word."

She grasped the glass like an anchor.

"I can imagine what state Rafael must have been in. His sun rose and set on Elanora. But we couldn't come and see him.

"Things were very dangerous in Madrid. Angel had his work cut out protecting our other son and son-in-law from arrest. You never knew from one week to the next who was wielding the power."

Her hands shook, and she lifted the rejuvenating brandy to her lips once more.

"You must have heard what Madrid was like. Queen Isabella played her favorites and left the prime minister or whoever to govern. It was a perilous place to be."

She exhaled.

"It's only now, a year after Angel's death, when I've got all the family back in Scotland, that I could devote time to coming here.

"I knew after all this time of silence it was unlikely Rafael had survived, but I had a secret hope… For a miracle, you know?"

She drew a handkerchief from a reticule at her hip and wiped her eyes, as if noticing for the first time in minutes that her face was wet.

"What did you hear about it? How did you hear?"

Alvarado spread his hands wide and let his broad shoulders and lift and fall in a gesture of helplessness.

"A photographer mentioned it. He died in Sacramento. His friend said he lost the desire to live. He simply ran out of steam, working as a photographer right to the end, I believe."

Fanny stared at him, her eyes wide with pain, but inside a frozen numbness consumed her.

Alvarado continued in his soft voice.

"Ohh… it was a few years ago now, I think. He married again, so I heard, anyway, but he never truly recovered."

"His photographer colleague said, *'Su muerte la dejo accent destrozada.'"*

He died of a broken heart.

Alvarado gave a solemn nod and repeated in a whisper. *"Su muerte la dejo accent destrozada.'"*

Fanny gazed down at the backs of her wrinkled hands, and she and Alvarado settled into a companionable silence.

Then she lifted her head and fixed Carlos with a bleak stare.

"You're right. I'm sure he died of a broken heart. But what of his beautiful children? The twins? Were they ever found?"

Alvarado gazed at her with deepest pity in his big brown eyes.

Wordlessly, he shook his head.

Then, one word. "No. I don't believe so."

"What about Graysie, the oldest one? She didn't die in the coach crash."

"Graysie? Oh, yes, she's a well-known singer here now. Come to think of it, I've heard little of her lately, but she used to appear in shows around town."

Fanny finished her glass of brandy and dabbed her wet face.

"Well, Alvarado, I was hoping to catch up on local news, but I wasn't expecting so much of it all in one go. I think you'd better see me back to my hotel. I need to sleep on it."

Carlos Alvarado gently reached out and restrained her arm as she rose from her chair.

"Just before you do, Marquésa. One last thing."

She raised her head expectantly.

"We didn't finish the conversation about Angel's land. Who was his partner in it? Do you know?"

Fanny took a deep, resuscitating breath.

"The Valaquez family, I believe. Hernandez, the governor's brother, was his great friend. Is he still alive?"

Alvarado shook his head. "Hernandez? No, he died not long ago. And his son, Emmanuel, was gunned down in a barroom brawl a few months before that."

Fanny's mouth screwed up in a grimace.

"We thought it strange that no one has ever contacted us about the land. Do you know if they'd begun proceedings to renew their legal claim, and what's happened to it?"

"Hernandez had been muddle-headed for some time before he died. Emmanuel was the only son I knew of. He didn't amount to much, I'm afraid. Too fond of the drink."

"Isn't there anyone else in the family I could talk to?"

Alvarado made to rise. "I'll make it my business to find out, and we can talk again tomorrow.

"All I'd say in the meantime is, don't make any official approach to the Land Claims office or anyone else, until you've got yourself properly lawyered up. The land sharks prowl that place, waiting to pounce on the innocent."

"That bad, is it?"

"And worse," said Alvarado, the beetling brows lowered over his sour face.

"Look out for a young lawyer called Ewan Campbell. He knows his way around the old documents and he's one of the few honest chaps around."

He gazed into his empty glass and glanced back up into Fanny's expectant face.

"Being knowledgeable doesn't mean he'll always win, mind you. He fought for some of his own family lands for a decade and the court finally found against him just last month."

As Fanny rose, her legs momentarily wobbled and then took up her weight.

"I doubt I'll sleep a wink, but I must try to get some rest," she said.

"And then tomorrow, I'll do my best to track down Graysie Castellanos."

Alvarado gave her his first genuine smile in the last thirty minutes.

"Oh, that one's simple, Marquésa. I'm sure she'll be at the Mathew Brady portraits show later this week. As you know, her father and Brady worked together in New York. It's highly likely she'll be there."

Finally. Something's going my way.

Fanny started for the door, her legs feeling ten years older than when she'd walked in here an hour ago.

She paused against the doorjamb and uttered a silent prayer.

Please Lord, let me finish my race strongly.

Twenty-two

Graysie stared at the woman in the doorway of her Lick Hotel suite and grabbed wildly for the door frame as her knees buckled under her.

She gasped and righted herself, her eyes filling with tears, because before her stood an image of what Rafael would have looked like if he'd lived to grow old.

The straight, finely modeled nose, the piercing dark eyes under elegantly arched brows and a high forehead. Even given the fact that the person standing before her was a woman, an older but still beautiful woman…

She could see her stepfather in every feature, even the shell-like ears that shone with fine ruby earrings.

Her breath caught in her throat and she dashed the back of her hand to her right cheek to brush aside the tears.

"Marquésa…" The word came out of her throat, thick and strangled, blocked by the lump that had formed there.

"I'm very sorry," she gasped, her hand going to her mouth. "It's such a shock to see you. You're so like…"

She couldn't voice his name.

My father. Rafael.

She swivelled back into the room, unable to hold in the shock, the unexpressed grief rolling over her like a mountainous ocean wave.

She fell into the arms of her rock, her husband Nathan, who'd stood back, silently watching, and she sobbed into his shoulder.

Nathan stroked her back consolingly and shot a conspiratorial look at their visitor.

"Give her a few minutes," he said in a deep whisper.

"It's a lot to come to terms with in a short time."

***

Truth was, Fanny had decided within minutes of returning to her hotel room the previous night that she would not wait to lock eyes on her granddaughter Graysie Castellanos at a public show like a photography exhibition.

The last time she'd seen the child, she'd been a babe in arms, and the reunion was far too private and tender to take place in a hall of curious bystanders.

She'd made a quick check with the hotel concierge—did he know where Graysie Castellanos stayed when she was in town?

She guessed she'd be here for the photographic show, and couldn't believe her ears when he advised her they were staying in the same hotel.

Another quick errand thanks to Juliana—a note delivered to Graysie's rooms—had set up this meeting the next morning.

She suspected neither of them had got much sleep because of it.

Nathan indicated with his head that she and Juliana should please come in.

"We'll only be a moment. Please, make yourselves comfortable."

She and Juliana settled themselves on a gold velour couch, and a young woman who was probably a nanny or governess appeared followed by two of children.

An imp with dark, corkscrew ringlets and a mischievous smile, and a smaller, sturdy blond lad Fanny could see bore a close resemblance to Nathan.

Nathan shot her a quick smile and said, "Marquésa, we're proud to present our children, Minette and George."

Children… my great grandchildren… Oh my goodness.

Fanny clasped Juliana's hand as a wave of dizziness momentarily unbalanced her.

She put her hand to her brow.

"Thank goodness I'm sitting, or I might have fainted with excitement," she said, smiling at the children.

"I'm very pleased to meet you."

"And their governess—Nanny Blanchett," Nathan said.

The children regarded Fanny with solemn eyes.

"My mummy is from France," said the dark-haired moppet. "Where are you from?"

Fanny smiled. "I'm from Scotland and Spain. Have you heard of those countries?"

"Of course," said Minette, with a little skip on the spot. "Sissy always reads me stories about faraway places."

Nanny Blanchett took her hand. "We're off to the park now, little one. Say goodbye to the Marquésa. We'll see her another time."

Graysie lifted her head, her cheeks still wet.

The little girl's face puckered. "Are you all right, Sissy? Why are you crying?"

Sissy? Whose child is this?

Graysie gave her an adoring glance and turned to take her in her arms.

"I'm crying because I am happy, my darling Minette. Sometimes we do that, you know."

Minette's pink cheeks creased into a giggle.

"That's silly," she said.

"We've got a very special visitor. Marquésa Fanny is my father's mummy. And she's been living a very long way away, so we haven't seen her for ages."

The child's face sobered. "I see. So, you're happy and sad at the same time. Like I am sometimes because my mummy isn't here anymore."

"Exactly like that, my sweet imp."

She glanced across to the governess. "Nanny Blanchett, how about you take the children downstairs for ice creams and then to the park, and they can say hello to the Marquésa later on? Give us a chance to catch up in the meantime."

The governess dipped her head with a smile and moved to gather the children to her side.

"Who wants a chocolate ice?"

***

In the silence that fell after the children's departure, Graysie sank into the couch opposite her visitors, and leaned forward with a great sigh.

"So sorry about getting weepy," she said. "It's all been a shock and you so look so like Rafael..." Her eyes flickered uneasily.

"I have a great deal to tell you, and some of it may be uncomfortable for you, so please, don't be embarrassed if you too find yourself overwhelmed.

"We've got two lifetimes to catch up on… And a lot has happened…"

She took a deep swallow.

"The first gut-wrenching thing I have to tell you, right up front, is that I am not Rafael's daughter. Not his biological daughter, you understand.

"In every other way, he is still my adored dad."

She tipped her head on one side, hesitating.

"Did you know this at the time of my birth?"

She curled her mouth up at the corners in an apologetic curve and then rushed ahead.

"Because I didn't. He was always my treasured pa to me, growing up. I've only discovered the truth recently."

Fanny glanced sideways at Juliana and said: "I never knew for sure, and I didn't feel it was my place to ask. But let's say it doesn't surprise me. Rafael was always such a tender-hearted man."

Graysie nodded, her eyes shining.

"That he was. I wish he was still here for some amazing news I have for you next." She took a deep breath.

"We found the twins," she exclaimed.

"They've come back from the dead!! And they're both wonderful people, here in San Francisco, so you'll be able to meet them."

***

The Marquésa Fanny de Castellanos y Ordonez was a resilient Scotswoman with a lifetime of diplomatic training that enabled her to mask her emotions and give nothing of her true feelings away.

But when she heard the words "We found the twins," the despair that had swept over her the previous night at the long-suspected confirmation of Rafael's death was swamped with giddy joy.

Her hands came up to her mouth and she cried out.

"You what?" She twisted her head this way and that, unable to sit still, finding it difficult to breathe or believe.

"The twins?" She expired the words in a long breath. "Here? In San Francisco"

"That's right. Here." Graysie's pink face shone with an inner elation. "Isn't that wonderful?"

"Oh, my dear Graysie, you couldn't have told me anything that would make me happier. And more amazed."

As they'd been speaking, Nathan slipped in, followed soon after by a hotel staffer bearing a tray of coffee and cookies. Graysie beamed.

"Let's get the morning tea served, and then you can hear the whole remarkable story."

***

Hours later, after Fanny had got to know the children a little and the coffee tray cleared away, Fanny turned to Graysie with a tender smile.

"We both need some quiet time before tomorrow's exhibition," she said. "I expect that will be an emotional time as well. I'm having a private reception beforehand. I'd love for you to attend."

Anticipating her next move, Juliana opened a reticule and drew out a stiff white gold deckle-edged card and a fountain pen and handed them to the older woman.

Fanny flattened the card on her knee and wrote on it with black, flowing strokes. When she glanced up, Graysie was staring at her, her jaw dropped, and her green eyes wide open.

"Ohhhhh." Suddenly, her hand flew to her mouth.

Her nose stung with the horrible smell of bleach. Her fingers twitched with the tickling softness of kitten fur, although she knew there was no cat in the room.

"Heaven's above, I've just remembered something," she cried.

She reached out and gingerly took the invitation card that still lay on Fanny's knee and gazed at it.

"Yes. I thought so. It's exactly the same. All these years later. It's the same handwriting."

She clasped her hands together in wonder.

"You wrote to Father. One day, it came to his studio."

She paused, and closed her eyes tight, as if seeing a scene in her mind's eye.

And then she opened them again, sparkling bright and clear, staring straight at Fanny.

"You wrote him a letter, and I got into such trouble over it."

Twenty-three

So Rafael is dead.

The miracle Fanny had long prayed for was not to be. She needed time to grieve for the son she would never see again, before she could pick up the pieces of her life and carry on.

A son finally confirmed dead, yes, but a whole family of descendants to rejoice in. Fanny's heart expanded in delight.

The only stone in her shoe was the realization Angel had died, not knowing his family in California was doing mighty well, despite the setbacks.

She sunk her shoulders beneath the hot rose-scented bathwater and let go once and for all of her dream of seeing her firstborn son alive again.

On the marble shelf that ran around the Lick Hotel bathroom, cedarwood candles flickered, providing soothing light and a calming aroma.

She submerged all but her face and breathed in its healing perfume. As the minutes ticked by, the tension in her muscles drained away, and a bright clarity of mind replaced her dark confusion.

Graysie had explained everything to her so well. Temptation

Thompson, always in Graysie's mind. "Mrs. T." The punishing "second wife."

They'd never married, Graysie had assured her.

The woman's jealous reaction to the letter with the Royal Spanish emblem the child had recognized was something special.

It was a simple matter to conclude that she'd resented a ghost and had withheld all the letters she'd sent.

"Father was lost without my mother and the twins," Graysie recounted. "They forbade me to mention Elanora's name, because Mrs. T. would fly into a blue rage and threaten to quit. His photography was his life after mother died."

Tears leaked into the bathwater as Fanny recalled Graysie's face as she'd spoken of life after her mother's death. Her fresh cheeks were scored with deep lines of grief.

"Rafael was loving to me when he remembered I was there, but much of the time he was in his own world."

Fanny squeezed water from the fat sea sponge over her head to wash away the tears.

She'd known the chances of discovering Rafael was still alive were slender to nil, but she'd continued to hope for the impossible.

Now she had to lay to rest her fantasy of him coming through the door and sweeping her off her feet, his powerful arms at her waist as he whirled her around, both of them laughing hysterically.

How many times had she lain awake at midnight and imagined just such a scene?

She'd felt the smooth touch of his favorite leather jacket against her cheek as he pulled her close and hugged her. She'd breathed in his familiar woodsy green cologne, a mix of cedarwood and geranium.

Recalling that fragrance, thinking of him buried deep in his grief. Receiving none of her comforting words, ignorant to the torrents of love she'd poured out on dozens of pages that had never reached him…

She touched her cheeks and realized she was weeping all over again.

A dam that had remained locked for two decades had finally burst open.

She could offer an open-eyed, heart-bared lament for her firstborn. He'd already been ferried across the crystal river, the river of death, and had probably welcomed the journey.

She pulled herself up out of the bath, and as the delicious water streamed off her body, she imagined herself reborn. She was like a goddess, risen from the depths.

The old is gone, and the new is come.

***

When Fanny summoned Juliana later that evening, her niece instantly sensed something had changed.

Her aunt sat in a cushioned bath chair, her legs stretched comfortably in front of her, but despite the conveyance, she'd never looked in better form. The dark cloud of sorrow that had hung about her like a winter storm had gone, replaced by pink-cheeked zeal for getting things done.

"You don't have to tell me I don't need this chair, bairn," she said with a twinkly smile that lit up her peat-bog brown eyes.

"Don't worry. I'm practicing for tomorrow night, and jolly comfortable it is too. I might decide to get one for occasions where I'm expected to stand around for a long time."

Juliana laughed. "For someone who's always protesting about not wanting to be treated like an old lady, it's certainly a surprise. What's behind it?"

"I've got an extremely important night tomorrow. And I want to be sure I'm at my best for it."

"Tomorrow night? But isn't that the night of the Mathew Brady Photographic Exhibition? I know you were looking forward to it, but has something changed? You didn't seem this excited about it yesterday."

"Of course, something has changed," Fanny said. "You were there yesterday. You heard what Graysie said.

"I'm going to meet grandchildren I've never seen before and I want to look my best for them."

"But… but…" Juliana stared at her aunt, her stomach hollowing out at her joyful face.

"I thought the news that Rafael was dead would be the last straw for you. You seemed to hold on to that hope like it was a lifeline.

"Now that line has been destroyed, and you have risen like a nymph in a Botticelli painting, all freshness and light. How is this possible?"

"Oh, my dear, you might know your classics, but do you know your Old Testament? Do you recall King David, when his first son with Bathsheba died? Do you recall what he said from the depths of his grief?

Juliana stared. Her tongue locked in her mouth.

"He'd refused to eat a bite. He was in such intense distress while his son struggled to live. But after he died, he got up and washed and prepared to eat. And when his astonished attendants asked why, do you know what he said?"

Juliana shook her head, still unable to find the words to speak.

Fanny shook her head in mock disapproval, her eyes sparkling like a fresh spring.

"You really should know your Bible better, my dear."

She took a long pause and then spoke, her voice coming out in strangled snatches.

"But now that he is dead, why should I fast?" She hesitated and dabbed damp eyes.

"Shall I be able to bring him back any more? I shall go to him rather: but he shall not return to me."

A long silence stretched between them, as if they were both making mute farewells to a man who'd disappeared long ago.

Then Fanny pointed to a nearby chair. "Come sit and listen. I've sworn Graysie to secrecy. I want to surprise this new grandson of mine. Rafael's son. We've got a lot of planning to do."

Twenty-four

"No Isabella tonight?" Two parallel worry lines furrowed between Graysie's brows as she stepped forward to greet Alex.

He paused at the entryway of the Brady exhibition to breathe the air of hallowed ground, preparing himself to see the work of one of America's most famous photographers.

Mathew Brady had made a name for himself during the Civil War, photographing battlefield scenes never before caught on camera, and before that capturing the portraits of the nation's most prominent leaders, war generals and every US president of his time bar one.

Black and white portraits positioned on stands filled the Lick House ballroom. Alex's excitement elevated with the reverent background buzz coming from the show's first arrivals. They were already flitting among the exhibits like early bees in a flower meadow.

His half-sister Graysie loitered, obviously awaiting his arrival. Despite the anxious pitch of her inquiry after Isabella, she too vibrated with pent-up excitement.

"No Isabella, no. Sebastian's only been back a couple of days. She's loving having him back so much. She's staying home."

He shot Graysie a lazy grin. "If I give the show an excellent report, she might come later this week. She says photography is my thing, not hers. Why?"

Graysie responded with an unconvincing shrug. "Nothing. I wanted to make sure she's well, that's all."

He glanced around, eager to get started on his examination of Brady's work. Well, Brady and his band of jobbing photographers. He knew hired men whose work Brady had claimed under his studio rights had taken many of Brady's pictures.

"I gather this is mainly Mathew Brady's non-military stuff, isn't it? From what I see looking around, that's the case."

Graysie nodded, and again he was struck by her sense of burning anticipation. "That's right," she said. "There are some fascinating family photos I want to show you."

It was well known that Brady had extended himself financially, capturing the war pictures, investing a fortune in printing up plates he expected the government to buy from him once hostilities ceased. After all, he'd recorded an epochal conflict.

But a cash-strapped Washington resisted the purchase, and private collectors didn't want to dwell on the gruesome carnage after the war ended.

Rumor had it Brady was close to bankruptcy, and this show was touring the nation to raise funds for the impoverished artist.

Graysie hung on his shoulder, seemingly reluctant to let him go.

"Have you already looked around?" he asked. "You must have got here early."

She shrugged. "A quick look," she said. "I think you'll really like it." She hesitated.

"Can I walk with you?"

He hesitated.

She gazed at him, her eyes darting with mischief.

What is this?

"There's one I'd like you to see," she added. "But no hurry. Take your time."

Alex laughed out loud.

"Graysie, you might be a wonderful singer, but you're a lousy actress. You need Rosie to give you lessons."

She halted mid stride and stared. "What's that supposed to mean?" she growled.

"Look, never mind. For goodness' sakes, let's get this over so I can wander through here at my own pace. What is it you want to show me?"

"There's a portrait here I want you to see. And I want to be with you when you do. Can I conduct you to it and then leave you in peace?"

He searched her face for clues, but her dancing eyes and pink cheeks gave nothing more away.

"Is it good news or bad?" he asked. "I'm not sure I can stand any more negativity. I'm still fending off a murder charge, I hate to remind you."

She burst out laughing. "Oh, for goodness' sakes…" She took him by the elbow.

"Let's not waste any more time talking. Come with me."

She wove her way to the other side of the room and drew up before a historical wedding portrait.

"What? You want me to look at a wedding shot?"

"That's right," she said. "Cast your photographer's eyes over this one."

He leaned into the daguerreotype frame. From the clothes the couple wore, he guessed it had probably been taken twenty years ago, long before the Civil War.

So, this was one of Brady's early efforts, from when he'd opened his New York studio and the daguerreotype was the latest thing.

He leaned in and absorbed every detail. A handsome wedding party, an older couple who were probably the parents of the bride, and a radiant young woman beside her dark-haired groom.

His eye traced the detail of the faces, and a strange sense of familiarity sent tingles up his backbone. He'd seen at least one of these faces before.

He glanced at Graysie and clutched at her arm to steady himself as the light-headedness threatened to topple him.

"That's..." He struggled to breathe. The words stuck in his throat.

"That's our mother..."

The family study on his wall. The daguerreotype he'd rescued from Durant's Sacramento studio.

"It's the same woman as in that one on my wall. The one with us all in it except Rafael. That must be him..."

The words tumbled forth, sounding dreamy, wondrous.

"That is a photo of my father. Taken by the great Mathew Brady."

He exhaled a disbelieving breath.

Graysie's exquisite face glowed with the satisfaction of a mission accomplished.

He turned back and stepped closer to examine every detail, and his eye was caught by the identifier posted on the wall beside it.

New York, February 1848: Mr. and Mrs. Rafael de Castellanos y Ordonez, with the groom's father, the Spanish ambassador to Mexico, the Marqués Angel de Castellanos y Ordonez, and the bride's aunt, Miss Gloria Grayson, a well-known New York educator.

"I don't believe it," he said. His heart pounded in his chest, and his eyes swung wildly to Graysie, standing beaming beside him.

"You kept this a secret? Why didn't you tell me? When did you know?"

"Just yesterday. And sorry. I was sworn to secrecy."

"To secrecy? By whom?"

He ran the back of his hand across his brow, fending off a choking sensation, like he was running out of air.

She took his arm consolingly. "Alex, I'm sorry I couldn't warn you. But now, there's someone I want you to meet."

Twenty-five

Alex did a 180-degree turn following Graysie's lead and saw two older grand dames parked on a lounge suite close by. One of them he already knew.

"Countess! My sincere apologies. I didn't see you there. Graysie was demanding all of my attention."

He stepped forward, took Christiana's hand and kissed the back of it in the courtly manner he knew delighted her.

"Are you the culprit who's spinning secrets with my sister?"

Christiana's smile spread from ear to ear on her worn face.

"Not me, my dear boy, but my friend here."

His eyes trailed to the other woman, seated on a matching gold couch at right angles to Christiana's.

A majestic older woman with piercing dark eyes and bountiful raven hair, without a hint of white despite her age, gazed back at him.

She nestled in a blizzard of purple silk ruffles on the top of a bodice that fell to a V-shaped waistline, neatly fitting the lady's slender waist.

His eyes traced from her waistline to her face, and he saw her sparking intelligence tracking his every move. Embarrassed at having been caught checking her out, he stepped forward, arm extended.

"My apologies." He laughed. "Forgive me. You've quite taken my breath away."

Her elegant brows raised in delight, and the slanting aristocratic cheeks creased into a warm smile.

She scooched along the couch and tapped the space next to her. She indicated he should sit next to her, close enough to touch thigh-to-thigh.

Countess Christiana interjected.

"Alejandro, may I present the Marquésa Fanny de Castellanos y Ordonez?"

"Sit here, Alejandro," the Marquésa said, in a voice that brooked no denial.

"Graysie, you can sit on the other side of the Marquésa," the Countess added.

Graysie dipped her head to the other woman with warm affection.

Feeling more set up than ever, he glared at Graysie with laughing eyes.

"What have you got me into, oh sister mine?"

He laughed uneasily.

"Since when has Countess Christiana been one of your acquaintances?"

She dipped onto the couch in one graceful swoop, smiling apologetically as she did.

"Since yesterday," she replied simply.

Alex glanced at the other woman seated the other side of him.

"Alejandro," Graysie began, her mouth puckering in a self-conscious half smile.

"May I introduce you to our grandmother, and your father Rafael's mother, the Marquésa Fanny?

Alex stared, the air whooshing from his lungs like it was escaping from a suddenly ruptured balloon.

For long seconds, eyes wide with disbelief, his ears ringing, he processed what he'd just been told.

My grandmother?

He stood on unsteady legs and half bowed.

"Marquésa…Forgive me. I… I… I'm overwhelmed."

He plopped down in the space she'd marked out for him. An iron clamp was squeezing his lungs, and a whirlwind swirled in his brain.

A Spanish Marquésa? Why have I never known about this?

The noblewoman stretched out a wiry arm and clasped his hand.

"Alejandro. I know this is a lot to take in."

She spoke perfect English with a slight Scottish accent.

"Believe me, you are no more astonished at discovering you have a Scottish grandmother than I was discovering I had a grown—and marvelously handsome—grandson.

"I hate to be predictable, but you look just like your father."

She withdrew her hand from him and placed it on her heart, as if seeing him was bringing on palpitations.

Graysie stirred at her side and whispered, "Are you all right, Fanny? Can I get you water? Or something stronger?"

Fanny. I missed her name before. I was so shocked.

And Graysie was already on familiar first-name terms with

this phantom from the past.

"No, no, Graysie. I will be fine. Like Alejandro here, I'm finding our reunion rather breathtaking, that's all."

She tilted her head to Alex, and for a moment she looked like a beady-eyed blackbird.

"We have a great deal to catch up on, Alejandro. Forgive me for taking you by surprise. I couldn't resist. And it's not Graysie's fault we caught you on the hop. I swore her to secrecy."

She swiveled to smile at Graysie, then turned back to him.

"I came here to settle some family business, and to satisfy myself once and for all that Rafael was dead. We've had no word of him—or any of you—for years…

"We just didn't know. The last we heard, you and your sister were missing after that dreadful accident.

"I wanted to find out as much as I could, and it seemed the only way was to actually come here.

"I didn't know what joy, as well as sorrow, awaited me. And now we have the luxury of discovering one another's stories. I really don't know where to begin."

Twenty-six

"Everything ready?"

Dionisio Garcia tried to ignore the loud blowfly buzzing up and down the window, trying to escape the stuffy office.

He had a message to deliver, and he wanted no distractions. He planted his feet slightly apart, hands clasped behind his back in a confident stance, and glared. A man seated behind an enormous oak desk in the Land Claims Court anteroom on Clay Street took up all his attention.

Elmer Green's narrow foxy face flickered with irritation at the interruption. His pale oddly yellow eyes behind wire-rimmed glasses were flat and cold, the combination of bad humor and cynicism, making him look ten years older than his twenty-six years.

His hand, which held a gold-nibbed pen, stopped moving across the paper before him, but he didn't put the instrument down.

His mouth opened and Dionisio jumped in before he could object.

"There's been a change of plans, Elmer… I've been talking to Bram, and he wants to take a different approach on the Los Putos claim because of Alistair's death."

Green's eyes narrowed in suspicion. He put down the pen and laced his fingers in front of him and flexed, eying Garcia with a flinty stare.

He gestured to the chair set on the other side of his desk.

"Why should the boy's death affect anything? He's been set on getting his hands on the place for years now. He's spent a lot of time and money on it, lining it up with the city fathers and all. They're ready to let it drop into his lap."

Despite his own cool bravado, Dionisio could feel his cheeks reddening.

Damn the fellow for questioning me. I'm the client.

He slumped down into the seat, as casual and arrogant as he liked.

"The old man was doing it all for Alistair. For the next generation of his heirs. Now Alistair's gone. He's happy for me to take it over. After all, I am the only descendant on the Valaquez side."

"You?" Elmer barked the word, questioning the whole proposition.

"That's right. Me. I've done the work on the deal for starters. He'd never have found out about the Castellanos heir without my digging."

He pushed back from his chair, suddenly feeling antsy sitting at eye level with the cold-blooded bureaucrat who'd only got the job because of his father.

The corners of Elmer's mouth twisted in distaste.

Dionisio leaned onto the desk and stared over the bare, circled dome of Elmer's prematurely balding head.

"Old lady Castellanos is back in town," he said, his heart

beating faster in anticipation of Elmer's response.

It was instantaneous. Elmer Green reared back, pushing away from the desk with his hands on the edge in front of him. His jaw dropped open, revealing narrow, pointed teeth.

"She's what? No one's heard from them in twenty years. Why is *she* back?"

Dionisio's skin tingled with the power of knowledge. He made it his business to stay ahead of the game.

He shrugged, a masterful display of nonchalance.

"Who knows? Probably to see an exhibition of old photos going on display at Lick House."

"Old pictures? What old pictures? And why are they of interest?"

"Who cares?" Dionisio got up and ambled over to the windows that looked out on the street in calculated disinterest.

There is no need for him to know she's reunited with the grandson.

They'll be all over this court case next week if they find out it's being heard.

He swung back to Elmer, still sitting at his desk.

"Thing is, I'm going to need that birth certificate we've already had the foresight to prepare. The one that shows I'm Hernandez Valaquez's legitimate son."

Elmer's already washed-out complexion faded to an even lighter shade at his words.

"But... But... my man hasn't done the final work on it."

From across the room, Garcia caught the whine in Elmer's voice.

He prowled back to his seat like a jungle cat and leaned in.

"Then you'd better make damn sure it's ready. The hearing's next week. That's what Bram's been paying for all these years. To make sure the purchase goes through with no last-minute hitches."

Elmer's eyes shifted nervously from the desktop to Garcia's face.

"So, whose name goes on the final settlement documents? I thought this was always set up to be in the name of Abraham Gordon?"

"That's what's changed. It's now to be in the name of Dionisio Garcia Valaquez. Understand? And not a word to anyone. You know what this town's like. I don't want the Callestanos gang hearing a whisper of this."

Beads of sweat broke out on Elmer's prominent forehead.

"And Bram's fine with that?"

Dionisio swaggered across to the sideboard decanter and poured two glasses of whiskey.

He gazed out the window, unwilling to meet Elmer's eyes.

"Legitimate, illegitimate. What's the difference? I deserve recognition for all the unpaid work I've put in for Bram Gordon."

He took his first long swallow, standing with a decanter in hand, and topped his glass up again before putting the decanter back down and returning to slap the second glass in front of Elmer.

"You're not losing your nerve, are you Elmer, old chap? I'd hate to see you come to the same end as Emmanuel Valaquez, wouldn't you?"

The whiskey in Elmer's glass trembled, and his finger pads turned white with his tightened grip.

"You've all got your payouts on this deal," Garcia said, staring the shaking registrar in the eye.

"I'm the only one still waiting."

Well, me and Castellanos.

But with any luck, it will have all gone through before they even hear about it, and then it will be too late to appeal.

Twenty-seven

Come along and meet the gang…

Magdalena's invitation was like catnip to her feline instincts after Rosie's bruising encounter with Alex the day before.

Even Ewan Campbell had been sanguine about any dangers Alex might face when she'd tried to explain her fears.

"The main issue was O'Halloran threatening to arrest him," Campbell reassured her.

"Now that we've got him playing along, and extra security arranged, Alex should be fine. Please don't worry about it. We don't need your help."

She'd objected, but she'd failed to make them see sense.

Idiot men!

With Sebastian and Isabella snuggled up like new lovers now he was back home, Rosie sat around feeling as useless as a third arm, and as restless as a caged lion.

Which was how she came to be nursing a very warm ale at a big round table in the Cats and Dogs Bar on the fringes of Chinatown with Magdalena. A wide group of her friends and acquaintances surrounded them, all drinking and laughing at an after-show wind-down session.

She knew how it was to come off a performance at midnight, charged with energy. No one wanted to go home to bed when they'd just seen the curtain close to an excited audience.

Magdalena was already talking about finding her a place in the show, which meant they'd be together every night.

Many of the show's performers and behind-the-scenes operators—stage hands, producers, musicians—were included in the jolly company, along with a few incongruous hangers-on—businessmen and lawyers, giddy young women, all stage struck in one way or another.

As Rosie nursed her ale, intent on making it last all night, she told herself it was the perfect chance for her to pick up on any street talk about Alistair's death.

Without anything definite to go on, that was the best she could hope for, she rationalized. She might pick a morsel of random gossip that turned out to have a crumb of truth.

Dionisio Garcia was glued to Magdalena's side, assuming the role of the Big Cat of the pride with his natural ascendancy.

They made a handsome pair, Magdalena, with her vibrant laughter and exotic flashing beauty in shimmering red skirts, and the conquistador. Tonight he was at his dramatic best, in a theatrical black cape, gold braided matador's hat and the ever present tight black leather pants.

Magdalena turned to Rosie. "Now your arm is getting better, why not stay on here in San Francisco for a while? You're tired of that night riding routine, aren't you? You can do better than that. Leave it to me."

Magdalena sat to her right, occasionally whispering new information about the group into her ear.

"That guy opposite you—that's Elmer Green. He's a court registrar, thanks to his important daddy."

Rosie looked guardedly across the table, where Green was engaged in deep conversation with the man on his left.

He had a narrow, mean face, and pale, cold eyes framed by thick glasses which magnified their emptiness.

"Looks a bit of a cold fish," Rosie commented.

Magdalena laughed. "I thought that too, but he must have hidden depths. He's tight with Dionisio, so he must have red blood somewhere, though it's hard to tell exactly where."

They giggled at their companionable naughtiness.

"Is that girl sitting next to him his wife?"

"Good Lord, no," said Magdalena. "She's in the show. He's single. I get the impression he's planning to marry well. Elmer does nothing without deep calculation. Mr. Spontaneity he is not."

Rosie laughed quietly again. Being out with this crowd was better than sitting at home alone at Isabella's, and she might even discover something useful.

"Did Alistair come to these nights when he was here?" she asked, suddenly alert to a possible paramour in the crowd.

"All the time," Magdalena replied without hesitation. "Bram too, sometimes. Not as often."

"And did Alistair have a girlfriend?"

Magdalena pointed to the far end of the table, where a girl with translucent peach skin and midnight black hair sat. She surveyed the crowd with faraway eyes and appeared to speak rarely.

"Celadine Martin. She's a dancer. French. You might have seen her around?"

Rosie shook her head.

"I don't think so. She's a beautiful girl."

Another sudden thought occurred. "Does she speak English?"

"Some. Not a lot. Why?"

"Just wondering," said Rosie with a shrug. "I'm curious about what happened that night, that's all."

Magdalena's eyes widened in shock.

"The night he was killed? Oh, Rosie, don't."

"Don't what?"

She knew she was playing deliberately dense, but she couldn't help it.

"Don't ask questions here about that night. People are terrified to talk about it."

"And why is that, do you think? Have they got something to hide?"

Magdalena darted a worried glance sideways to Garcia, but he was engaged in a raucous drinking contest with the man on his left, and didn't notice.

"Everyone has their secrets," said Magdalena. "Promise me you won't ask."

"Why?" inquired Rosie, acting deliberately dense.

Pinpoints of perspiration dotted Magdalena's brow.

"Just understand. You'll be asking for trouble, and there'll be nothing I can do to protect you."

Twenty-eight

Isabella, eyes brimming with happy tears, gazed across her dining room table and shot her twin a trembling smile.

"Alejandro," she breathed.

"We have to call you that from now on, in honor of our Spanish family. How could we have been so ignorant for so long?"

She stretched out one hand to take Fanny's wrist.

The other she rested lightly on her stomach.

"To be able to link the generations like this—touching you, dear Marquésa—and your coming great-grandchild… I can't explain how much that means to me."

Alex—or Alejandro, as his sister and grandmother insisted on teasingly addressing him—had "done a Graysie" on Isabella. He'd surprised her with an unannounced visit with Fanny the morning after the Brady show. It had given him great pleasure to introduce her to the unborn child's great-grandmother.

He knew the coming child had raised many questions in Isabella's mind about their own family history, ones neither of them had until now been able to answer.

Fanny's arrival left Isabella overwhelmed. As the two women

made their initial exchanges, he'd slipped off into his own astounded musings.

One short sleep had not given him enough time to grapple with what he'd heard from Fanny last night.

His grandfather, a Spanish aristocrat who'd spent his last years in Madrid in the service of the Spanish queen, named—funnily enough—Isabella?

How had I not known this?

Not that it meant anything in California.

Once the Americans won the war against Mexico and took California as part of their spoils, Spanish titles ceased to have any status in either country.

But still.

His ignorance shamed him.

And Fanny was a highly unusual Marquésa, one with a down-to-earth Scottish take on Spanish court life.

He pulled himself back to the present where Isabella was gazing deliriously at Fanny, her hand at her throat, her words choked.

"I can hardly speak because of my happiness," she half gasped, half laughed.

"I'm so happy you came to California. That's all I can say."

She placed her hand back down on the table, and Fanny reached over and gave it a loving squeeze.

"That makes two," she glanced at Alex "possibly three of us," she laughed.

"I never dreamed my visit would have such a happy outcome."

There was a long, contented pause, and Alex rejoined the conversation.

"I feel bad. I never thought to investigate further," he said.

"It thrilled me to hear about my father, the photographer, because it reflected my own interests, but that was as far as it went. It didn't occur to me to look further back. I suppose my life was so blessed with Hector, I never felt the need to do it."

Fanny gazed at him with shining eyes.

"One thing I will be grateful for till the day I die is that you both were so fortunate with the families you ended up in. You got a great second start in life after that awful disaster."

"We did," Isabella said. "But it's not the same as having a real family. Especially when you're about to introduce the next generation. Now I'll be able to explain to our children where we come from."

Fanny turned her attention to Alex.

"Alejandro, tell me about the other night when those men broke into your house. I know you've explained the bare outlines. But I want to hear the whole thing again, from start to finish, leaving nothing out, not the tiniest detail. We've got to get to grips with what's going on here."

Before he spoke, Isabella jumped in.

"Would it be all right if I asked Rosie to join us? She's turning herself inside out, trying to work out what's going on.

"She's worried I'll be affected by it, too. She's such a darling friend, and she's got a magnificent head on her shoulders..."

She shot an appeal to Alex, who pulled a face.

"What's wrong?" she asked. "Don't you like Rosie?"

"Rosie's okay," Alex said in a flat, lukewarm voice. "I think she's making too much of it, that's all. It was probably plain bad luck they chose my house, and O'Halloran is realizing that, I think."

"O'Halloran?" Fanny asked. "Who's he?"

"The deputy who was all set to arrest Alejandro for murder," said Isabella. "Alejandro's been in hiding for the last week while Sebastian got things sorted out, but they're still not settled. Alejandro is a suspect in O'Halloran's mind."

She fixed Alex with worried eyes.

"If Rosie is making too much of it, I suggest you're not taking it seriously enough."

Fanny's jaw set in a determined line.

"Is Rosie here?"

At Isabella's nodding assent, she said immediately, "Then, by all means, ask her in. You can't have too many bright minds on a sticky problem, and this one sounds serious."

She shot Alejandro an apologetic smile.

"Besides, if she's Isabella's best friend, I want to meet her."

***

Fanny Castellanos glanced from Rosie to Isabella, intelligent inquiry lighting up her sea-blue eyes.

"So, how did you two meet?"

Isabella's translucent creamy skin flushed a delicate pink.

"I hate to admit it now, but I had a momentary rush of blood to the head and ran away from home to join the traveling road show," she said with an embarrassed giggle.

"I was so naïve!"

She shared a conspiratorial grin with Rosie. "I got a berth with Lotta Crabtree's troupe. I met Lotta in Grass Valley and I was star-struck. I thought Huldah was mean when she wouldn't agree to me joining them."

She shook her head. "My poor stepmother. She knew best all along.

"I was incredibly lucky to land Rosie as my bunkmate and guide. I hate to think about the trouble I could have got myself in without Rosie."

She flicked a smile to Fanny. "But that's a whole other story, for another day. For now, let's just say Rosie has been an incredibly loyal and helpful friend.

"She's taking a break from the show because she badly sprained her wrist. I've loved having her here, especially when Sebastian was away."

Fanny turned her searching eyes on Rosie.

"Alejandro here is complaining you're making too much of the intrusion in his home the other night. Tell us what you make of it. I'm interested to hear your thoughts."

Rosie glanced mulishly at Alex.

"He seems to want to see it as a random attack. 'They'd been drinking and hit the wrong house' kind of thing.

"I don't agree with that. I'm dead certain they knew whose house they were in and they were after him for something.

"Whether they intended to kill him, I don't know. But I can't shake the idea they had a purpose in going there. We've got to find out what that purpose was."

Fanny nodded, her brows furrowed in serious thought.

"And what do you think it was? The purpose, I mean?"

"This man named Dionisio Garcia came to Isabella's house after Alex went into hiding. He threatened her and me about Alex.

"He more or less said we weren't to do anything to help him, or we'd be in for it."

She shot an emerald-eyed dart at Alex.

"I don't know about him, but anyone who threatens Isabella, I'm taking them seriously. No one's going to get near her, if I can help it.

"I've asked around, and Garcia was Alistair Gordon's close friend—maybe his closest friend. He does a lot of 'minder' jobs for Bram Gordon, Alistair's father."

She glanced around the circle, who were now captivated by her story.

"Bram Gordon is one of the biggest offenders around her for gobbling up the old Spanish land grant ranches. He's made it his specialty to buy up disputed land.

"Places where there's been a long court case, and the current owners are bankrupted and can't afford to keep fighting any longer. He steps in and gets it for a song."

Alex's fingers went to the collar of his shirt, and he tugged at it uncomfortably.

"You didn't tell me that."

He glared at Rosie, aware the blood was pounding in his temples, and that Fanny and Isabella were gaping, but he couldn't help himself.

If Rosie gets injured, or worse yet, killed because of me...

"And what do you mean, you 'asked around?' If this Garcia character is as dangerous as you say he is, I don't want you messing with him, or anywhere near him."

Rosie's emerald eyes flashed.

"Who said I was 'messing' with him? I tried to tell you the other day. I know his close woman friend, the actress Magdalena da Silva. You said she was 'too dramatic' because she's on stage. You were dismissive of the whole idea…"

He held her angry gaze, but could find no words in response. She was right. He had accused her of being "too dramatic."

Fanny's steely, calming voice cut the air between them.

"Rosie, I'm getting the impression you think this attack might be linked to some land claim. Is that right?"

Rosie's rebellious stance immediately softened.

She hunched her shoulders in defeat.

"It seems like a reasonable suspicion, yes, but Alex and Isabella both say they've got nothing to do with any land claims.

"Hector left an extensive business behind him, but Alex is certain none of it involves pastoral farming, nothing like it. Nor Isabella either."

She screwed up her face in a frustrated appeal.

"I can't shake the feeling Garcia is involved somehow. I even suggested to Alex he might have been the second guy who was there with Alistair that night, but he pooh-poohed that idea, too."

Alex wriggled uncomfortably in his chair.

"I didn't exactly pooh-pooh it."

"Oh? What did you say to me, then?"

Rosie's voice had a triumphant edge.

He hesitated.

What did I say?

"You said I was 'letting my imagination run away with me.' Those were your words."

She turned back to Fanny.

"He wasn't interested, but I can't let it go. I can't stand the thought of someone targeting Isabella, and maybe whatever it is involves her too. Who knows?"

"Who indeed," said Fanny with steady intensity. "Because Rosie, I believe your hunch is correct. Isabella might be in danger too."

Alex sat bolt upright. "She might? How?"

Isabella sat forward in her chair, both hands on the table, her mouth open.

"Yes. How?" she said.

"Because I didn't come to California only to follow up on dead leads to my eldest son. I also came to see what happened to land that Angel had a share in long ago, before California was American.

"I promised Angel I would look after it, and this is the first chance I've had. Sounds like I might be right on time."

Rosie let out a wail of protest that sounded like "Ohhhhh… Noooo…"

Fanny gazed at her in concerned amusement.

"What? You're not happy to be proved right?"

"It's not that, Marquésa. Of course. We all like to be proven right."

She darted Alex a triumphant look that was as clear as poking her tongue out in her intent.

"I'm worried because if that's the case, you might be in danger too.

"You all might be. From what I hear, Bram Gordon takes no prisoners. His motto is 'Kill or be killed.' And he always wins."

Twenty -nine

A Week Later

Rosie shot an understanding smile to the pretty young Irish girl serving drinks at the raucous next-door table. She gave her a silent hand clap as she executed a quick sidestep to avoid being groped by a drunken patron.

Rosie had served enough drinks herself to appreciate that the lass had to accept unwanted attention as an annoying but inevitable part of her job.

It feels wrong to be sitting here as part of this bawdy mob, she thought.

I'd much rather be at home sipping tea with Isabella.

She gazed down at her pot of beer, going flat on the table in front of her.

On her right, Magdalena gave her a quick prod in her ribs. "You're quiet tonight, Miss MyHoney—are you all right?"

Miss MyHoney. A spoof name for the Irish surname Mahoney, one role she played in the Magdalena's variety show. A humorous rendering of a popular Irish surname.

Rosie flicked her a grateful glance.

"I'm fine, Maggie, really I am. I'm tired, that's all. I've got to get used to working six nights a week. I'm eternally grateful for the opportunity you've given me."

She'd joined Magdalena's vaudeville entertainment a week ago. She'd been out every night since, taking part in the after-show ritual of drinks and chatter about who did what and who got the most cheers at the curtain fall.

If Magdalena was unquestionably the star of the stage production, the after-party drinks were Dionisio's show.

They followed a predictable routine. Magdalena settled and gazed at Dionisio with adoring violet eyes. A secular Madonna whose main purpose in life was to pay homage to her man. Meantime, Dionisio scattered jests and flirtatious comments far and wide.

And no one received more of these romantic sallies than Rosie. She suspected her rejection of his demands on his first visit to Isabella's had lent an edge of challenge to her continued presence at the table. Garcia hated nothing as much as being rebuffed, she guessed.

And while his attention stung like nettles, it also suited her purposes.

She despised going home with her head full of dull chatter and her clothes stinking of cigar smoke. But she was determined to find out why Alex had been attacked.

And she was convinced Dionisio Garcia knew the answers to both those questions better than anyone else.

The late-night bar was pulsing with the day's stored heat and a rising tide of inebriated voices that competed with the band of Spanish guitars. The cast occupied a table at the center of the action. She glanced around her, satisfying herself the regulars were all there.

Magdalena was on her left. On the other side of Magdalena, Dionisio. On Rosie's right, the looming void of Garcia's mate Elmer Green, who rarely spoke but watched everyone with suspicious eagle eyes. He'd drifted to her side of the table, and she wondered if being involved in the Land Court gave him any secret insights.

Every night, one of Dionisio's female camp followers injected herself into the seat on his other side. Garcia tormented Magdalena by paying her rival an outrageous amount of attention.

Tonight, it was Lula, a fiery redheaded flamenco dancer, who enjoyed baiting Magdalena. She hardly bothered to conceal her amorous designs on the man who sat between them.

It's all so predictable. The battle of the queen bees. Any minute now we'll witness a *"crimen pasional."* At the very least, a cat fight with nail gouging.

She allowed herself a grim little smile.

"What's so funny?"

Elmer Green leaned into her space and fixed her with gimlet eyes that delivered a shock right down her backbone.

She coughed and brought her hand up in front of her mouth.

"No…nothing," she stammered.

Her eyes scanned his face. He actually wasn't bad looking. He had a firm mouth and finely arched brows and chiseled cheeks. But his sour personality tainted everything about him.

"Tell me," she said. "Why do you come here night after night?"

His pale eyes fluttered, as if he'd been caught off guard by the unexpected question.

"I'm invested in Garcia," he said. "And I want to safeguard my investment."

Another ripple of surprise tingled at the back of her neck.

"Invested? I don't understand. In what way, invested?"

He stared, considering whether to answer her question, and she could pick the moment when he switched off.

"It's private," he said. "My business." His jaw locked shut.

He stared for a few more seconds; she guessed regretting he'd ever started the conversation. Then he fell back in his chair and lapsed into silence.

***

One bright side of Rosie's new employment was that she'd be able to resume her payments to her family in New York by the end of the week.

Whenever she thought of her sister Eilish scrambling to earn enough to feed their mother and the younger children, her stomach churned.

The pay here in Magdalena's show was much better than her turn with the Crabtree troupe, and she was doing all she could to make a permanent place for herself.

The Remarkable History of Fun and Laughter, as it was called, was drawing full houses and looked set to continue for months.

They presented a mashed up, revolving program of

Shakespeare parodies, acrobats, singers, clowns, and an elephant named Mr. Sweeney.

The general tenor was parody, and Rosie's role was to play the pretty—and riotous—Irish colleen, Miss MyHoney, to Magdalena's dramatic and grand Spanish Countess Catalina, with material hastily assembled and purloined from any number of sources, including Lotta's rambling carnivale.

The audiences loved it as long as they were sending somebody up, and Magdalena and Rosie worked as perfect foils.

Magdalena was the aristocratic, dark-haired, romantic Latin. Rosie was her cheeky, redheaded Irish offsider, all fireworks, songs and laughter.

One of the show's standing jokes was that whenever Magdalena got mad with her, Rosie broke into song. If the audience wanted a song, they chanted for Magdalena to castigate Rosie, and these exchanges were becoming high points of the show.

In a skit titled "The Irish Boy and the Yankee Girl," she appeared—poorly disguised—as the male love interest, billed as "The only lady in the country who does an Irish character in male attire."

Amazingly to her, after only a week in the show, she was already attracting attention on the street. When they came to the Cats and Dogs Bar each night, chants of "Paddy Paddy Paddy" greeted her, accompanied by the banging of tankards on the bar. Many times, the patrons called for her to sing "How Are You, Harp of Erin"—a song she and Magdalena sang together.

The point of it all was, as she'd explained to the Marquésa Fanny and Izzy, to gather intelligence on what Dionisio Garcia was up to.

Practically every night he was there, pinned to Magdalena's side. He kept his possessive eye on the star of the show while he misbehaved under her watchful gaze.

Her elbow suddenly jogged as Magdalena rose abruptly. Rosie clasped her mug more tightly to stop beer from sloshing into her lap and glanced to her friend sideways.

"What's wrong?"

"*Te pasas,*" Magdalena muttered through gritted teeth.

He's gone too far this time.

Rosie glanced to the other side of Magdalena.

Garcia was in a passionate clinch with Lula. Or was it Lula in a passionate clinch with Garcia?

Magdalena thrust back her chair, unloaded a string of Spanish invective on Dionisio's head, and stormed out.

Garcia turned momentary attention to the spectacle, and then pushed Magdalena's chair aside and moved into her intimate space.

Lula shrieked in protest, but he ignored her. He drew his arm around Rosie's shoulders, as if she needed protecting, and leaned down to whisper in her ear.

"*Bomboncita! Qué bonita estás!*"

Sweetie. How pretty you are… She froze under his touch.

Oh, no…What the heck do I do now?

Magdalena will hear about this.

You're here to win his trust, remember?

But not at the expense of our friendship.

"Dionisio, no," she said, laughing, as if he was playing a joke, gazing up into his eyes.

But Garcia wasn't gazing back at her.

He'd lifted his head, and his face was dark with anger.

"What's he doing here?" he hissed.

She followed his line of sight and saw Alex, standing outside the ring of the crew's chairs, staring at her, eyes narrowed in disgust.

She glanced from Alex to Dionisio and shrugged.

"Goodness knows," she said. "He's nothing to do with me."

Garcia threw back his head and roared, his white teeth flashing.

"Magnifico."

He clapped his hands to attract attention.

"More drinks, everybody. The night is young."

Her eyes flicked to where Alejandro had stood moments before, but all she saw was his retreating back.

Thirty

As her hired hack neared Isabella's front gate, the strung-out tightness in Rosie's head and shoulders dissolved into lightheaded exhaustion.

Home. At last.

The plaque on the gate glimmered in the faint moonlight.

Gardenvale

In honor of Alycia Stockton's wonderful garden.

She couldn't remember when she'd last felt such a sense of relief at the sight of a familiar front gate.

Maybe never.

She stepped down, paid the driver and tiptoed wearily up the sidewalk to the front gate.

No need to advertise to the entire household what time I'm finally home.

She slipped her hand over the familiar latch and stepped into Sebastian and Isabella's front garden, catching the fresh sweet fragrance of jasmine.

A dark shape loomed up from the darkness and her heart leapt to her mouth. Her footsteps froze.

"Whoooo… Whaat…." Her breath was raspy in her throat,

and then she recognized the shadow.

"Alex… What on earth…?"

She let out a gasp of relief as a furious rush of anger flooded her tired brain.

"What are you doing here?" She spat out the words in an urgent whisper.

"For goodness' sakes. Are you stalking me or something? First the club. And now here?"

She wiped the back of her hand across her eyes.

I don't believe this guy. Who does he think he is?

For half a minute, the fury galvanized her. But then her mind and limbs sagged under a renewed wave of exhaustion.

"Stalking you?" His tone was corrosive.

"Why in heaven's name would I want to do that?"

He shook his head, his dark locks flopping over wide-open eyes that shone white in the night gloom.

"I was curious to see how far your betrayal would extend, that's all." His usually warm voice was laced with contempt.

"You lectured us all about what a dangerous fellow this conquistador is, and now you're snuggling up to him? I wanted to get my facts right, that's all.

"What is he? Some blackguard out to kill me, or your latest lover?"

His fury slammed into her like the blows of a sledgehammer.

"My latest lover? How dare you?"

Her legs set up such a tremor she was frightened she'd slump to the ground right there in front of him.

But she'd be darned if she was going to let him see it.

"Why should you care, anyway," she hissed at him, still

maintaining a whisper, but furious with it.

"You belittle everything I say. A few days ago, you decried my suggestion he was involved with Alistair Gordon, Bram's son.

"And what business is it of yours what I do in my private life? I haven't noticed you've been interested in much except yourself."

He stared, and adjusted his mouth as if he was going to reply, but then thought better of it.

A long silence hung between them, and then he spoke.

"Believe it or not, I am interested. I don't want you to court unnecessary danger. For goodness' sake, Rosie. You can't trust that devil, surely?

"If you thought he was capable of murder last week, what's changed that you're snuggling up to him now?"

She saw red again.

"I. Am. Not. Snuggling up to him," she enunciated. "No matter what it might look like. And already I'm hearing snippets and rumors that might help us."

As they'd been talking, Isabella's cat had appeared on the front doorstep and stalked its way daintily across the lawn. When it reached Alex, it wound itself around his ankles, meowing as it did so.

He leaned over and took the long-haired blue-gray moggie in his arms.

He let out a long sigh as he drew the animal to his chest and snuggled it under his chin.

"Come inside. Let me make you a cup of cocoa. And tell me, what rumors?"

His sudden change of mood threw her off balance.

Her hands dropped to her sides like leaden weights. She stiffened her back to stop herself from collapsing to her knees.

"Alex, I am exhausted. I have nothing left. Can't we do this some other time? I'm sorry. I'm all out of puff."

He stared across the path, reluctant to give up.

"Rosie. I've said it before. I don't want you to put yourself in danger."

She shook her head.

"Not tonight, Alex. I can't handle it tonight."

And she turned and dragged herself up the front steps, praying their confrontation hadn't woken the household.

Too bad if he hates me, she thought as her key slipped into the front door lock.

This is just how it's got to be.

Thirty-one

Alex watched as Rosie dragged herself up Izzy's front steps, her shoulders sagging as if she was under a tremendous burden.

His heart lurched in his chest and he spontaneously brought his hand to his rib cage to calm the palpitations.

He bit down on his bottom lip, suppressing the rage that roared in his blood every time he thought of Rosie cuddling up to that arrogant blackguard Garcia.

The varmint was mussing her hair! And she was smiling, as if she loved every minute!

I'm not jealous, he told himself, ignoring the red spots that danced before his eyes whenever he thought of that cozy scene.

I'm extremely disappointed, that's all. I thought she was better than this.

Where was her friend Magdalena, anyway?

Surely, she wouldn't betray Magdalena?

Well, she did, didn't she? Just as well you found out what's she's really like before it's too late.

Too late for what? It's not as if I'm interested in her…

The cat dawdled around his ankles, meowing.

He stood in the darkness and saw a glimmer of lamplight

from the windows of Rosie's bedroom.

He picked up the cat and cuddled her warm back against his cheek. Her soft fur tickled his chin.

The light in Rosie's room clicked off.

She's going to sleep, no problem. I wonder if she's dreaming of him?

Oh, for goodness' sake, Alejandro, what's wrong with you? She's only a woman. What does it matter?

Reluctantly, he put Isabella's cat down on the lawn.

I need to get home myself. No point in standing around here.

He glanced up at Rosie's window one last time and then slipped out the gate.

I have to get a satisfying sleep myself. But tomorrow I'll find out exactly what "rumors" she's talking about.

Not that I've got any desire to see her again, the traitorous little cow.

But I owe it to the rest of the family.

Thirty-two

Dionisio paused mid mouthful, his fork loaded with a tasty hash brown and a rasher of bacon, and gazed across the hotel breakfast table at Bram Gordon.

"The heir's not a problem. He's a lightweight pretty boy who's only interested in photography. But his grandmother is a different proposition."

Around them, San Francisco's bankers and merchants, real estate developers and railway tycoons and their richly garbed families broke their fast with oat cakes and coffee, a full cooked grill, or fresh fruit and pancakes.

The tinkle of silver cutlery on porcelain, the aroma of roasted coffee beans and tomato ketchup, of fresh apricots and perfectly browned toast, provided a predictable start to another day in their sheltered lives.

One day I'll be like them. One day soon.

Dionisio waited patiently for Bram to answer him.

The old man's face was hatched with dark grooves that hadn't been there a month ago.

Garcia hesitated before pushing the fork load of food into his mouth, but he decided not to wait any longer.

Grief, he thought as he shoved it in, and then chewed and swallowed it down contentedly.

That's what grief does. Ages you overnight.

One good reason not to get too attached to anyone.

He's getting more haggard by the day.

He'd cornered Alistair's father in his Lick Hotel suite to bring him up to speed with the new developments—his first and most important task of the day.

He intended to make him understand the threat the fancy Marquésa represented to the successful outcome of their land claim case.

He rested his fork on the side of his plate and sat back contentedly, savoring the surroundings and, at this moment, pretending he belonged here.

A pleasing glow flushed through him as he recalled how Elmer Green was all lined up to carry out his wishes.

Now he had to organize Bram.

The aging magnate gazed distractedly at his plate, seemingly only half listening to what Dionisio was saying.

"Bram. Are you listening to me?"

His voice carried a peremptory bark he hadn't intended. He softened his approach to sound more appealing.

"It's important. We don't have to worry about the son, Alejandro, as he's taken to calling himself these days.

"He doesn't know one end of a horse from another and he's not interested in ranching. He's got as much money as he needs from the dead senator. But his grandmother…"

Bram stared directly at him over the white linen cloth decked with a crystal bud vase filled with spring flowers, some of the old keenness quickening in his penetrating eyes.

"What about her? The Marquésa?"

"From what I hear, she's on a 'life after death mission' to find out if Hernandez sold Angel out while he's been away. She's made the 'deathbed' promise… That kind of thing… She's here to sort things out."

Bram swallowed, but stayed silent.

"Old Castellanos might have back been in Spain ever since he was a young buck, but he hasn't forgotten California. Of course, his son died here too."

Gordon's eyes glazed over.

"Well, you know all about that. She's on a Hail Mary visit to see to their business affairs here. And now she's discovered there's a new Castellanos brood, she's all fired up. She's got that pesky lawyer Ewan Campbell on the case."

"So what?" said Gordon, picking up a cup and staring into the bottom of it. He reached out for the silver coffeepot at his elbow.

"I don't recall when I drank that coffee, but it's empty, so I 'spose I must have done."

He poured a fresh brew, the arching fountain from the spout narrowly missing the spotless starched cloth.

"He's nothing to be afraid of," Gordon said. "We beat him last time, didn't we?"

Bram blinked angrily.

He's so used to winning he can't countenance losing, Dionisio thought.

Quite the opposite of me. I've lost so many times I know how tough it is to win.

"This time round, it mightn't be so easy," Dionisio said.

"Especially if they start raising questions about Emmanuel's death."

"That's your problem, boy. It's why you'll never amount to anything. You take far too many unnecessary risks. And my son died because of it."

Not this again.

"Bram, I told you. He was all fired up. I couldn't stop him."

Bram held a piece of toast in the palm of one hand and clumsily smeared it with a knife of honey with the other.

An awkward silence stretched between them.

When Bram looked up, his Arctic eyes were icy and calculating.

"The guy you call a useless pretty boy proved himself a pretty sharp hand with his gun that night. And you ran away as fast as your legs could carry you. Leaving my son to die alone."

"He was already dead, Bram, I told you. Did you want me to get it too?"

"You know what, Garcia? I don't give two hoots what happens to you, or to that damned land claim. It cost me my son. As far as I'm concerned, the whole thing can go rot in hell."

The ice in Bram's eyes lodged deep in the pit of Dionisio's stomach.

I've lost him, he realized with a shudder. He's mad with it.

Just as well, I've already taken precautions against something like this happening.

He might be right on some things, but he's wrong about that.

Men like me have to take risks, or we never get out of the mud we were born in.

And neither Rich Man Gordon nor the Oh So Grand Marquésa are going to stop me from getting Los Putos.

It's mine by right. And I'll risk anything to grab it. Even my life.

Thirty-three

Despite the upsetting scene with Alejandro, Rosie slept late and missed breakfast. She'd stopped thinking of him as Alex. "Alex" was Izzy's friendly brother, an acquaintance. "Alejandro?" He was an entirely different creature. One she disliked and felt drawn to in equal measure.

It was lunchtime when she finally made it downstairs, bathed and clothed in a new gown Magdalena had given her, an Irish green satin which she'd shortened and taken in around the bust.

She examined herself in the bedroom mirror before she traipsed downstairs to face the Marquésa and Fanny, unsure of the reception she'd receive. Had Alejandro already called around and told them of her perfidy?

The green dress did wonderful things to her eyes. She had to admit it. You'd hardly guess she was still feeling overwhelmed by doubts and wracked by guilt at playing up to Dionisio. She plumped up her golden curls and smiled at herself.

There.

She was looking as good as she could in the new dress, and

the gloomy headache she'd woken up with eased as she spun to the door and made her way downstairs before she lost her nerve.

She found Fanny and Isabella taking coffee on the veranda that overlooked the garden where she and Alex—Alejandro—had argued last night. Her stomach fluttered uneasily as she breathed in the jasmine she'd smelt then, reminding her of the embarrassing scene.

At the sound of her soft steps, Isabella turned with a quick smile.

"Rosie! Come and join us for coffee… Are you hungry? I'm sure Betty will bring you something from the kitchen if you are."

The nervous tremor in her stomach instantly eased.

Isabella seemed her usual lovely self.

Not fed up with me, then.

Rosie turned to acknowledge Isabella's grandmother.

"Marquésa…"

Fanny's chin dipped.

"How many times do I have to tell you, I'm Fanny when we're home with the family, Rosie, and that includes you?"

She gestured to the cushioned seat on a bamboo couch beside her.

"Please. Sit down."

Rosie turned to Izzy. "Just a coffee, thanks, Izzy. No food. I'm not hungry."

Isabella rang a silver handbell on the coffee table before her.

"Betty will be here any minute. How did last night go?"

Alejandro hasn't got in first with his version, then.

The rock in Rosie's stomach returned.

"Good in one way. And not so good in another."

"Oh. Take a deep breath and tell all. We're expecting Alejandro at any minute, but we're dying to hear it all, aren't we, Fanny?"

Isabella regarded her gran with a piercing intelligence, and it struck Rosie how much like Fanny she was.

Both formidable adversaries.

If Isabella wasn't made of such stern stuff, she might never have found Alejandro in the first place.

She launched in on her account of last night's events, including the tiff between Magdalena and Dionisio and his subsequent play for her attention.

She paused mid-sentence, eyeing them uncertainly, as they waited with bated breath for the next revelation.

"I went along with it," she said. "I felt awful for Magdalena, but I had to. The whole point of being there is to win his trust so he'll confide in me. So, I had to."

Her stomach cramped with nervous tension.

"The thing is, Alex turned up at that exact moment, and he wasn't impressed."

She pulled her mouth down in a grimace.

"He was waiting for me when I came home and he was furious."

Her eyes filled with tears and she clenched up inside, determined not to let them see how upset she was.

She sounded like a frog croaking, her throat was so tight.

"He accused me of awful things, Izzy, and I couldn't explain. I'm not proud of my actions, but it's essential we find out who's attacking Alex and why, and this is the only way I know to do it."

Her eyes searched Isabella's face for signs she was shocked or disappointed, but her friend sat there, cool and unmoved.

"I kept him at arm's length. I didn't get carried away or anything. But Alejandro now has a terrible opinion of me."

Izzy chewed her lip, deliberating.

Fanny sat unmoved, with her hands lightly clasped in her lap.

"And have you found any worthwhile information so far? We don't want you risking your reputation, Rosie… Or losing a good friend."

Rosie lifted and lowered her shoulders in frustration.

"I'm getting hints, Izzy. I definitely think it's worth continuing. But nothing definitive, if you know what I mean."

"What hints?" Fanny had been silent for so long it was a surprise to hear her voice, low and considered.

"Well. For a start, there are rumors that Garcia had fallen out with Bram Gordon since his son's death.

"Garcia still speaks as if he's front man for Gordon's ranching operations, as if nothing's changed. He seems to have a tight relationship with the registrar of the Land Court, a young guy, Elmer Green. His father is one of the court judges. I wonder what goes on there, and why they're apparently such good friends.

"They are very different. Garcia is flamboyant, and Green is quite the opposite. He's often surly and the rest of the time hardly says a word. He doesn't seem to enjoy the party atmosphere.

"And when I asked him why he came to the club, he said the strangest thing."

Betty Butler swept in at that moment with fresh coffee and an extra cup, and Rosie paused while she placed the tray in front of Izzy.

"Anything else, Mrs. Russell?"

"All lovely, Betty. Thank you for the freshly cooked oatmeal cakes."

When she left the Marquésa leaned forward.

"What did Mr. Green say, Rosie, that struck you as odd?"

"He said he'd invested in Garcia and he wanted to safeguard his investment. When I asked what he meant, he backed right off, as if he regretted admitting to anything."

"He wants to safeguard his investment." Fanny turned over the words on her tongue thoughtfully, as if tasting each one for meaning.

"I quite agree, Rosie. That shows something possibly tricky. Not the thing you'd expect from a man in his position. Well done."

The tension in Rosie's stomach eased, and she smiled.

"I can't shake the conviction this is mixed up in the case. Garcia and Gordon are all about land. And this rumor that they've had a falling out?

"It would definitely back up my other hunch—that Garcia was the other man there with Alistair on the night he was killed."

She put down her oatcake and sighed.

"Alex doesn't seem to want to accept it, but it all fits. Even the sparkly braid Kaleo found, probably from a Spanish jacket?

"That's what Dionisio wears often, the old ranchero stuff. It's like he wants to be an old-time ranchero. He's got the garb and the sidearms. He needs the land and the cattle to complete the picture."

She heard a rattle in the hall, and immediately the nausea rose in her throat.

They're expecting Alejandro. Is this him?

Her ear tuned to the steps. One set was definitely a heavy male tramp. Could be Alex? But the other was an uneven gait, halting, uncertain.

A footfall she knew exceedingly well, from many years of painful trial.

It can't be.

She stood to her feet, ears cocked, her heart racing, arms stiff at her sides, her throat thick with excitement and disbelief. She trained her eyes on the French doors that opened onto the veranda from inside.

Alex stepped through the gap and stood to one side, like a major domo hesitating on the threshold to welcome an important guest.

His eyes found hers, and they burned with derision.

She flinched, and her eyes sought the space beside him, the open door.

Stepping into that gap, holding herself tall and proud despite the walking stick in her hand to support her trailing, weak leg, was her sister Eilish.

The air gushed out of her. Dizziness rolled in like a fog, and her knees gave way from under her.

As she pitched forward, she'd one last thought.

It can't be.

Thirty-four

A dose of Fanny's smelling salts had brought her around, but as Rosie lay back on the drawing room sofa cushions, staring up at her younger sister, her stomach roiled in queasy waves that weren't quelled by the fierce joy burning inside her.

Eilish… here.

She still couldn't believe it.

It had been—what?—three years since she'd left her standing alongside their brother on a crowded New York railway platform. That day she'd boarded the train that would ultimately bring her West.

She couldn't believe the transformation her sister had undergone in those years.

When she'd left, Eilish was a pale-faced seventeen-year-old, three years younger than her, withdrawn and insecure from years of being shut up in their dingy tenement.

The withered leg that had forced her to wear calipers made it hard for her to get outside, because she couldn't navigate the stairs.

Her disability resulted from a severe illness as a toddler. They'd never had the money to have her condition properly diagnosed or treated. It meant she was at home for much of the time, any chance of schooling hampered by poor health and her lack of mobility.

Now, she used a walking stick for balance, and she'd gained a lot more leg strength. She entered the room with an upright poise Rosie hadn't seen in her before, but that wasn't the biggest difference.

She'd grown taller. She'd outstripped Rosie by an inch or more in height. And although she looked weary from her travel, her dewy rose-petal complexion glowed with an inner light.

The abundant auburn hair that had always been her most attractive feature was her crowning glory, tumbling around her shoulders in exuberant waves. Her brown, green-flecked eyes shone with a confidence and purpose she'd lacked before.

"Eilish, you've turned into a beauty since I saw you last, you sneaky thing," Rosie declared with a gust of laughter, leaning across in an awkward hug.

"How did you do it?"

Eilish gave a light shrug and a wide smile.

"I met someone who gave me a chance at life," she said.

"Not a man?" Rosie's stomach lurched at the thought.

She's so naïve…

"Noooo," Eilish guffawed. "Not someone. A couple," she corrected.

"Anna and Leonard Rosenbaum. They set up schools for the poor on the East Side—one of them on Bleecker Street near us—and they took me on as a teacher's assistant."

She gazed at Rosie with sparkling eyes. "Anna's been wonderful.

"Not only has it enabled me to contribute to the household expenses, but even more importantly, she's helped me to catch up on my learning."

She reached out to Rosie with a hand that was warm and alive with excitement.

"Sitting in on the kid's classes helped, and Anna's also been giving me free lessons."

She threw back her head in delight.

"I've discovered I'm not the dummy I thought I was."

She squeezed Rosie's hand affectionately.

"It's made such a difference."

She halted, suddenly nervous. "And then when I got Isabella's letter, saying she and Alejandro wanted to invite me out here, that they'd pay all my traveling expenses—well, it was like heaven smiled on me."

Rosie's heart lurched in her chest.

"Isabella wrote to you?"

"Yes. She didn't tell you?"

Eilish's face crumpled into a worried frown.

"You don't mind, do you? Me being here? I promise not to be a nuisance. This health setback I've had recently? It's just a setback, that's all. Nothing permanent."

Rosie lifted herself into a more upright sitting position and grasped her by both shoulders.

"Darling Eilish, you'd never be a nuisance. I'm surprised, that's all."

She bit her lip, shame eating her up.

What did I say to Alex?

You only care about yourself.

And even then, he was planning this special arrangement.

Her cheeks flushed at the memory.

"I'm going to have to eat humble pie with Alejandro. I got quite the wrong idea about him."

Eilish's eyes quietened into solemn pools, deep with pain she understood so well.

"The wrong idea? In what way?"

Rosie flinched. "I accused him of being taken up with himself. Not caring about others."

She flexed her jaw.

"And now he's done this for us. How embarrassing."

"You're not angry, are you?" Eilish stuttered on the question, her eyes narrowed in distress.

Rosie's wide-open eyes met her sister's worried ones.

"No, of course not. I'm overwhelmed that you're here, that's all.

"It's my fault for not taking the time to understand things better. I've been too hasty in forming my opinions."

And too full of myself to listen. I'm the one who's blind to others.

She winced, and they lapsed into a long, thoughtful silence.

Then Eilish cleared her throat and said haltingly, "I'll never be able to repay Alejandro for his kindness, but I don't want to take advantage. I plan to pay my way.

"Anna and Leonard have friends here in San Francisco who operate a similar school to our one in New York, and they've already said they'll give me a job."

She gave Rosie a wry smile.

"I'll be able to send some money back home to help Mother and brother Liam out."

A gentle tap at the door stopped them short; their heads turned in unison to see who was interrupting them.

The door opened into a narrow gap and Alejandro peered in.

His hazel eyes brightened as they settled on Eilish's smiling face.

"Sorry to disturb, Eilish, but Izzy's asking if you'd like to freshen up before dinner. She's having a rest herself. She says we'll eat in an hour."

His jaw tightened as he turned his gaze on Rosie.

"Is that okay with you, Rosie?" His eyes were wary.

Expecting me to be difficult?

Rosie swallowed the lump that lodged in her throat and choked off her words.

She glanced at Eilish and noted the sparkle in her eyes as she took in Alejandro's dark length as he leant through the door frame, half in, half out of the room..

They're already pals, she thought, and an emptiness opened up inside of her.

I'm such a fool.

First Magdalena, then Alex.

I'm making a habit of biting the hand that feeds me.

She pushed herself forward on the sofa and made to rise.

"Thank you for what you've done for Eilish," she said, more stiffly than she'd intended.

"And Izzy's plan sounds fine. We'll take a quick rest. I'm sure Eilish's weary after her long journey."

And you already know I didn't get home till dawn.

Alex remained standing, his shoulders stiff, his eyes watchful. He gave her a formal nod.

She didn't blame him. Her "thanks" had come across like a routine civility, cool and automatic.

Not at all how I'd meant to sound.

Alex switched his attention to Eilish and gave her a warm, welcoming smile.

"Welcome to San Francisco. We're delighted to have you here."

Her cheeks flushed a deep pink as he pivoted on one foot and left the room.

Eating humble pie is going to be a lot harder than I thought. I don't even know where to start.

Thirty-five

Dionisio gazed at the young woman at his side with his lazy bedroom eyes. They were the sexy eyes he'd found most women couldn't resist, and he leaned over and breathed heavily into her right ear.

She pulled back sharply, her hand coming up to her ear with a light slapping sound, her face registering shock.

He gave a whiskey-fueled laugh.

"What's wrong, sweetheart? You're not shy?"

Her arms went tightly to the sides of her skirts, as if she were expecting him to rip her dress off, and her eyes teared up.

He shook his head in disgust.

"Don't worry, darling. I'm not paying for anything I can get for free."

"And I'm not selling, so that's good," she said hotly, swinging around to walk away.

He grabbed at her arm and held her back.

"Fiery little cat, aren't you? I like hot-blooded women."

She wrenched at her arm, attempting to break his hold.

He let go of her suddenly and took a step back, his hands raised in a gesture of surrender.

"Hey, hey. Don't be like that," he said in a more moderate tone.

He glanced around them, but no one was taking any notice.

Couples whirled around on the small dance floor. Beyond the dancing, women nestled on scallop-backed sofas beside attentive men, sipping drinks, giggling, getting acquainted.

The Red Fox Fandango, his favorite "party room," provided an innocuous setting for light entertainment, with pretty girls to chat to. It also provided a prelude, if customers desired it, for a visit to the bedrooms upstairs.

It was a tastefully designed meeting place, supplied with endless numbers of "party girls" to encourage the clients to buy drinks and sometimes other favors as well.

"Your boss won't like it if I give you a poor report," he said teasingly. "The least you can do is get me to buy some more drinks."

She glanced around fearfully, as if expecting the hostess for the night to be looking over her shoulder.

She was a pretty blue-eyed brunette with a button nose and perfectly sculpted pink lips. Obviously new to this game, but he found her fresh-faced innocence refreshing.

"What's your name, anyway?" he asked. "Mine's Dionisio."

"Violet," she said, a little too quickly.

"Well, Violet, let's find somewhere quiet to talk. I'll get us both a drink and you can tell me your life story."

She stared up at him with a calculating glint.

Innocent, but not stupid, he thought.

"I promise. I won't eat you. You'll be safer with me than some of these other Lotharios."

He gestured around them. "What do you reckon?"

She sighed resignedly and allowed him to lead her to a corner love seat.

***

Dionisio didn't really understand why he'd felt the need to bury himself in his cups after the depressing talk with Bram Gordon earlier in the day.

Did he expect he'd accept him as a surrogate son and welcome him with open arms?

He wasn't that simple-minded. He knew Alistair's death had gutted him, but he hadn't expected his lethal bitterness, his resigned despair.

The man is giving up on life when victory is at his fingertips.

He was a master at buying up vacant properties where no known heirs remained, but where city rates and other costs had been racked up and the property left in debt.

Bram did a deal with the city fathers to pay all the accumulated costs and take over the property for a song and a prayer. He'd done it before, so why not again?

Dionisio had seen to it that no heirs remained to be found. Except he hadn't expected Alex de Vile's inconvenient appearance.

It hadn't counted before, because the dude did not know he was in line to inherit. But now that the family matriarch was in town, that must change.

Castellanos had been ignorant of his family heritage until the old grandmother arrived. He was pretty sure of that.

But who knew what he understood about it now? And they

couldn't wait around for a court hearing to find out.

If he turned up there next week as a rightful heir, it would blow Bram's plans right out of the water.

He says he doesn't care now, but will he still feel that way when I step in to take over?

Garcia flexed his shoulders, reminding himself of who he was.

I haven't come this close to getting my hands on a sizeable chunk of land, only to have it ripped from my fingers.

I've already put a lot of time and money into arranging this double cross.

He surfaced from his tipsy musings to eye the little piece seated beside him.

"Cat got your tongue?"

She gazed back up at him with a perky grin.

Feeling more confident now I'm not trying to rush you off to bed, I see.

He reached out and gently stroked her cheek. Her eyes flashed wide like a shying mare, but she remained quiet in her seat.

"Just thinking about how cruel life can be," he said. Except the words didn't quite come out right.

"Not jush," he corrected. "Just."

Her face lit up with amusement.

"It's all right. I know you're drunk. I don't mind. So long as you don't get abusive."

He laughed in response. "You are a cheeky puss, aren't you?"

She ignored the friendly jibe.

"Why do you say life's cruel?"

"Ahh, little girl. You wouldn't understand."

"I might. Tell me."

"I done a lot of things for the big man and he's acting like he owes me nothing. And it gets me all humdurgeoned."

"Humdurgeoned? Why let him give you the needle?"

He took another swallow, though he knew he didn't need any more to drink.

"Good queshtion."

"What did you do for him?"

She regarded him with blinking periwinkle eyes.

"I killed a man…. Two men, actually. Nearly three."

The skin around those blue eyes went white, but she held her nerve.

"Were they bad men?"

"Mmmm." He licked his lips while he considered the question.

"One of them was a no-good son of a gun. No one will miss him. The other? He was my dearest friend."

Her ruby red tongue shot out, and she licked her top lip nervously.

"So why did you kill him?" she asked, her eyes under wrinkled brows flickering across his face.

He shrugged. "It was an accident," he said lamely, though he instantly knew it was a lie.

"He got in the way. That's all."

"Oh. How sad," she said lightly. "Will you go to hell?"

He stared into her innocent face, and an irrepressible wave of laughter engulfed him.

"You little devil," he slurred. "You're ash bad ash I am."

He was certain she gave him a knowing smile, before he ran out of breath and the world went black.

Thirty-six

Two-and-a-half-year-old George threw up his arms as Fanny entered the playroom, jumping up on both feet and grinning wildly. He'd already worked out when Fanny came to visit a small treat appeared. A bonbon or an iced gingerbread biscuit always followed.

"Gam Gam," he cried, his arms up for a cuddle, whooping with laughter.

Fanny swooped down and gathered him up in her arms, smothering his dewy, soft-pink face in smoochy kisses as she laughed with him.

The children had only known her a week, but already they were a family. She held him in her arms until he started wriggling and then put him down again with a teasing rush. He guffawed and clapped loudly.

"Oh, to be his age again."

Fanny's voice held a note of pained longing as she crossed the room to engulf Graysie in a warm hug.

"Not a care in the world. Long may it be so," she said with a wide smile.

"How are we all this fair day, Graysie, my love?"

"As busy and gorgeous as ever," Graysie chuckled, drawing six-year-old dark-haired Minette to her side.

"Say hello to Gam Gam Fanny, darling."

Minette gave Fanny a shy smile.

"Does this mean we are going to the park again?" she asked, holding Graysie's hand and looking from one of the adults to the other with shining eyes.

"Would you like to go to the park?" Fanny asked, leaning over to peck Minette's cheek. "Perhaps we'll see the ducks again."

Minette jumped up and down with excitement. "And feed them again? Have we got any spare bread, Sissy?"

Sissy. The name she'd adopted for Graysie long before her mother Francine had died tragically and Graysie had taken over her care.

"Why don't you go and ask Nanny Blanchett to get some from the kitchens?"

***

Half an hour later, the governess was supervising the children as they fed ducks at the pond side while Graysie and Fanny sat on a bench seat in the morning sun.

The trees were a vibrant high summer green, the gardens a riot of bright yellow goldenrod and red pineapple sage that scented the air with a fruity sweetness.

Fanny stretched her arms along the back of the park bench and leaned back contentedly.

"It's been such a blessing to get to know you all this last week," she said with a wry smile in Graysie's direction.

"You'll never know how grateful I am you've delayed going back to Grass Valley so I can see a little more of the children before I leave."

Graysie patted her hand affectionately. "It's been marvelous for me to get to know you too," she said. "Rafael was the dearest father to me until Mother died. I'll never forget that."

A vacant peace fell between them, the words that came to both their minds unsaid.

Until Mother died.

"He worshipped Elanora," Fanny said. "And because you were her daughter, he adored you too. He never once acknowledged you were not his child, although I'm sure he knew it."

Graysie gave a sad smile in agreement.

"He always made me feel special. It was that awful woman he took on as a housekeeper who spoiled everything."

Another long silence. The blistering sun was making Fanny feel sleepy. Warm air caressed her neck. The silence was broken only by an occasional bird call, and the faint sound of creaking pram wheels and children's laughter as the nannies brought them out to play.

"What was her name? You've only referred to her as Mrs. T."

Fanny could sense Graysie's shudder.

"Temptation Thompson. I always thought of her as the hated Mrs. T. She claimed she was a widow, though now I've grown older I wonder about that. Nothing got her madder than being called Thompson. She so wanted to bask in Father's glory."

Fanny fought back a sudden rush of tears.

"Did she love him, do you think?"

Graysie gazed at her with her watery gold and green eyes, her face a picture of considered thoughtfulness.

Then she winced and shook her head from side to side.

"Honestly? I think Father kept her on because he needed someone to look after me when he did his photographic trips. He'd no clue how awful she was when he was away.

"He had to travel to keep the money coming in. He couldn't work and look after me at the same time. And she put on such a good act of being nice to me when he was around."

She grimaced.

"He vanished into his work after Mother died. It felt like it was all he had, really."

Fanny swallowed hard, years of stored grief and rejection making themselves felt in her throat.

"I've often wondered…" She struggled to get the words out. "Do you think Rafael ever got any of the letters I sent him?

"Did he know we loved him and worried about him? And if he did know, why didn't he ever reply? Did he remember us? His father and he were so close.

"They shared their passion for photography, for a start… Angel was so proud of Rafael, his pioneering work. Did he know that? And if he did, why did he never reply?"

She glanced away to the pond, where the children were still happily engaged with the ducks.

"Or did he think we'd forgotten about you all, that we didn't care?"

Once she'd begun to speak, the floodgates opened. She'd

tortured herself, kept quiet on her fears for so long, and now she was confessing her doubts, facing up to her grief.

Graysie hugged her into her shoulder as the tears trickled down her cheeks, and she did not hide them.

"I told you about the one letter I saw, and how furious she was about it," Graysie said. "It was a forbidden topic, as far as I was concerned from then on. Did she ever show it to Father?"

She laced her fingers before her mouth and gave a deep sigh.

"I don't know. To be fair, I just don't know. But I suspect not. Any mention of his previous life got her angry. She wanted to think it all began with her."

Fanny sat in silence as the tears dried.

This afternoon peace, sitting here saying nothing to Graysie, is healing, she told herself.

A sudden thought pierced her mellow mood, like a hatpin in her scalp.

"Is she still alive? This Temptation Thompson? Do you know if she's still alive?"

Graysie gave a reluctant smile and shook her head.

"I've no idea. She drove me out after Father died. I ran away because she only wanted me for the money I made from singing. Once I escaped her clutches, I never wanted to go back. Why?"

"One of those silly things, I suppose. I'd like to hear from her own mouth whether she ever gave Rafael my letters. Or whether she stole all of them. To me, that's about the cruelest thing anyone could do."

Graysie considered her words, her mouth downturned.

"She was capable of it. Believe you me. But did she actually do it? Honestly, I don't know."

Thirty-seven

"Turn your head a little further to the right… further… stop! That's exactly right. It shows off your beautiful profile to perfection."

Beautiful profile?

Rosie ground her back teeth as she watched Alejandro duck under his photographer's cloth to focus on the third of this morning's portraits, one in a series he had planned to take of Eilish in his Montgomery Street studio and later, out in the garden.

He'd explained some of the finer technical points of the session to them when they'd arrived. Well, if Rosie was strictly honest with herself, he explained it all to Eilish, in a charming, intense conversation which barely acknowledged Rosie's presence.

She was here as Eilish's companion and Alex's assistant, the "go-to" girl who tweaked at the fall of a skirt, helped Eilish with costume changes, tidied her hair or added a hat or other props.

Flowers on a table, a book to lie open at Eilish's elbow. She was there to organize the shot however Alejandro desired. The less she said, the better. The more invisible she was, the more appreciated she'd be.

And through the entire session—they'd been going nearly three hours so far and were due for a refreshment stop shortly—Alejandro had been complimentary and encouraging of his model's work.

"You've such a beautiful, calm presence, Eilish," he said early on. "It's hard work when the subject is tense and fidgety. I have to spend all my mental energy making them feel comfortable. With you, I can simply focus on the work."

Rosie's spirits sagged. She let out a long, silent sigh and noted to herself he'd never asked her to sit for him. But was that at all surprising?

Even before their major falling out over Dionisio, she'd been combative and too free with her opinions. No wonder the man was ignoring her.

She hated it, but being a silent observer certainly helped her develop a keener appreciation of his work.

He'd explained it all so thoughtfully to Eilish; how the new tin type process he was trialling published the results within minutes, rather than hours, and also made it much easier to shoot photos outdoors.

They'd taken shots of Eilish stretched out on a chaise longue in a "come hither" pose in fluid white satin, her glorious mane of auburn hair flowing around her shoulders.

Eilish, with her elbow on a stack of books on the occasional table next to her chair, hand resting on her chin, looking pensive, with her hair tucked under a coquettish felt hat.

And now, perched forward in a calfskin-covered armchair, her arms folded along the upholstered arms, the royal blue of her dress providing an interesting contrast with the light background.

Each shot required costume changes and adjustments to her hair. A touch of rouge and lip gloss, applied by Rosie, a shadowy presence, who'd obeyed all of Alejandro's directives without question.

He was the artist, she was merely the "go-to" girl—she understood that.

"I've got a breathtaking model at my disposal," he said to Eilish. "And I don't want the opportunity to go to waste. You never know. We might take something good enough to enter a competition."

His eyes glided over Rosie as if she wasn't in the room.

I deserve this, Rosie thought. I'm probably lucky he didn't throw me out altogether.

Eilish was regarding Alex with a dewy-eyed adoration.

Who can blame her? He's brought her out here, he's paying for her to see a specialist to check if anything can be done now about her leg, and he's making a fuss over her.

No wonder she's in love with him.

She switched her attention to Alejandro. who was emerging from under his camera hood, his fine-featured face alive with his passion for his work.

"That's wonderful, Eilish," he called, a broad smile on his sculpted lips.

"We'll take a break and then do a few shots in the garden before it gets too hot to sit out there."

He paused.

"Come to think of it, one with a parasol would be nice."

"Could you dig out a parasol for the after-lunch shots, Rosie?" He glanced briefly in her direction but did not hold eye contact.

"I'll see what I can do," she replied gamely.

Eilish slipped out of the calf hide chair and fell into step with Alex as they went from the studio to the dining table, where Alex's housekeeper was serving lunch.

Neither took any notice of Rosie trailing along behind them.

***

Magdalena gave her the same cold shoulder treatment as Alex at the show that night.

I shouldn't be surprised, she thought disconsolately, as she pulled on her costume in the ratty dressing room to which they had suddenly demoted her.

Obviously tittle-tattlers had got in the star's ear and told them Dionisio fell over Rosie with amorous intentions after she left.

When she arrived for the pre-show briefing, one of the assistant stage managers drew her aside and told her she'd no longer be sharing with a dressing room with Magdalena.

"Magda wants her privacy, love," Ned advised. "Says she is sick of people hanging on her coattails."

He blushed as he registered the implications of his words and stammered his excuse.

"Not that she'd be talking about you or anyfink. She just wants a bit more privacy."

"I understand," Rosie said with as much composure as she could muster.

The show that night was awful. Magdalena delivered her lines with passion and fury but addressed them over Rosie's head, refusing to make eye contact.

Goodness knows what the audience in the penny dreadfuls think of this show, Rosie thought grimly to herself. There's not much I can do to rescue it when she's determined to act as if I'm not here.

As the audience caught on to the tense atmosphere, there were more regular calls for their song, and Rosie tried to camp it up more than usual to make amends.

But in bed that night she lay stiff as a board on her back, gazing at the ceiling.

She'd made enemies of two of the people she'd valued the most, and right now there wasn't a thing she could do about it.

She needed to keep close to Dionisio and his friends. to work out what was really going on and to protect Isabella and Alejandro from further harm.

And if that meant she had to be a foul smell in their nostrils, then she'd have to wear the cost.

Especially now she was so heavily indebted to Alex for "rescuing" Eilish. He'd already made an appointment for her to see a physician about her condition, to discuss if anything could be done to ease her pain and strengthen her weak side.

She rolled over in Isabella's soft bed, the one she usually found so comfortable and encompassing. But not tonight. She pulled her arms close around her, seeking the feeling of succor she usually enjoyed in the safety of this room.

Instead, she was on edge, her legs and arms twitching with a nervous energy she couldn't fidget away.

It's wonderful they're getting on so well together, she told herself stoutly. I'm thrilled for her.

He's generous in doing this. I'd never be able to give her the same chances and I'm not in the least bit jealous.

When this is all over, what will I do? Go back to the Crabtree Circus?

As a fretful sleep descended, the last image that floated into her mind was of Eilish and Alex, gaily processing out of his studio, with her trailing behind like a wet dog hiding from a thunderstorm.

Thirty-eight

They'd eagerly consumed the cherry clafouti dessert and the wait staff were serving steaming hot coffee from silver pots as they sat back, replete and sleepy, in their dining table chairs.

Fanny stood at the head of the 12-seater table and tinged with a spoon on a crystal wineglass to get their attention.

"I love being able to host you all for a family dinner. I never in my wildest dreams imagined it happening," she said, as she paused and glanced around the circle with wide, sparkling eyes.

"But I have a more serious purpose in calling you all together tonight."

Her eyes traveled from Alejandro to Isabella, from Graysie to the Russell men, then to Eilish and Rosie, included as special family guests.

Finally, Fanny's gaze alighted on the lawyer, Ewan Campbell, seated next to Eilish.

"With the exception of Rosie and Eilish, you all have some direct involvement in what I am going to say next, but perhaps Ewan, most of all among you, will appreciate its significance."

All eyes switched to Ewan, who gave a contented "cat got

the cream smirk" as if he already had a good warning of what was coming.

Rosie, who sat on the other side of Eilish from the sandy-haired lawyer, whispered in her ear: "I bet the Marquésa has already picked his brains on this. I'd wager it relates to land. That's Ewan's speciality."

Eilish's face pinkened, and she sent her a wordless message with her deep brown eyes.

Keep quiet! You're embarrassing me.

Rosie smiled to herself.

Nothing's changed between us.

I'm still the noisy interloper and she's the perfectly behaved guest.

Eilish slanted her eyes sideways to check on Ewan's demeanor and he flashed her a warm smile.

My sister's charming all the men, thought Rosie. She's certainly a lot more popular than I am.

"Ewan will add some thoughts of his at the end, but first let me outline the situation as I understand it."

Rosie's eyes gleefully shot an "I told you so" message to Eilish, who raised her index finger to her lips in warning.

Fanny hesitated, seeming to consider how to begin.

"Many years ago, before I met my husband, and when this land was Alta California and this town was Yerba Buena, Angel was granted a 50 percent share in a Spanish land claim with one of his good friends, Hernandez Valaquez.

"The land was north of here near Sonoma, ten thousand acres along the Los Putos River. Beautiful river flats suitable for ranching with good grass, as well as drier, less fertile areas.

"Hernandez was the brother of one of the early Spanish governors, and it wasn't hard for young adventurers with good connections to acquire vast stretches of ranching country in those days.

"For Angel, it was all part of the adventure of being young and free in a big new land.

"But as you all know, that period didn't last long for Angel. He was called away to a life of diplomacy which he loved, and he faithfully served his Spanish sovereign one way or another for the rest of his life.

"Hernandez stayed and for some years kept at least some cattle, before he too was drawn into other pursuits and gradually lost interest.

"I gather he couldn't make it pay. He racked up debts. He may have even sold some of it without contacting Angel about it. We don't know. We lost touch, and not just with Hernandez."

She paused, her face crumpling for a moment. "With Rafael, too. To think our darling son died here, and we didn't know it for so long. Even when I sent him letter after letter. We never heard…"

She swallowed hard and blinked tears away.

"When Angel was lying in with his last illness, his mind returned to California. Thoughts of Rafael possessed him. He became feverish, torturing himself about his unknown fate.

She glanced at Alejandro, who sat next to Seb, a tense forefinger rotating the cup in its saucer in front of him, eyes narrowed in concentration.

Rosie's breath caught in her chest.

"Most of all, he wanted to know what happened to you,"

she said, casting her sorrowful, deep brown eyes from him to Isabella

"He remembered the land he'd acquired all those years ago. In fact, he couldn't forget it.

"A desire to reclaim it for the next generation possessed him. He wanted to pass it on, either to the daughter or son who'd remained with us in Spain, or any descendants Rafael might have in California.

"He made me promise I would do my utmost to see it was restored to the family."

She spread her palm out upwards in a gesture of surrender.

Trapped in a private bubble, a tense silence hovered over the table, the nearest sound the low scraunch of Alejandro's cup in its saucer as he continued to inch it in circles. More distantly, Rosie caught the faint clink of crockery from the hotel dining room.

"So, here I am. The first part of my mission is completed. I've discovered our darling Rafael's fate, and reconnected—to my utmost delight—with his family.

"Now, to satisfy my darling husband's unquiet spirit, I want to complete the second part of his commission."

As Fanny spoke, a deep calm crept over the gathering's strained silence. Alejandro removed his hand from the cup and rested his elbow on the table.

When she finally fell silent, no one spoke.

Then she turned to Ewan and said, "We've already canvassed some of this together, Ewan. Tell everyone about your thoughts on this situation."

Ewan stood and gazed around the group, his face quiet and serious.

"I've always suspected the attack on Alejandro was connected to a land claim, but we didn't know where to look. I had no idea it might be linked to the Valaquez issue.

"It's clear now why Alex might have been a target. What surprises me is how they knew Alejandro was Rafael's son."

He paused as a hotel staffer approached their table.

"Anything else we can get you, Marquésa?"

He glanced around the table uncertainly.

"Would the gentlemen like brandy?"

Fanny waved a courtly arm. "Give us another fifteen minutes, Anastasio. Thank you."

Ewan waited until the man was out of earshot and continued.

"Alex has been known publicly as the senator's son his whole life. His true origins were only discovered recently, and they've always been a private family matter, haven't they?"

He picked up an inch-thick file of papers and waved them in the air, as if to demonstrate the mystery.

Rosie glimpsed an official looking document with a stately seal on the top of the pile.

"Whoever it was who attacked him knew more than we did about his family heritage—until now. With what the Marquésa is able to tell us we've got a new start.

"It gives us very clear lines of inquiry to follow up on—but we've got virtually no time to do it. The case is due for its final hearing next week, and the general feeling is it's a foregone conclusion. Bram Gordon will get ownership.

"Since Hernandez's son Emmanuel died a few months back, until Fanny and the twins turned up there were no other recognized heirs.

Ewan slapped his paper file back down with an air of resignation.

"Even if you appear in court, it's not a foregone conclusion that Angel's interests will be recognized. The court might decide too much time has passed to unwind things. You might have missed the boat on that one, I'm afraid, Fanny.

"Bram's got the judges and other administration staff nicely tied up with a bow, if you ask me. That's the way he operates. He'll pay them into submission."

Alejandro jumped up from his seat.

"I can't believe we sorted through all those old claim documents and never recognized what was in front of our noses. What can we do to stop it all from going to the Gordons?"

He stared around the table with passionate eyes.

"That's what you'd all want, isn't it?"

"Absolutely," said Graysie. "I doubt Rafael knew anything about this, but he'd want you and Isabella to have your interests recognized, I'm certain."

"It seems so wrong that Bram Gordon can corrupt the process," agreed Nathan. "And especially galling that his son tried to kill Alex. Now we know it was to prevent him from discovering his rights."

"Worse yet, that they're trying to pin his death on you," said Isabella with vehemence.

Ewan glanced at Fanny.

"Sounds like they're right behind you, Fanny. We show up in court and fight. We've got a heck of a lot of preparation to do before we're ready to face those judges, though. And very little time."

Alejandro stripped off his dinner jacket, unbuttoned his cuffs, and began to roll up his sleeves.

"What are you waiting for then, Ewan?"

He met Fanny's startled eyes. "Firstly, dear Gam Gam, we need a full account, as detailed as you can make it, of what you understood occurred. And the signed claim documents, if you have them."

"That I do," Fanny said with a broad smile. "Your grandfather was nothing if he wasn't a perfect diplomatic recorder."

Thirty-nine

Rosie hovered in the schoolyard, feeling like an interloper, watching as Eilish greeted and farewelled mothers and nannies who arrived to collect their children from class.

Lessons were over for the day, and some children lingered in the yard, playing at hopscotch or tossing balls, while others ran to their mothers' sides to prepare to go home.

A small tousle-haired boy with brilliant blue-gray eyes fringed by dark hair hung off Eilish's free hand as she negotiated her way across the schoolyard.

They threaded their way through a stream of visitors there to collect their offspring, eager to hear good reports of the day's activities.

The child gazed up at her sister as if she were his sun and moon, his adoration plain in his engrossed expression.

She's been here barely more than a week and she's already winning hearts.

Add his name to the list. Alejandro, Ewan, this little fellow, whoever he is. Who's next?

Eilish caught sight of her, and the surprise and delight in her eyes immediately shamed Rosie's gnawing envy.

You're just peeved because you've taken it for granted you're the show pony of the family, and see what's happened?

Eilish has grown into her deserved place as a true champion.

They meshed in a joyous hug, and her sister immediately leaned down and whispered to the small boy.

"Fergus says hello," she said. "His mum will be here any minute."

"Hello Miss Rosie," Fergus piped up, his enormous eyes latched on hers. "You're Miss Kelly's sister, aren't you? She's told me all about you. How clever you are."

Rosie's throat gurgled in unexpected pleasure.

"She said I'm clever, did she? Do you think she wants something? Sweeties, perhaps?"

He folded into Eilish's skirts, giggling, as Rosie thrust her hand into her pocket and drew out a chunk of caramel candy wrapped in waxy paper.

"Like this one, just for you."

He gazed at her hand in awe.

From his thin worn shorts and patched but heavily washed shirt, she guessed the kid didn't get many treats.

He glanced uncertainly to Eilish, seeking permission to take it, and she smiled and nodded down at him.

"Yes Fergus, you can take the candy. We're not in class now."

His little fingers shot out and peeled the toffee out of Rosie's palm with the delicacy of a butterfly landing on a flower. He tore off the paper and placed the candy against his lips. His luminous eyes widened with pleasure.

He's never tasted caramel before.

Rosie lifted her eyes to her sister's face, her brows raised in a hidden query.

Where does this little gem come from?

"Fergus's mum is a clerk at the courts and sometimes she has to work late, so we keep company together until she gets here," Eilish said in explanation.

As they'd been standing talking, Rosie became aware the yard had fallen silent as the last remnants of the class departed with their mothers.

"Do you think we've got time to learn a new song before Mummy comes?" she asked.

Fergus's angelic face lit up, and Rosie crouched down on her haunches to meet him at eye level. She launched into a fun Irish song from Magdalena's show about a little red fox that breaks into the hen house—"Madairin Rua."

The chorus—in Gaelic—always amused audiences.

An Madairin a Rua, Rua, Rua, Rua, Rua

An Madairin a Rua ta granna…

The child stared in wonder as she danced a few steps back and forth beside him, then broke into peels of delighted laughter.

I've forgotten how much fun it is to be around children, Rosie thought as she laughed and sang.

I've forgotten a lot of things.

Like how much I love my sister.

She sensed the moment Fergus's attention was distracted away from her mad caper and she stopped singing and turned to the street.

A pretty but tired-looking young woman crossed the yard, hands clasping the side of her face.

"I'm so sorry to be late again, Eilish,"she called. "I hate to keep you waiting."

Eilish 's smile was full of understanding.

"You know I love having extra time with Fergus, Diana. It's no problem at all.

"You haven't met my sister, I don't think. Rosie Kelly. Rosie. Meet Fergus's mother, Diana Gilligan."

Fergus tugged at his mother's hand. "Rosie gave me a candy, and it was am-az-ing."

Diana glanced down at her son and rubbed at his sugar-caked chin with her thumb.

"I can see she did," she said, laughing.

Her eyes were moist when she gazed into Rosie's face.

"He's never had candy," she said, a soft Irish lilt in her voice. "You've made his day."

"And she sang me a song," said Fergus, his eyes sparkling. He turned to Rosie. "Can you sing it again? I want to learn it."

"We have to be going, Fergus," Diana said. "Perhaps another day."

Eilish jumped in. "Why don't you come to visit tomorrow and teach all the children the red fox song?" She grinned at her sister. "I'm sure they'd all love it."

Rosie gave an answering smile. "Nothing to stop me if you'd like that, I suppose. I'm not likely to have my job in Magdalena's show for too much longer."

Eilish frowned. "Oh? Why not? I thought you were getting good houses. What's happened?"

"We're still getting good houses, but Magdalena's got a

snitch on me because of Dionisio."

"Dionisio? What's he got to do with it?"

"Magda and Dion had a fight, and he started paying me attention—not that I wanted him to. And now she's got it in for me."

Rosie became aware that their visitor, Fergus's mother, was silently gaping at the overheard conversation.

She turned to the young woman. "Sorry. You don't need to know all about my woes. I'd be happy to come back and teach the kids few songs, that's all."

Diana continued to stare, a bewildered cast to her face.

"Dionisio? As in Dionisio Garcia? That same one?"

Rosie studied her conflicted expression.

"The same. Why? Do you know him?"

Diana's eyes flickered toward Fergus, who was holding her hand and watching the adults carefully, his avid curiosity plain to see, taking in every word.

She doesn't want to say anything those flapping little ears will pick up on.

Rosie made one of those intuitive snap decisions that can change lives.

"I'll tell you what. Why don't we go get a meal at Grandma's Kitchen? My treat? I'm sure it will help with your budget, and I'm new to town.

"In return for dinner, I could use some local advice about who's who and what's what. Is that okay with you?"

Diana's face betrayed doubt, but Fergus jumped up and down excitedly at her side. His enthusiasm appeared to swing her decision in Rosie's favor.

"He's excited about eating out," she said. "We never do that."

***

They settled in Grandma's Kitchen and ordered cottage pie followed by apple shortcake.

Fergus sat wide-eyed, totally immersed in the bustling scene, watching the servers with laden trays delivering food to the tables, and listening for the loud calls from the kitchen whenever a new order was being dispatched.

"Lamb's fry and bacon for Table Six." "Grilled sole coming up for Table Eleven." "Here it is—fish stew for Thirteen."

Under the cover of the excitement, Rosie and Diana conversed freely.

And after they'd covered the "getting to know you" preliminaries, Rosie told Diana about escaping New York and joining Lotta Crabtree's show, and Diana described her job at the Land Claims Court.

My guardian angel is sure looking after me today.

Rosie shot a "thank you" heavenward—and whether Diana knew it, they got down to Rosie's business.

"You know Dionisio then?" she asked, working to sound as casual as she could, though she doubted she'd fooled Diana for one minute.

"I've seen an awful lot of him this last couple of weeks because he's always drinking with Magdalena after the shows. He rarely lets her out of his sight."

Diana smiled knowingly. "I know who he is. Everyone at the court does, because he hangs around there so much. He wouldn't have a clue who I am, though."

Rosie raised her brows in cheeky skepticism. "Really? A pretty girl like you?"

She grinned. "I've got the distinct impression he makes it his business to know all the pretty girls, and you'd certainly qualify."

Diana's startling blue eyes dropped to her plate, and her cheeks reddened.

"Oh, I'm sorry. Me and my big mouth. Have I said something wrong?"

Diana stared straight at her. "No, no, not at all. It's just me. I keep a very low profile around the court because of someone else there."

A strange conviction took hold of Rosie.

"Not Elmer Green, by any chance?"

Her hectic pink cheeks darkened to crimson.

"How..." She coughed, struggling to get the words out. "How did you know?"

"A hunch, really," said Rosie. "He's always hanging around Dionisio, and yet they are so different. I've wondered why."

She hesitated, and seeing that Fergus was engrossed watching the next table where two small girls dined with their parents, continued.

"He's often at the post show drinks too, though he hardly ever says anything. That's why when Elmer said something a bit odd, too, it made me think."

"What did he say?" asked Diana with intense interest.

"Oh, something about 'guarding his investment.' He said he had a lot invested in Dionisio and he was guarding his investment."

Diana chewed her lip. The corners curled up in a way that signaled she'd tasted something sour.

"Elmer's trying to make a name for himself as one of the town's 'top men' so he can marry well. It's very important to him because his father's a judge and he wants to prove he's living up to his expectations.

"He's made it clear he won't marry 'just anybody.' They have to be 'somebody.'"

"Is that so?" said Rosie, amused at sour-faced Elmer having grand notions about future wives.

"And what's their business, do you know? Dionisio's and Elmer's, I mean."

Diana flushed, but shook her head in denial.

Some conflict here. Does she or doesn't she know?

"Something to do with land," she said. "They're always huddled together in Elmer's office, and they don't like to be disturbed."

The server came with their cottage pie, together with green beans and tomato ketchup.

Fergus asked if he could sit with the girls at the next table, who he recognized from play school, and Diana had a quick chat with their parents and they agreed.

"Do you know which claim they're talking about?" Rosie asked after they'd got him re-located.

"Oh, I'm pretty sure it's more than one. Garcia's been working for Bram Gordon for years. They seem to get what they want in court most of the time. The commissioners love them because they make knotty problems go away.

"A lot of the deals they do are on deserted land that's piled up enormous debts. You know, places where the original owners aren't occupying it and squatters have taken over?

"When they settle on a place like that, everyone who's owed money gets paid out, so the town loves them. The squatters? They don't have any rights, so who cares?"

"Ohhh… I understand," said Rosie. "It's annoying for the bureaucrats when that kind of thing is left in a mess."

Diana looked around her, as if checking for eavesdroppers, but the background noise in the busy family café drowned out their voices to prevent anyone overhearing them.

"You're quite right, if it was all done according to the law, but I don't think it is."

"What do you mean?" Rosie asked. "How could it not be all right?"

"If you created false documents, for example, and from what I hear, that's what they do."

The blood in Rosie's veins turned cold.

"False documents?" she asked in a squeaky voice.

"Like what?"

Diana shrugged. "Like birth certificates, ownership documents, signed sales agreements. The possibilities are endless…"

"What makes you think they do this kind of thing?"

"I don't just think, I know," Diana said hotly. "I've seen them."

A storm of excitement cascaded inside Rosie. Her heart sped up as she fought to caution herself about expecting too much from this revelation.

"Golly gosh," she said, battling to sound casual and playful.

"You hear stories, but I never really believed things like that happened."

"When people want something desperately enough, they do," Diana said.

"More than anything, Elmer wants to climb the social ladder, and to do that, he needs money. In San Francisco, that's what talks. Money."

Rosie detected a note of bitterness in the girl's voice, and her blood sung in her veins.

She's got a personal axe to grind here. I've struck gold.

"Is that right?' she replied, pitching her voice to sound naïve and amazed. "I'm new in town. I had no idea."

She paced herself, ensuring she didn't sound too eager.

"You must see a lot of Elmer Green in your job. What's he like? Do you work for him?"

Diana's face lit up with a powerful emotion, but Rosie found it hard to identify exactly what she was experiencing.

Is she angry? Or embarrassed? Or both?

There was a long, awkward silence. Her companion glanced to the next table, where Fergus still played happily with the girls.

"Not now, I don't. I'm in records now. I used to be on reception. I had a lot to do with him then. Before Fergus was born." She hesitated, and glanced around again.

Whatever it is she's hiding, it involves Fergus.

"He doesn't know I've got the job in records. If he found out, he'd probably try to get rid of me. I'm very careful about him not seeing me."

She flicked Rosie a resigned grin.

"You ask what he's like? He's an absolute cad. He'd sell his own grandmother if he could see an advantage in it."

Rosie pulled a sympathetic face. "Oh Diana, I'm so sorry you had to work with someone like that."

She paused, and let her tender feelings flow across the gap that separated them like a healing balm.

Then she added, "So, he's selling stuff—information or whatever—to Dionisio, to Bram Gordon?"

"To them and anyone else who's willing to pay," she said, the bitterness no longer concealed.

Rosie could tell by the briskness of her pace that she'd decided to spill the beans.

"We were engaged. He thought I was wonderful," she said. "My blue starry eyes, my hair like a thunderstorm… It didn't matter that my family were ordinary people. I was beautiful, sweet-natured, everything he wanted in a wife. He loved me. That's what he said."

She nervously fingered a spoon that lay beside her plate.

"He loved me all right. Until I got in the family way. Then I was rubbish. He turned his back on me. And Fergus."

She threw Rosie a wicked grin. "But I got my revenge. When I say I've seen evidence of what he's up to, I don't mean I've laid eyes on it and put it back in the files. I took notes."

"Notes? Like what?"

A veil fell over the face that momentarily had been openly gleeful.

She glanced around nervously.

"I can't say. I'd get into big trouble if anyone knew what I've done. But one day…"

Fergus distracted her attention. He was pushing back from the table next door and turning to come back to her side.

"Mum…" he whined.

"Can we go now? I'm tired."

Darn it. That's it for tonight, I guess.

"This one is on me," Rosie said, voice ringing with a bravado she didn't feel. "It's been lovely to talk. We'll have to do it again soon."

Forty

"I thought I should warn you, Marquésa. Bram Gordon will present some kind of fake documents to the court. Of that, I'm certain. But I can't say yet what documents they'll be."

The Marquésa Fanny di Ortonez Castellanos gazed into the Irish girl's dazzling green eyes and marveled again at her intrepid spirit.

She's so delightfully unaware of her own attractiveness. Beauty and brains in one lovely body.

The older woman had interrupted her mid-afternoon rest to hold this audience in her Lick House rooms. Apparently, Juliana's message that Rosie Kelly wanted to see her with important news had intrigued her enough to break her routines.

They were barely a few minutes into their conversation when Rosie convinced her the information was worth her sacrificing her private nap.

The Irish lass's cheeks flushed with excitement, her urgent gold-flecked eyes sparkled. That glorious crown of red hair was like an aureole highlighting her flawless peaches and cream complexion.

Why on earth can't Alejandro appreciate her? I don't know.

Or rather, she corrected, why won't he admit he notices?

Fanny waited a few heartbeats before responding and Rosie took a deep breath and rushed on, radiant with youth and health.

"I appreciate it sounds vague right now, Marquésa. I didn't like to push Diana too far too fast, in case she took fright."

She wrung her hands together, her lips parted to display strong white teeth.

"I divulged nothing about your family business. It wasn't my right to share private matters, so Diana doesn't know you might be interested."

She momentarily closed her eyes, as if she was gathering her thoughts.

"Could I introduce you to Diana, and you two talk directly? Then she'd understand how important any information she has might be."

She swallowed hard and stared at Fanny expectantly.

Fanny let a long silence fall as she went over Rosie's suggestion in her mind.

"Your resourcefulness amazes me, Rose Kelly."

Her smile reached across the gap separating them, and she could almost feel the younger woman melt with her approval.

"Truly, you are a remarkable young woman."

Rosie gave her a jerky smile, as if hardly able to believe her ears.

Then she shook her head in denial.

"I've got the luck of the Irish," she laughed through the hand she'd raised to her mouth.

"I did nothing except respond to a gorgeous five-year-old. Fergus is an adorable child. You have to love someone who can raise a charmer like him."

She took up a cushion on the sofa beside her and gave it a couple of nervous slaps before stuffing it back behind her backbone.

"Is something bothering you?" Fanny asked. "You're anxious."

"I know Alejandro's been skeptical about Garcia, but I've always felt in my bones that he's muddled up in this somehow. I think I've mentioned it before.

"That's why I've tried to win his confidence. Why I accepted Magdalena's invitation to join her show. It was because of Alejandro being accused of that Gordon boy's murder."

She licked her lips again and shuffled awkwardly on the sofa. The cushion behind her back slipped, and she readjusted it again.

"Diana says Elmer Green and Garcia cook up a lot of business together.

"I'd bet my back teeth some of it relates to that Spanish claim your family has an interest in. And that would throw a whole new light on why those men broke into Alejandro's house, and what their motivation might be."

She pushed back confidently, smiling up at Fanny as she did.

"And now we might get our hands on documents that might prove it."

Fanny's lady-in-waiting Juliana tapped on the frame of the open doorway, but Rosie didn't notice the interruption.

She sailed on happily with her mission to accomplish.

"I'm seeing Diana when I go to the school to give the kids some singing lessons tomorrow. I'll push her for more details."

Fanny's majestic poise eased, and she shot Rosie an amused smile.

"Singing lessons? You are a young woman of diverse talents, aren't you, Rosie?"

She turned to Juliana. "What is it, Juliana? We haven't quite finished here. I can be with you in another few minutes."

"Not you, Marquésa. There's a messenger here for Miss Rosie. He says it's urgent."

Sam Butler's portly form shadowed Juliana in the entryway.

Rosie jumped up in alarm.

"Sam! What are you doing here? Isabella's all right, isn't she? Nothing's happened?"

Isabella's factotum shook his head but maintained his solemn demeanor.

"Nothing like that, Miss Rosie. Someone came for you with a letter and said it was urgent. Miz Isabella knew you were here and thought you should get it immediately."

He bobbed into a light bow in Fanny's direction and she gestured him into the room.

"Of course, Mr. Butler. Please come in."

Sam crossed the room and placed the paper in Rosie's outstretched hand.

She bit her lip as she ripped it open and read it; her face was still and expressionless.

Then she glanced up with a sigh.

"It shouldn't surprise me, I suppose. They've sacked me from the show. Magdalena is refusing to share the stage with me. They're going back to the script they were using before I joined."

Her eyes drifted to the carpet at her feet.

Fanny clapped her hands indignantly.

"Oh Rosie! I'm appalled. From what I hear, you're the life and soul of it. And I didn't have time to see it while you were in it. What on earth are they thinking?"

Rosie heaved her shoulders in a weary shrug.

"Honestly, I've been expecting it. Last night was awful. Magdalena refused to address any of her lines to me."

"What's happened? I thought you were good friends."

"Dionisio happened," said Rosie dejectedly. "She got the pip over him."

She grimaced. "I couldn't tell Magdalena why I was really there. She might have been tempted to tell Garcia."

She shrugged again.

"Magdalena's the star. She's fully within her rights. I'll just have to grin and bear it."

She attempted a brave smile.

"Anyway, now we've found Diana, buttering up Garcia isn't so important. We might do without him."

Fanny's lively curiosity sparked alive within her.

"It's a shame you have to lose the chance to do what you love, Rosie, but I'm sure there'll be other opportunities."

She hesitated. "Have things improved with Alejandro?"

"Not one bit," Rosie said with wide, candid eyes. "He doesn't acknowledge I exist. He's gone off with my sister Eilish."

Curioser and curioser, Fanny thought.

It takes old eyes to see what's going on here. Young ones clearly don't have a clue.

"My commiserations," Fanny said.

"You can tell your friend Diana I'd like to meet her. Why don't you invite her and this delightful little fellow Fergus for dinner tomorrow night, here at Lick House? Just you, me and them."

She turned to Juliana, who'd shown Sam out while they'd been talking and had quietly slipped back into the room.

"What time do young children like to eat, Juliana?"

Juliana's eyes drifted to Rosie, her brow raised in a query.

"About 5:30?" said Rosie. "I took them to Grandma's Kitchen last night. Now Lick House? That's really a step up."

Fanny glimpsed Rosie's usual sparkle and purpose in those amazing green eyes as she rose to take her leave.

Why on earth doesn't my photographer grandson notice those eyes? Is he blind?

"Five thirty it is," Fanny said, turning to Julia. "Mark it in my diary. Would you be a dear? And let the kitchen know."

Forty-one

Alex mightn't want to listen, but his Gam Gam does…

Rosie practically skipped along the streets back to Isabella and Sebastian's house. Her singing heart drowned out the deep fear of being jobless again that lurked in the recesses of her soul.

How am I going to help support my maa? she wondered.

I can't worry about it right now.

As soon as we've got everyone safe and Fanny's settled her land claim, then I'll worry about how I'm going to make a living. I owe it to them for what they're doing for Eilish.

But in sight of Isabella's front door, her heels dragged.

Her singing heart plummeted and the fear resurged.

Oh, no. A repeat of last time.

Dionisio Garcia was at the front door, berating Samuel Butler, who was resolutely barring his entry to the house.

"Miss Kelly is not at home," he shouted in exasperation.

'No, no, no," replied Garcia, stamping his foot.

Samuel was unmoved by the childish display of bad temper.

"Return on another occasion, Mr. Garcia. I told you already. Miss Rose is not here, and Mrs. Isabella is not to be disturbed."

Rosie bolted for the garden gate. The clink of the latch

attracted the men's attention.

Garcia was in romantic cavalier mode. The trademark slinky black leather trousers molded his shapely legs. A white satin shirt overflowed his belt line, and the talisman red wood serape hung over one shoulder.

He whirled at the clink of the gate and spread his arms wide when he saw her.

"Hermosa Rosa," he cried, his face wreathed in smiles.

Beautiful Rosa.

She ran up the garden path as if he was the very person she'd been waiting to see.

"Dionisio! What are you doing here?"

He enfolded her in his arms. She breathed in his salty masculine odor as he pulled her to him for a few seconds and then she resolutely stepped back, out of reach.

"I can't live without you," he declared dramatically, plucking at the shawl around his shoulder like a bull fighter preparing for an encounter in the ring.

"Come out with me."

She gave an emphatic, negative shake of her head. "No, I can't. You've got me in enough trouble already."

"Trouble?" he barked. "What trouble?"

"You know very well what trouble. Magdalena's sacked me from her show, and it's all your fault," she accused.

"What?" he growled. "That woman… forget about her."

Samuel Butler coughed politely.

"Miss Rosa, do you wish to come inside?"

He glanced around nervously, anticipating admonishment for not managing the house guests better.

Isabella wouldn't care, Rosie knew, but Samuel was the perfect steward.

Hanging around on front porches talking loudly to random visitors wasn't acceptable in polite society.

You either sent them on their way or took them inside and conducted your conversation in private.

And if Alejandro caught them… Her insides cringed at the thought.

She turned to Garcia, whose broad shoulders crowded the porch space.

"Come inside, Mr. Garcia," she said. "We can talk better in the drawing room."

She raised an arched brow at Samuel, and he stood aside and shepherded them down the hall and into the sun-filled room.

"Can I bring you refreshments, Miss Kelly?" he asked when they were seated, her in a carefully chosen single chair, with Dionisio on the couch opposite.

"Thank you, Samuel. Coffee would be lovely."

She stared at the fellow across from her; he was a hunk of a man, his hair again tied back highwayman style at the nape of his neck, his dangerous dark eyes flashing with challenge.

He was a rebel, like her, someone who operated outside of normal social rules to make his way in life.

I understand that.

It would be so easy to fall under his spell. Except, she reminded herself, he's a fraudster and a cold-blooded killer.

And he's attempting to cheat the family I love, the very people who are helping my darling sister to heal and find a new life.

And what if the rumors are true, and he's fallen out with Bram Gordon? Where does that leave him?

A bag of wind, twisting in a storm.

Anemic, vacuous Elmer Green has probably got more clout than he has.

She regarded him through narrowed eyes.

"Why did you come here today, Dionisio? You've already cost me my job."

He widened his eyes in feigned innocence.

"Oh, *bebé,* don't be like that. You and me, we can make beautiful music together."

Rosie rolled her eyes in contempt.

"Oh, for goodness' sake, Dionisio. Don't play me for a fool. If you can't do better than that flash-girl talk, you'd better leave. Really."

She tossed her head like a short-reined horse, impatient to be rid of the bit in its mouth.

She caught the ripple of tightened muscles down his cheek as he ground his teeth in annoyance.

He opened his red lips, white teeth glistening, and then snapped his mouth shut again.

At a loss for words.

A pregnant silence hung between them, only broken when Betty bustled in with fragrant coffee.

Rosie realized with a rush she'd not eaten all day.

She savored the first sips of hot coffee, watching Dionisio over her cup. Then she went on the offensive.

"You talk big, Dionisio, but word around town is Bram Gordon isn't playing ball with you anymore. And without

Gordon's backing, who are you?"

She pierced him with a sharp eye.

"I bet that insipid Elmer Green's got more clout than you have. He's a colorless turkey. Never says a thing for himself, but he's likely pulling strings behind the scenes. Would I be right there?"

Dionisio edged uncomfortably forward in his seat.

"Thing is, I'm asking myself why I should give you any more of my valuable time and attention. You've cost me a friend and a job, and for what? To sit around and be flattered by empty talk?"

"Elmer Green," he spat. "He's nobody. Why would you take any interest in the likes of him?"

Rosie laughed. "I wouldn't. But I could say the same of you. Why should I make any time for you?"

He stared at her, as if no one had ever put the question to him before.

"I've got plans—big plans."

"Oh, yes? To do what?"

She saw the spearing temptation that glinted in his eyes, to let her in on his secret plans, to show her how clever he was.

And just as fast, she saw it quenched. He gritted his jaw more tightly, afraid he was about to let the vainglory run away with him.

He doesn't trust me with his secrets, she thought. And I don't blame him.

She rose as if she was leaving and he jumped in unison, reaching over and grabbing her arm to draw her close to him again.

She put her arms against his chest, ready to push him away, but before she could, the door to the drawing room burst open, and Eilish and Alejandro stood in the gap, mouths gaping.

Rosie pushed Dionisio aside, and then caught the ranchero's triumphant smirk as he turned to face the new arrivals.

He knows exactly what he's doing. He's alienating me from my friends.

"Rosie," Eilish cried, shock magnified in her voice. "What are you doing?"

Alejandro's mouth screwed up in the corners. He didn't need anyone to explain further.

"It's pretty clear what she's doing, isn't it?" he muttered.

"It's a pity she chose here to do it, that's all."

"What's wrong?" she responded. "I'm allowed to see my friends, aren't I? So what if we were having an argument?"

Eilish's surprise dissolved into bewildered confusion.

"Rosie. You said yourself this man was…" Her voice trailed off as Rosie took Dionisio's hand in hers. The confusion turned to disbelief.

"You're not… you're not siding with this man?"

"What if I am? Alejandro insists he's done nothing wrong. At least last time I asked, that's what he said."

She glared at him in defiance.

Garcia's hand was warm and alive. He leaned over and whispered into her ear and she suppressed a responding shudder.

She despised this man, but if worming her way into his confidence was the best thing she could do for Fanny and Isabella, then that's what she was doing.

What was it they said about Bram Gordon?

He won at all costs? Was that it?

Rosie straightened her shoulders and stared straight ahead, her jaw locked.

That's going to be my war cry from now on.

Win at all costs.

Forty-two

At the front door, Garcia leaned over her ear again.

His hot breath on her neck. She gritted her teeth.

Mia cara.

She giggled and spun away, playing the coquette.

He grinned, his eyes hungry.

"See you tonight. Usual place, usual people?" he said.

She gaped. "But Magdalena…"

"Magdalena is a drama queen. Don't worry about her. She'll get used to it."

Rosie was under no illusions that Magdalena's pulling power outshone hers by the magnitude suns.

As soon as she decides she wants Dionisio back, she'll only have to crook her little finger.

I'll have to work fast.

"Why don't you skip Magdalena's show tonight? It won't be nearly as much fun without me in it."

She gave an alluring shimmy of her shoulders and hated herself for it.

"Let's celebrate our understanding," she said, reaching up on tiptoes and smooching his right cheek with soft lips.

"You said it. Together, we'll make an impressive team. I was sick of the stage, anyway. Let's decide what to do next. You need a new partner if Bram's dropped you."

She felt rather than saw his body tighten at the throwaway line, and she ran her hand from his shoulder to his elbow.

"You don't need him, anyway."

He grinned and nuzzled her neck.

"That's what I adore. A woman who doesn't underestimate me. You've got a deal. I'll come for you at seven. And wear something sexy."

His eyes grazed her neckline, and she didn't miss the message.

Show your boobs more.

She patted his hand and swung back inside.

We'll see about that. In your dreams, beefhead.

She'd barely taken two steps back inside when Alejandro confronted her in the hallway.

"What are you playing at, Rosie? This isn't like the old you…"

She drew up abruptly and glanced up into his slim, expressive face, framed by restless dark curls that hung over dark deep-pooled eyes.

He wasn't breathing brimstone. His mouth twisted in a bewildered grimace, and a heavy sadness dragged at his shoulders.

Her heart did a painful flip.

Her pathetic charade was biting deep. He was deeply hurt. She got the impression he really cared.

In her mind's eye she saw him with a noose around his neck, and her sister in a wheelchair, the final awful outcome if she left things to roll along the way they were going.

Nothing cost too much to ensure those things didn't happen to the people she loved most.

The people I love most.

A lump the size of a boulder rose in her throat, cutting off air, making it impossible to speak for several long seconds.

Alejandro continued to gaze at her with tortured eyes.

Waiting for a reply. Hoping for reassurance that she wasn't doing what she seemed intent on: making a play for Dionisio Garcia.

It took every ounce of will she possessed to crack a bright smile across her frozen face and shrug her rigid shoulders.

"Playing at?" she echoed. "I guess that's the key word, isn't it? Things have got so boring around here. Isn't a girl entitled to a little excitement?"

She stepped sideways to walk around him. She knew she shouldn't maintain this charade for a moment more. But she couldn't resist glancing flirtatiously over her shoulder as she leveled with him.

His jaw had dropped open.

She hesitated. "After all," she said with a half turn in his direction. "I'm not welcome around here, am I? You've made that abundantly clear."

Head down, she made for her room, not daring to look back.

By the time she reached the top of the stairs, the tears she'd been holding back streamed down her cheeks.

That should do it. He'll hate me now. Eilish will look like an angel in comparison.

Forty-three

Rosie and Eilish sat in the empty waiting room of Dr. Guntner Schenk's North Beach surgery, staring silently at the fibrous flax-colored carpet. Their small talk had dried up as they waited for the goodly doctor to complete his current consultation.

Something's changed. It never used to be like this, Rosie thought. We always had something to say to each other.

She glanced across and studied her sister's somber expression, her hands clasped in her lap, eyes cast down, a frown playing across her brow.

"Are you nervous?" she asked.

"Not at all," Eilish replied. "If this doctor can do anything to help me get stronger and more mobile, I'll be indebted to Alejandro for life."

"Me too," Rosie chimed in.

"I can't believe there might be a cure. The New York doctors always told Mum there was nothing they could do."

"They also said they didn't know what caused it," Rosie pointed out. "So, how would they know?"

Eilish raised her eyes and flicked her a quick smile.

"You're right as usual, Rosie. As Mum always used to say, 'There are no flies on you.'"

Rosie held her gaze for a few seconds and then looked away.

Alejandro had made the appointment, the earliest that the popular physician had available. Dr Schenk would see Eilish about the impediment she'd struggled against ever since her earliest days.

"I asked a friend who worked in the Tenderloin district, who sees a lot of children with similar problems," Alejandro had told Eilish.

"She says Dr Schenk is the man to see for mobility and bone conditions. German medicine is much more advanced than ours in this area, so that's where you'll go. If anyone can fix it, he can."

But in the waiting room, they fell into a stale silence and it hung on, like a wet sheet on the line.

Suddenly, Eilish asked the thing Rosie had hoped they'd avoid.

"What's gone wrong between you and Alejandro, Rosie? You seemed good friends when I arrived, and now, only a week later, you aren't talking."

Eilish fixed Rosie with a steady eye that forced her to engage in the conversation she had been running away from.

"You're exaggerating," Rosie said with an uncomfortable shrug. "It's nothing, really. We never were particularly close. He's always struck me as rather a spoiled rich boy."

Eilish bit her lip.

"Spoiled little rich boys don't pay for a doctor for total strangers," she snapped. "What's wrong with you?"

The door to the doctor's rooms opened and a plump woman

carrying a young boy with a bandaged foot stepped out, followed by a white uniformed nurse.

"We'll let you know when Dr Schenck is doing his next surgery," the nurse said.

"Meantime, ensure Marcus gets plenty of fresh air and sunshine. Take him to the park to play."

The child's mother, dressed in a smart yellow dress with a black jacket, smiled in agreement.

"I can't believe the doctor can do something for him. Thank you so much!"

Eilish's eyes flicked to Rosie's, as if to say, 'What did I tell you? I'm so fortunate to be here."

The nurse held a clipboard on which she consulted her notes. "Miss Kelly?" Her intelligent eyes scanned them. "Miss Eilish Kelly?"

Eilish stood. "That's me. Can my sister Rosie accompany me in to see the doctor? She's got a much better memory for detail than I do."

The nurse smiled. "No problem at all. The doctor likes family to be involved."

***

Dr Gunther Schenck was a graying, grandfatherly man. Alejandro explained he'd arrived amid great fanfare as a passenger on the first steamship to enter San Francisco Bay, a few months after the 49er gold strike. He'd never left.

His courteous, lightly formal manner quickly set them both at ease and helped relieve the tension that had snapped in the waiting room minutes before.

He quickly got to the details, asking about Eilish's life, her childhood years, how much time she'd spent outside, what their childhood diet was like.

He asked her to stand and gently tested her ability to stand without the aid of a cane. He examined her shoes for wear and tear.

"We can tell a lot from the way you spread your weight," he noted, gazing over steel-rimmed glasses with kindly blue eyes.

At the end of thirty minutes of questioning, he relaxed into his spindle-backed chair and steepled delicate long fingers against his neat blond mustache.

"From everything you've told me and what I've observed, I don't think an operation is going to be the answer for you."

Rosie's heart plummeted.

No answer. Those were the only words her frazzled brain heard.

Eilish's face paled, and the tired lines around her eyes seemed more pronounced.

She gulped back her disappointment, and her hands automatically went to her skirts, signaling her readiness to depart.

She made as if to rise.

Dr Schenck's gentle eyes twinkled with bemused good humor.

"Are you going somewhere? Don't you want to hear the rest of my assessment?"

Both Kelly girls stared, as if given a reprieve.

"Your case seems to me to be a moderately treatable form of rickets, one amenable to alleviation with cod liver oil, nutritious food, and plenty of sunshine.

"If you're willing to follow the regimen I recommend, I believe you'll see a full recovery within six months to a year. I certainly would not advise you to return to your previous life in New York."

Eilish's hands stilled in her lap. Her eyes widened, and her face glowed.

"Full recovery…?" she stammered, "I can't believe it."

She turned to Rosie.

"Rosie! How can I ever thank you?"

Rosie shook her head. "It's not me you've got to thank. It's Alejandro."

Dr Schenck stood from behind his desk and smiled at them with paternal fondness.

"If only all the cases I see were as easy to fix as yours. Miss Kelly, we'd all be happy."

He gave them a wide smile.

"Make an appointment to come back and see me in a few days. I'll have a full treatment regimen written up for you by then. If you follow it diligently, you'll be a new woman a year from now, I promise."

Forty-four

When the lion-headed brass knocker thudded in the early afternoon, Rosie and Fanny were the only ones at home.

Isabella and Sebastian were out shopping for a nursery cot. Rosie suspected that was really an excuse to get away by themselves for a few hours. Perhaps take a romantic afternoon tea in the kiosk by the Woodland Garden's lake, and she didn't blame them.

Since Alejandro's near miss nearly two weeks before, the house had been busier than Grand Central Station.

Rosie's stomach got its familiar "rocks in my stomach" sensation whenever a visit from Dionisio was in prospect, so it was a relief for her when the housekeeper tapped on the drawing room door lightly, and put her head around the door frame, her face alive with inquiry.

She was waving a white envelope in her raised hand.

"Marquésa, a delivery for you. A letter."

Fanny Castellanos glanced up from her embroidery frame with a flicker of surprise.

"For me? Whoever could write me letters here?"

She shot a conspiratorial look at Rosie.

"Open it for me, would you, dear girl? I'm in the middle of finishing Red Riding Hood's cloak on this nursery cushion, and I'm making such good progress. I don't want to interrupt myself."

Rosie shot her an understanding smile. As the reality that Isabella was expecting her first child settled over them, they all, in their different ways, were laying plans for the baby's arrival.

Rosie realized when the child came, Isabella would need the guest room she was staying in for the baby's nurse. Despite Isabella's polite protests, she would have to find alternative accommodation or leave town.

As Betty Butler crossed the room and placed the newly delivered letter in Rosie's hand, her skirt brushed the yellow jonquils that sat on a pot on a side table, releasing the creamy fragrance of late spring in the room.

"Smell that," said Fanny. "Soon it'll be winter and I'll be heading back to Scotland." She pulled a sad face. "I plan to stay until Isabella's baby is born, but then I suppose I'll have to go."

Rosie shot her a sympathetic smile and tore open the envelope. On one sheet of fancy pale pink writing paper, someone had scrawled a few explosive words in black ink.

Rosie abruptly folded the paper in two and glanced up at Fanny, who was staring at her, embroiderer's needle poised above her fabric.

"What's wrong?" she asked with a teasing chuckle, "You look like someone's asked you to eat a rat."

"Not a bad analogy," Rosie said gruffly. "I suspect that metaphorically, that's exactly what someone is asking you to do."

Fanny tucked her needle into the cushion cover and stretched out her open palm to receive the letter.

"Who's it from?" she asked lazily.

Rosie shook her head, pushing down a sense of rising panic. "Someone called Temptation. Temptation Thompson. Do you know her?"

Fanny's hand froze around the paper. "Temptation?" she yelped. "Are you sure?"

Rosie shrugged. "That's who she claims to be. Why?"

Fanny spread the paper sheet out on her lap and stared at the words before her.

"Temptation Thompson." She whispered the words to herself.

"Who is she?" Rosie's words came out garbled, her throat was so tight and dry.

"She's the woman who probably knows more than anyone about what happened to Rafael," she said. "But until now, I haven't known where to find her."

Rosie jumped up, her legs wobbling under her. "You're not proposing to meet this woman? She could be dangerous. It might be a trap."

"And I'll never know if I don't go," she said, her fingers tight on the paper.

"Fanny! No!" Rosie's voice was a rising wail.

"If anything happens to you, I'll never forgive myself. And Alejandro will blame me, too."

"You, Rosie? Why on earth would he blame you?"

"Because I've been encouraging Dionisio to hang around like a lovesick calf. It's likely Temptation isn't even alive, and he's using her as a lure to draw you in."

"And why would he want to do that?"

"Because he's trying to steal Castellanos land, that's why, though Alejandro doesn't believe me."

The words strangled in her throat.

"It might be a trick to abduct you."

Fanny shook her head.

"Oh, Rosie, I think you're imagining things."

Fanny's voice rose a few notes with indignation.

Rosie stood, her fists balled up in frustration.

"Why won't anyone take me seriously? You're just like Alejandro. He won't believe me either."

Fanny gestured for her to sit down.

"You're giving me a headache, standing like that," she said.

"And why won't Alejandro believe you?"

"Because he's got a thing against Dionisio."

The mangled words fought their way out of her throat and flopped to the carpet like stranded kippers.

Before they landed, she knew deep down she was wrong.

He doesn't have a thing against Dionisio. He has a thing against me throwing myself at Dionisio.

And he's right. What am I thinking?

Dionisio failed in his attack on the son, so now he's going after the mother. And no one but me seems to get it.

Forty-five

The Marquésa Fanny di Ortonez Castellanos gazed at the beautiful Irish girl who remained standing before her, her fists clenched, her brow set in a defiant question mark.

This girl has captured Alejandro's heart, but neither of them knows it yet.

"What is going on between you and Alejandro?" she asked, her voice querulous. "You can barely exchange a civil word, and yet you've so much in common."

Fanny's frustration leaked out into her words, and a heavy silence fell between them.

Rosie sank back into the chair she'd popped up from minutes before and sighed.

"We just don't get on," she said, her voice flat and weary. "Never have."

Fanny's mouth tightened.

"Why not?"

Rosie gave a wan smile and shrugged. "A lot in common? Not really, Marquésa. I'm a poor Irish girl from New York struggling to establish a stage career. He's the son of a wealthy senator. Not exactly the perfect match."

Fanny's frown deepened, and her brow ached. "Alejandro's father was a Spanish nobleman, and I was the daughter of a Scottish laird with modest estates. That didn't stop us from having a long and fulfilling marriage."

Rosie gazed at her with admiring emerald eyes for a long minute and then shrugged.

"We got off on the wrong foot from the start, and it's gone downhill since then. I'm indebted to him for his generosity to Eilish. I can never repay him for that."

Her smoldering eyes flashed, dangerous with unshed tears.

"But day to day? We don't see eye to eye, that's all."

She glanced away and pulled back her shoulders, presenting a staunch front, unaffected by the breach.

Fanny warmed inside. For a young woman who was so convincing on stage, she made a terrible job of masking her true feelings in real life.

Rosie flicked a curl out of her eyes and continued with the faked indifference.

"Alejandro and Eilish seem to get on very well," she said, in a falsely bright voice that cracked halfway through the sentence.

"Maybe that will come to something."

Fanny laughed. "Rosie, my dear, if you can't see what's right under your nose, I'm not the one to tell you."

She folded up the embroidery which had gone unattended for the last few minutes and turned to stash it in the work basket beside her.

"What are you doing?" Rosie's voice surged in alarm. "You're not seriously considering going to meet this woman, are you?"

Fanny's heart surged at the girl's obvious concern, but she shook her head and continued to prepare to depart.

Join me at St. Stephen's for evening prayers. And come alone…

That's what the note said.

I can't lose this chance to discover more about Rafael's final years.

Maybe she's got his diary. Or all my letters…

Rosie jumped to her feet again. "You can't, Marquésa. It's dangerous, I tell you. You shouldn't trust Dionisio and I have a creepy feeling he's behind this."

Fanny's heart surged at the girl's obvious concern, but she shook her head and continued to prepare to depart.

"She says she'd got some papers of Rafael's for me. Maybe there's a diary? I know Father Stephen at St. Mary's. He's always there for the evening prayers—for vespers and compline. No one would dare make trouble in the church with him around."

Rosie rose to her feet, shaking her head, alarm etched on her bonny face.

"He might take you away somewhere else. Who knows what he might do? It's too risky."

Fanny sank back down onto the sofa. "Sit down, Rosie, and I'll explain why I have to go."

She patted the seat beside her. "When you hear what I've got to say, perhaps you'll understand."

She stared at her wrinkled, folded hands and her mind traveled back to the last time she'd seen them, in New Orleans on their way to California, her debonair eldest son and his exquisite young bride.

"They were so in love, Elanora and Rafael. It was written on their glowing faces. And I truly thought that day that my precious son had found his future. They came to stay with us for a few months before they moved on to California."

She picked at one nail restlessly, recalling what happened next.

"Angel got the royal command to go back to Madrid. The Bourbon-Anjou house was in turmoil, and the new young queen desperately needed a steady pair of fatherly hands to guide her through.

"They urgently recalled us. We had no time to visit Rafael and Elanora here. Of course, we didn't know we'd never see either of them again."

She twisted her hands in her lap, releasing some of the tension that charged her veins whenever she spoke of Rafael and Elanora.

"All these years, I've held on to a slim hope Rafael might still be alive, even though so many of my letters went unanswered.

"I told myself I must have had the wrong address. I didn't question why they hadn't been 'returned to sender.' For a long time I kept hoping by some miracle he was still alive."

She gazed up into Rosie's sparkling eyes. She'd almost forgotten she had an audience.

"Now I can talk to the woman who was there. We know from Graysie's story that she took delivery of one of those letters and she probably never passed it on. I'm sure in my heart if Rafael had received it, he would have replied."

She shook her head, and a driving energy rose through from the soles of her feet to the top of her head.

"I suspect from then on, she made it her business to intercept them. I'm not going to go back to Scotland without talking to this woman. It will make a mockery of everything I've lived for all these years if I fail in this. I hope you understand."

Rosie reached out and gently clasped her fidgeting hands. An instant calm filled Fanny from the young woman at her side.

"I've got to know why she did it," Fanny whispered. "I want to see her, face to face, and hear what she says. That's the only way I'll feel I've done my utmost. I'll feel satisfied."

She gave a strangled laugh. "Well, maybe not exactly satisfied, even then. But as close as I can get to it."

Rosie leaned forward and, in a strangely formal gesture, kissed her lightly on both cheeks

"I understand. But what about Diana and Fergus? We're having dinner here with them this evening? She'll be so disappointed if she can't come."

Fanny put her face into her hands and sighed.

"I'm sorry, Rosie. We are going to have to defer that to another night. Get Betty to prepare a food parcel from leftovers we have in the kitchen.

"Would you be good enough to deliver it and explain? We'll meet another night. This is too important to ignore."

A peculiar heaviness fell over Rosie as she stood up to go to the kitchen.

"I can do that, but I'm still not happy about you going to that meeting alone."

"I won't be alone. I'll take Juliana with me. Besides, it's in a public place. The cathedral, for goodness' sake. And there will be people around because they'll be starting evening prayers.

"What could happen to me there?"

I hate to think. And Alejandro will be furious with me. Again.

Rosie tried to ignore the ominous pounding in her chest, as if her body was warning her not to go along with Fanny's determined plans.

"I'd better get moving and find Diana," she said. "I won't stand in your way, Marquésa Fanny. But for goodness' sake, don't get yourself killed or Alejandro will never speak to me again."

Forty-six

The soft candlelight from the wall sconces was still bright enough to pick up Temptation Thompson's Criss Cross wrinkling. A hatchet of weary bitterness.

Fanny felt a flicker of compassion for a woman plainly battered by life. It couldn't have been easy, being a woman on her own, fighting for a place in an unforgiving new land.

But her feelings of tenderness hardened with her next breath, as she gazed into granite eyes sparking with malice.

Fanny recognized the haunted desperation that veiled those sallow cheeks. She'd seen it many times before in the Madrid court, the visage of a fortune hunter disputing the roll of the dice.

Temptation Thompson was a woman who wasn't here to give, but to take.

Fanny adjusted her expression to one of distant kindness and held her breath for the coming swindle.

She's going to attempt to sell me a pup. Rosie was right after all.

Temptation leaned at an insolent slant against the end of one of the white oak pews, her arms folded defensively in front of her chest, dawdling in her silence.

She'd been pretty once, Fanny could see, with a small nose that once would have been cute and a full mouth. But bitterness had stolen the good looks, replacing beauty with a dour unhappiness that leaked from every weary line.

She wore a utilitarian blue serge skirt and white blouse. Uniform for the middle-aged women who worked as shop assistants, cooks, and housekeepers.

A matching blue headscarf partially obscured her thin white-blond hair.

When she completed her scan of the near empty church, her suspicious eyes devoured Fanny, taking in her white and gold brocade gown embroidered with the royal crest, the tiered skirts trimmed in red satin.

Her gaze lingered on Fanny's large pearl drop earrings—a gift from Queen Isabella.

A bent-over old woman Fanny has seen every time she came here shuffled in through the entry and headed for an altar lit with candles that ringed the perimeter.

These altars were the reflective spots, where worshippers could pause and light a remembrance candle for loved ones who had passed on.

On her heels, a young mother stumbled in, eyes adjusting from the sunlight outside to the nave's holy dimness. She hugged a newborn baby wrapped tightly in a tartan wool rug.

"We'd better find somewhere more private to talk," Fanny said to Temptation. "They're about to start evening prayers."

As if on cue, Father Stephen emerged from the vestry space behind the altar and turned to survey the nave. He spotted Fanny, gave a quick wave and strode toward her.

"Marquésa," he cried, a wide smile spread across his broad face. "Are you here for the Angelus?" He consulted a pocket watch tucked into his vestments.

"The bells will ring in four minutes."

He looked expectantly at Temptation, and Fanny made smooth introductions.

"Father, this is Temptation Thompson. She was acquainted with my son Rafael and has kindly agreed to share some details of his life here in California with me."

Father Stephen thrust out his hand with a cordial grin. "So kind of you, dear lady. Thank you for your generosity."

Temptation shook his hand and muttered a greeting through scowling lips.

Fanny turned her full attention off the priest.

"We'll slip to the back corner so as not to disturb anyone," she said. "Good afternoon to you, Father."

"The bells will ring at just before six p.m., remember?" Father Stephen called after them. "I don't want you to get a shock."

Fanny led the way to the back of the red-carpeted nave. They settled on a pew tucked into a corner screened from the rest of the church by a board carrying details about missionary work St. Mary's was supporting in Tahiti.

"I might be Irish, but I don't go along with all this religious stuff," Temptation sniffed. "God did nothing for me."

"Well, that's a shame," said Fanny. "Did you ever ask him to?"

Temptation scowled.

"So, you're Rafael's mother. I've always wondered what you'd look like."

She twisted her mouth in a graceless smile, revealing pointed yellow teeth.

God forbid my darling boy allowed this woman to step into Elanora's shoes. He must have been in a terrible way to even have her in the house.

"That's correct," Fanny said lightly. "I am the Marquésa Fanny di Ortonez Castellanos."

Temptation tossed her head and the blue scarf slipped further back, showing more of her faded, straw-blonde hair.

"How did you know I was here? In San Francisco, I mean."

Temptation's eyes skittered toward the confession box in the corner diagonally across from them.

"I read it in the newspaper," she said, her tone defiant. "It wasn't supposed to be a secret, was it?"

Fanny ignored the affronted tone.

"And you knew Rafael?"

"Knew him?" Temptation snorted. "I kept him alive. Fed him. Picked up after him. Washed his dirty sheets. Him and his snotty-nosed daughter. And never got so much as a thank you for any of it. She always thought she was better than the rest of us."

She indubitably is, Fanny thought.

"She didn't even come back to help me when she got famous," she said.

"You were his housekeeper, is that right?"

Temptation scowled. "That and a lot more."

"Oh? Like what exactly?"

Temptation ignored the question.

"He didn't look much like you, except for the dark eyes,"

she said. "His father must have been a good-looking man."

Fanny chuckled inside at the backhanded insult.

All she said was, "His father was a very fine man. Dead now, just like Rafael. Can you tell me what happened to him?"

Temptation's face flushed pink, and she screwed her eyes shut, as if the topic was still painful.

"He gave up, that's what. He didn't have the backbone to keep going. I picked a dud. That's all."

Fanny's stomach rolled over in protest at the contempt implicit in her words.

Imagine waking up with this every day.

"And you know this how?" she asked, keeping the statement as neutral as possible. Another long pause, and a baleful stare. Then Temptation sighed.

"I was there every day, wasn't I? I saw what went on."

"Then you will have seen the letters I sent, too. Did he ever get to read any of them?"

"Not if I could help it," Temptation scoffed. "I wasn't going to get left behind while he skipped off to his royal family. That's for sure."

Fanny sighed, and the temperature of the blood pounding at her temples heated several degrees.

"You didn't consider that having loving support from his mother might have made him feel better? Might have even given him more 'backbone'?"

Fanny relaxed her gritted teeth before she spoke.

"I told you. He would have dumped me and taken the girl and gone."

They stared at one another in ill-disguised dislike, and then

Fanny asked, "Do you still have those letters?"

Temptation gave a triumphant smile.

"I do. And I figure all dolled up as you are, you'll be more than happy to pay to get them back."

Her eyes had a greedy gleam.

"I've got a diary of his too, where he confided all his pathetic little secrets. If you want that as well, it will cost you more."

Fanny's hot temper threatened to boil over.

"And how can you prove it was actually Rafael's? That you haven't made the whole thing up?"

Temptation stood, her eyes searching down the nave toward the altar, and then back to the corner confession box.

Is she looking for someone? Expecting someone?

Fanny sensed a change in the air. The bells were about to chime and the Angelus begin.

The housekeeper suddenly switched her attention back to Fanny.

"You can inspect the letters. You know what they look like because you wrote them. If you're satisfied with them, you'll have to take my word on the rest."

"And how much are you expecting to be paid to return stolen property to its rightful owner? I should get the superintendent on to you, not pay you for the return of my own private papers."

Fanny heard the creak of a chained lantern swing, far away, up in front of the altar, and the rising fragrance of sacred incense filled her nostrils.

The church taught that incense was emblematic of prayers rising to heaven. A sweet smell like precious myrrh enveloped her, momentarily making her dizzy.

She wiped the back of her forearm across her forehead to banish the light-headedness that folded around her like a blanket.

Then, another smell invaded her senses, an odor of tobacco and men's cologne.

She struggled to her feet, and an iron grip clasped the top of her arm. Her eyes flew open, and she was staring into the overripe face of a past-his-prime Latin troubadour.

Her eyes filled with the sight of tumbling black locks, fat red lips, and overblown rose cheeks.

"There'll be no more talk of calling the cops, if you don't mind," said Dionisio Garcia, for she knew instantly this is who it was. He held her in a fierce grip, pressing his stifling bulk unpleasantly into her side.

And right at that moment Fanny's ears rang, as the bells in the brick tower overhead broke into tumultuous pealing.

Under cover of the noise, Dionisio hustled her toward the double doors, which were curiously empty of crowds of last-minute worshippers.

She was being abducted, and she was helpless to stop it. No one would hear her protests above the deafening echo of the overhead bells.

Forty-seven

Rosie wrenched open the monogrammed door of the shiny black carriage parked at the kerb outside St Mary's on 660 California Street. She jabbed her index finger in the chest of the woman in the back seat.

"What are you doing here, Juliana? Why aren't you inside with the Marquésa?"

Juliana, who'd been slouched down half asleep, squealed at the interruption.

"She insisted on going in alone! I tried!

At that moment, the bells began tolling, and she covered her ears with her hands.

"What could I do?" she yelled above the clanging. "She insisted she went alone."

Rosie glanced around wildly. She'd hoped to head Fanny off earlier than this, but getting the food to Diana and Fergus took longer than she'd intended.

Pigeons which seconds before waddled at the foot of the cathedral stairs, searching for crumbs, fluttered off. An elderly woman leaning on a cane made her way step by slow step up to the cathedral's double doors, focused on getting in before the service started.

Rosie turned back to Juliana. "How long has she been in there?"

Juliana shrugged. "Ten, maybe fifteen minutes, I guess? Why?"

"She told me she was coming after evening prayers. She was meeting Father Stephen at the end of the service."

Juliana's face twisted in confusion. "Nooo," she said slowly, shaking her head. "Señor Carlos told her she could have the use of his carriage for the entire afternoon. She always planned to get here early, before the service began."

"Have you seen anyone else go in there?"

Once again, Juliana's mouth curled in doubt.

"No one obvious. Just a few people who looked like they were headed for prayers. A woman with a baby. An older gent. No one suspicious."

Rosie stared up at the double doors. As the old woman reached the top, a verger monk pulled them wide open to admit her, as if he'd been waiting for latecomers like her.

In the dark gap behind him as the doors opened, Rosie glimpsed a bulky male and a flash of red, and she made an instant decision.

She whirled back to face Juliana. "Tell the driver you've got an emergency and you need O'Halloran. Police headquarters is down the street." She flung her arm in the general direction. "Tell him the Marquésa's life is in danger. Go. Now."

Juliana's jaw dropped open. "Go," Rose rasped. "Or it will be too late."

She fled, taking the stairs two at a time, slipping in behind the old lady just as the doors closed.

She sheltered behind the old woman and the priest, who greeted her. She paused for her eyes to adjust to the dim interior, swiveling to take in the view.

She immediately spotted a cluster of figures not far away, near the confessional. Dionisio was clutching Fanny's arm in a way that, at a glance, could be seen as a younger man helping an old woman, with a second female figure beside them.

She circled around them on tiptoes, keeping herself facing toward Dionisio's back.

The monk and the old woman were moving away from the entry. He guided her to an aisle seat a few rows down the nave and then continued to Father Stephen, who was beginning the prayers.

O God, come to our aid.

O Lord, make haste to help us.

And an Amen to that, Rosie thought to herself, as she saw Dionisio turning obviously toward the doors. She buried her nose in a leaflet hanging on a wall rack, the words a blur as she strained her ears to gauge what was happening behind her.

The bells were still chiming, making it hard to hear anything else.

Keeping her head in the pamphlet and turning slowly, she watched as Dionisio thrust Fanny toward the doors. A woman she presumed was Temptation Thompson straggled behind them.

Her blood ran cold as Dionisio dipped his free hand into the woolen sarape that crossed his chest and he drew out a small black object. A revolver!

Her body froze, but her feet kept moving. Watching the ground so as not to attract eye contact, she melted into the background like a wraith in Shakespeare's *Macbeth*. She focused solely on approaching Fanny's group from behind.

As they reached the doors and Temptation obeyed Dionisio's gesture to step around him and open the doors, she darted forward. She covered her mouth with her hand, as if she was about to puke.

As soon as she was level with them, she shouldered Temptation directly into Dionisio.

For a few precious seconds, his hand loosened on Fanny as Temptation barreled into Dionisio's gun arm. Fanny ducked away with the agility of a woman half her age. The bells stopped ringing, and the roar of a gunshot fractured the sudden silence.

Rosie felt a searing burn across her right side and pitched forward, smashing her head on the cathedral's unyielding tiled floor as she went down.

Then there was just blackness.

Forty-eight

Alex offered his grandmother a crystal tumbler of brandy from the silver tray on the drawing room cabinet, but she refused it with a silent shake of her head.

"I don't need brandy at three o'clock in the afternoon, Alejandro, and I wouldn't have thought you do either."

She frowned as she glanced around Isabella's cozy sitting room, with its buttercup yellow silk walls and double-hung windows opening onto the garden.

Isabella and Seb lounged on a sofa opposite Fanny's comfortable big armchair, their faces drawn into worried lines.

The exchange between Fanny and her grandson was becoming increasingly combative.

Across the room, next to the window, Eilish curled in her chair, looking like she wanted to disappear altogether.

"Ewan will be here any minute, Alejandro. I don't want him to see us quarreling."

Fanny's tone was mild, but her mouth tightened in disapproval.

They'd gathered to receive a briefing from Alex's lawyer on how last night's scuffle was likely to affect the court case due to be heard in a couple of days, and Ewan was running late.

"Please don't continue to make a fuss," Fanny said. "You had enough to say last night. Let's move on. I've got the message. You didn't like me going out without telling you. But that's all in the past now.

"Ewan will tell us what impact last night's events are likely to have on the court case. That's what's important."

She paused and flashed a smile across the room to Eilish.

"That and making sure Rosie makes a full recovery. That young woman was so brave. She deserves praise, not criticism. What's wrong with you?"

She turned her head like an inquisitive bird and searched Alejandro's cloudy face with piercing eyes.

Alex glanced into the amber depths of the glass, still half-extended in his arm, and provocatively bent his head and sipped.

He muttered something barely audible, but which could have been, "I don't know. The women in this family just run amok," as he ambled back to the fireplace, where he put the brandy glass down on the mantelpiece.

"I'm still furious that you took off on such an ill-advised chase without telling anyone where you were going," he growled. "You could have so easily been killed."

Fanny eyeballed him, her glare steely.

"But I wasn't, was I? Thanks to Rosie."

Alex shrugged.

"And that makes me just about as angry as you hightailing out of here without telling me. What's Rosie thinking, letting you go off alone, and not saying anything about it? You're both as bad as one another."

Fanny grasped irritably along the arms of her chair.

"If you're looking to blame someone, leave Rosie out of it. Castigate me. First, I made her promise she wouldn't tell anyone.

"And then, because I guessed she'd probably follow me anyway, even though I told her not to, I gave her the slip and went earlier than she expected. I got there some time before she turned up."

A squeaking noise from the hallway interrupted Fanny's words, and she turned her head toward the door.

Betty Butler tentatively pushed a cane wheelchair into the room. Rosie rested in the chair, her face burning red, her hands linked in her lap.

"Rosie," said Fanny. "You don't need to be here. You should be resting."

"It sounds like I need to be here to defend my honor," she said, darting a lethal stare at Alejandro.

"Last night was all my fault, was it? I suppose I shouldn't be surprised."

Alejandro shook his head in indignant denial.

"Not *all* your fault. But you must admit it was a tomfool thing to let Fanny get mixed up in."

Rosie shot a despairing glance at Fanny.

"I understand why meeting Temptation was important to Fanny," she said. "It's a shame it was a trap, as I warned her it probably would be."

Fanny gestured to Betty, who had paused with the chair just inside the door, not sure where to negotiate it next.

Fanny pointed to the big armchair next to her.

"Seb, Alejandro. Can you move that chair so Rosie can pull up next to me? The dear girl should be in bed, but we all know she doesn't like to miss out when things are happening."

Seb and Alex jumped up to obey Fanny's instructions and moved the vacant chair to make a space.

Fanny shot the Irish girl a tender smile and reached out to pat her hand as Rosie reached to her side.

Even seated, it was plain her slender form was thickened with bandages which wound around the middle of her body.

Isabella jumped up from the sofa. "Thanks so much for bringing Rosie down, Betty."

She glanced down at her friend, her eyes glossy with kindness, and quickly bent and kissed her on the cheek.

"I'm scared to hug you because I know you're sore all over," she said with a cheeky grin.

"But that blue maternity dress of mine complements your green eyes perfectly."

Rosie had been hugging her ribs, as if in discomfort, but she now raised her rounded fists and pumped them as if air punching Isabella.

"You're enjoying this, you *turrible* person," she said with a flashing smile and an exaggerated Irish accent. "You just wait."

They settled her in place, and the room lulled into an awkward silence.

Rosie sat back quietly and surveyed the scene. Her emerald eyes, lacking their usual sparkle, settled on Alex's sour mouth.

"I know you don't want me here, Alex. You think I've meddled too much already? But I can't help it. All the way through this thing, you haven't taken my warnings seriously or understood why I've been concerned."

She scanned the others for a response. Everyone was carefully avoiding meeting her eyes, not wanting to take sides.

"I heard what Fanny said as I was coming down the hall. And it's true. She didn't want me to go to that meeting last night. She wanted to honor what Temptation had said about going alone. But I had a bad feeling about it, and as it turned out, I was right.

"I'm glad we escaped with a few grazes and bruises. Nothing serious."

Fanny interrupted.

"It would have been a different story if you hadn't been there, Rosie. They would have taken me away long before the police got there. I'm so grateful."

She shot Rosie a loving gaze. "You were a total champion. You really were."

Alejandro grunted.

"I still think it was crazy to let her go without telling me," he said, his mouth set in a sullen grimace.

"But..." Rosie objected.

"I know. Fanny told you to keep it secret," he said. "Wrong call." He glowered.

"But I agree with Fanny. You were very brave to tackle that goon single-handed. If you weren't there, things would have ended badly. For that, I thank you."

His shoulders remained in their stiff rigidity, but he gave the briefest conciliatory nod to no one in particular. Certainly not to Rosie. They heard the tramp of footsteps in the hall, and Alex turned his attention to the door.

Rosie flicked Fanny a tremulous smile before the sitting room door opened again and Sam Butler ushered Ewan Campbell, who was thrusting an overstuffed briefcase ahead of him, into the room.

"Sorry I'm late, everyone," he said with a grim smile. "And now I'm here, I'm afraid I have little in the way of good news."

Forty-nine

Ewan Campbell stood on the other side of the mantelpiece from Alejandro, his briefcase stuffed with papers overflowing at his feet. He regarded the tight little group over the top of his gold-rimmed glasses.

Makes you think of a college professor, about to lecture his class, Rosie thought.

But he's a man who knows his law, and he's not to be underestimated.

Her restless heart settled in her tender chest cavity, as she sank into the chair and tried to ignore the dull ache in her side. Garcia's bullet had grazed her rib cage, but not penetrated deeper.

The bullet had broken the skin, Dr. Fisher had said. She'd suffer heavy bruising from the percussion, but her ribs and lungs were intact.

"Just don't push it too hard," the doctor said. He had kindly pale blue eyes and smelled of pipe smoke.

"You might have a mild concussion from hitting your head on the floor. If you feel dizzy or lightheaded, consult me again."

As the lawyer spoke, Rosie's eyes wandered to Alejandro,

standing a few feet away, drinking in the solicitor's every word.

She didn't want to look at him. Or come to think of it, have anything to do with him.

I'm sick to death of his continual criticism. I can't do a thing right.

But she couldn't seem to help it. Her blood hummed with longing as she grabbed furtive glimpses of him, as he leaned forward, one elbow on the mantel.

His other arm hung loosely at his side, but everything else about him was on high alert.

His eyes narrowed in concentration. A hint of a wry smile tilted at the corners of his finely sculpted mouth. A dark lock hung over his right eye, and he nudged it away with the back of his hand as she watched.

Her heart started up with a familiar thud. He was so darned annoying, but when she looked at him, she went all gooey inside. She couldn't control her feelings for him. She took in a deep breath and tensed as her painful ribs protested.

"The police have questioned Garcia," said Ewan, his voice deep and measured. "His story is that his gun discharged accidentally when Temptation Thompson thumped into him. And Temptation crashed into him because Rosie cannonaded into her.

"In his version of events, it was all Rosie's fault. The police have concluded no crime was committed."

He fixed Fanny with an ironic stare. "You were there for a sentimental meeting with Miss Thompson, who happens to be a friend of his, and Rosie interrupted it. He has no idea why."

Fanny gave a bitter laugh. "From what we know, that's

probably the best we can expect from this particular police captain. Let's move on to Los Putos, can we? Where do we stand there?"

Alex cleared his throat. "Hang on a mo', Grandmama," he said, turning to face everyone head-on. "He's not arresting Rosie for assault? On his past record, we should probably be grateful."

He threw a cheeky colluding grin in Rosie's direction, and she couldn't resist acknowledging it with a smile.

Maybe he's getting over his hissy fit.

Ewan pulled a handful of papers from his briefcase and waved them over his head.

"To answer your question, Marquésa, I now want to run over what I think our biggest challenge is going to be with this claim."

He surveyed the room. "I want to warn you of our weakest points for a start," he said.

"First, we're coming in late. They ruled on many of these claims in the 1850s and '60s. If a fraudulent claim has already been approved on the same block, there's little chance of getting it overturned, even if yours is authentic.

"That's because some of that land will have been sold on to other genuine buyers, and the courts have shown themselves unwilling to go back and unravel that can of worms. Common sense tells you why.

"Second, although the original papers the Marquésa brought with her strengthen the case—she has a copy of the original signed grant, and a hand-drawn sketch of the area granted - the *discenio*, as they called it—neither of the claimants ever occupied the claim for any period.

"And none of them is alive and able to give evidence or signed depositions on what occurred."

He flapped some sheets of paper in the air above his head.

"In contrast to that, Bram Gordon's lawyers have produced sworn depositions from Mr. Gordon about his purchase of Angel's share from Hernandez Valaquez, and he will be in court to give personal statements about his dealings with Hernandez."

He sighed. "Gordon may truly believe Hernandez sold him half the property.

"This is all simply to warn you that you may be in for a rough ride at the hearings. You need to be prepared for it."

A long silence followed as they all grappled with the implications.

Then Alex asked: "Is there anything more we can do to prepare ourselves for it? Any documents or similar that would help our case?"

Ewan shook his head and smiled grimly.

"I can't think of any," he said. "And Bram Gordon is as thick as thieves with the Land Court judges. Pretty well everything he touches with them is granted. Just saying."

Fifty

Rosie slumped in her wheelchair in a silence she hoped her friends would put down to exhaustion. Seb and Alejandro, one on each side of a wheel, hefted her, stair by stair, up to the second-floor landing so she could to return to her room.

For once she was too overcome by a sense of black defeat to keep up appearances. Her head dipped to her chest, and before departing the sitting room, she'd make her excuses for not attending dinner with the rest of the family.

"I'm exhausted and I think the doctor said I need rest," she'd said with a wan grin.

She wanted nothing more than to retreat gracefully and be alone.

As she'd listened to Ewan's state of the nation address, the last ounce of her bubbling energy drained away. She was a stranded jellyfish, flopped on the high tide mark as the waves retreated, incapable of doing anything.

Her head drummed with a heavy ache as Ewan presented his depressing conclusions. Her last skerrick of optimism leaked away as he made his final predictions.

Bram Gordon has got it sewn up. That's what his instructions amounted to.

After all my efforts, Alex's family is going to lose their land. And O'Halloran may still arrest Alex for murder.

I haven't repaid him for changing Eilish's life and bringing her hope.

All I've done is make him hate me because he thinks I'm stupid enough to fall for a cad like Dionisio Garcia.

As soon as Betty deposited her on her bed, she fell into an Irish bog of despair. She was like a rag doll, collapsed on the bed.

"I've done too much, Betty. I need to rest," she whispered.

"No dinner?" worried Betty. Rosie shrugged.

"Maybe a little of that potato soup I could smell downstairs. That's about all I can manage right now. Sorry."

Betty Butler gazed at her with piercing eyes.

"You don't want me to bring headache powder and water?"

Rosie hesitated. "Actually, how did you guess? That's about the only other thing I do need."

Betty flashed her a worried smile. "I can tell by the way you're all hunched over, Miss Rosie. You're not your usual bright self at all. Something is wrong."

She moved the chair into the corner. "I'll be back in two ticks."

With a relieved sigh, Rosie rolled onto the middle of the bed and wriggled up to the headboard pillows. She propped herself up and surveyed the room while she awaited Betty's return.

I'm outstaying my welcome here, she thought.

I've messed everything up. If Alex and Eilish are getting serious about one another, I can't stand to be here.

Her eyes wandered to the dressing table, where a

daguerreotype of Isabella sat in a bronze frame bordered with curlicues. Her friend was laughing, her mouth open, her eyes lit up with a secret joy.

One of Alejandro's pictures. So different from what others were taking, and intended only to be seen by close family members.

And Isabella! She was so happy! Married to Sebastian, her first and only love. And now they are soon to have their first child.

Rosie brought her knees up to her chest and waited for the griping cramp from her middle regions to subside before attempting to take another breath.

Just as soon as I've got over this rib bruising, I need to leave. But where? I can hardly face the thought of Lotta and more midnight riding. But what else is there? I've messed things up here in San Francisco by falling out with Magdalena.

She pulled a rug that lay across the counterpane up over her knees as Betty bustled back in with a headache powder and a glass of water in her hands.

"Here we are, Miss Rosie," she said, her tanned face drawn into a frown as she watched Rosie carefully for a reaction.

"Miss Isabella says she will come and see you before bedtime, just to check you're all right."

Rosie took the water and laughed. "Such fussy care... I'm fine. Just a little beat up, that's all."

Betty hesitated. "Do you want me to help you into your nightgown? Is there anything else I can do?"

Rosie shook her head and gathered the rug further up around her shoulders, tucking it under her neck. "I'm just fine,

Betty. I need rest, that's all."

Still, Betty stood near the bed, scanning her face.

Rosie glanced up, noticing the housekeeper's hesitation.

"Is there something else?"

Betty had clasped her hands together, and Rosie saw them tighten.

"Miss Isabella needs you here, Miss Rosie. Especially with the baby coming, and things still so, well… cloudy where her brother is concerned.

"If that policeman arrests him… Well, I don't know how Isabella will manage, her expecting a baby and all. Mr. Russell is a fine man, but it's not the same as having a female friend, a best friend, here.

"I'm just saying, Miss Rosie. Mr. Alex needs you too, even if he doesn't know it."

From the burning sensation climbing up her cheeks, Rosie knew her face was flushing red. Her jaw dropped open, and she quickly snapped it shut and took another sip of water from the glass, which dripped in her hand, spilling water onto the bedcover.

She shook her head vehemently.

"Oh now, Betty. I'm certain you're wrong there. He'll be glad when I'm gone. He can't stand me."

Betty struck her own cheek with her hand in a playful reprimand.

"Cursed I be if I didn't believe what my old eyes see," she said.

"Young Mr. de Vile needs you too. He just doesn't know it yet. Men can be so dumb sometimes."

Rosie clutched at her ribs as she took a huge breath and laughed.

"Ohhhh noooo, Betty. Don't do this to me… I can't laugh…"

She was gasping for breath, clutching at her painful ribs, and staring at Betty, all at the same time.

"It's true, Miss Rosie. No joke. I see him when others don't. When you're not looking at him, he can't take his eyes off you."

"Yes. Because he hates me. He thinks I don't know what I'm talking about. To him, I'm a troublemaker and a hussy."

She pitched a mischievous tilt of her head Betty's way.

"And I guess I am a troublemaker. I can't deny it. But I'm not a hussy, though. He's got that wrong."

She flicked Betty a conspiratorial grin.

"I had to play up to that awful man Garcia to get information, and Alejandro didn't like it. I don't blame him. The man is a serious challenge to good judgment."

Betty put back her head and roared with laughter.

"Now that's more like the Miss Rosie I know and regard highly. Don't let that girl get lost. And please, stay on for a little longer, until everything here is more settled. The household—all of us—needs you."

Rosie regarded her with sad, fond eyes.

"I'm not sure I agree with your conclusions, Betty, but I will stay a bit longer. And I'm going to continue to be an awful troublemaker, so I'll need your help with that. I don't think anyone else here is up for it."

Betty Butler gave another huffing laugh. "Samuel and I are reporting for business," she said. "Starting with keeping that awful Garcia man away. You just tell us what you need."

Fifty-one

Rosie knew exactly what she had to do. She languished in bed and allowed Betty to bring her soup for dinner, although her newly laid plans charged her with an excitement she found difficult to conceal.

Ewan's sobering summary of their chances of succeeding with the land claim had dampened the mood in the entire house. Alejandro sloped off to his own home straight after dinner and Seb retired to his office to catch up on paperwork for Basil's business interests.

Fanny, Isabella and Eilish all tiptoed upstairs to kiss her on the cheek and wish her sweet dreams before either returning to Lick House—in Fanny's case—or going to bed early.

"It's remarkable how tiring bad news can be," Fanny remarked with the faintest hint of a self-mocking smile.

"After what Ewan had to say today, we're all feeling a bit bashed up. An early night is in order all round, and it's good you've been taking it easy and having your supper in bed."

She scanned the room with a frown. "That is what you are planning, isn't it? A nice quiet night?"

Rosie did her best to suppress the smile that was threatening to break through at Fanny's fully justified suspicion.

"Sadly, there's nothing I can do to help anymore," she said. "And anyway, Alejandro is so fed up with me, I wouldn't dare interfere."

Fanny shook her head, her eyes screwed up in frustration.

"He'll get over it," she said. "He's mainly sick with worry about your safety. He just doesn't realize that's what's at the bottom of his bad moods yet. Don't worry. He'll come out of it."

Rosie gazed into Fanny's lovely face. The careworn crinkles around her eyes and mouth made her even more precious, because she'd paid for those lines with concern for those she loved.

However, the Irish girl tipped her head to one side to show her disagreement.

"I don't think so, Fanny. I got off on the wrong foot with him and I've never made up the lost ground. We've disagreed about how to proceed all the way along."

Fanny leaned over to kiss the top of her head and enveloped her in her warm, rose-scented fragrance. So much more than the contents of a perfume bottle, she thought. A fragrance interwoven with wisdom, kindness, and wit.

I'm going to really miss you when I go.

A cloud of fatigue engulfed her, and she didn't need to fake the yawn that came naturally.

"You're tired, sweet lass. You must be exhausted after last night. I'll let you get some sleep. But don't forget—I owe you my life and I can never say thank you to you enough."

Hot on Fanny's heels, Isabella and then Eilish presented themselves to say "Goodnight" and ask if she needed anything before they turned in.

"I am perfectly comfortable," she assured them. "I'll be asleep before you reach your own beds."

***

She waited a good half hour before slipping out of bed, holding the bullet-grazed side of her ribs with one arm, as she fought her way gingerly into a heavy overcoat.

After spending the day tucked up cozily in bed, she knew she'd feel vulnerable in the cooler evening air. The coat was still hanging off one shoulder when Betty tapped softly on the door and stepped into the room.

"Rest of the house has gone down early," she whispered with satisfaction. "And a good thing, too. They're all a bit down in the dumps after Mr. Campbell's visit. It will do them good to have a sound night's sleep."

She cast a steely eye over Rosie. "And you, young lady, are going to be wrapped up good and warm before Samuel takes you out. Where are your winter boots?"

After scrabbling for boots and scarves and gloves and tucking an extra layer in under her coat, she satisfied Betty she was well enough protected to be let out. They tiptoed down the stairs, Betty leading the way, and Samuel glided out of the kitchen to meet them.

"The coach is all hitched up and ready," he mumbled under his breath. "After you."

The short ride to Diana's rented one bed-roomed lodgings

with a tiny kitchenette and shared bathroom gave her just enough time to question the wisdom of the whole idea.

As far as she could see, the only way the Castellanos family were going to see justice in the corrupt Land Claims system here in California was if Diana had some devastating evidence of forgery in documents relating to their case, and was willing to expose herself and her spying activities to the court.

The first hope—that she had something that would make a difference—was unlikely enough. But asking herself to step forward and disclose her activities? Rosie shivered at the thought.

If it was her, with the responsibility for care of a son, would she be willing to take the risk of possible charges for interfering with court records? All to present evidence on behalf of people she barely knew?

I guess it depends on how badly she wants to get revenge on Elmer.

She braced herself to stop from slipping off the leather seat as they went around a sharp corner, and winced.

He certainly deserves his comeuppance, after the way he's treated her.

If she has the evidence we need, and she will put herself on the line for Fanny, what can I offer her in the way of a sweetener to make it worth her while?

She was still turning that thought over in her mind when Samuel drew the coach to a slow halt and offered her a welcome hand to get down.

"I'll sit here and wait," he said with a quick grin.

"Don't worry. I'm not leaving you."

Impulsively, Rosie ducked her head and planted a quick kiss on his cheek.

"You don't know what this means to me, Sam," she said. "If it works out, Alejandro will owe you a nice fat bonus."

Fifty-two

Land Court Judge Jacob Green peered over his gold-rimmed glasses and banged his gavel on the bench he sat at with two fellow judges.

David Munster, a ruddy-faced genial fellow, and a relatively new appointment to the bench, sat on his left. Richard Sullivan, on his right, was Green's deputy and had been on the Lands Court for a decade. He was thin and pale, with a stiff formality that contrasted, like chalk and cheese, · with Munster's easygoing style.

At a desk in front of the bench sat a stenographer and the court registrar, Elmer Green, ready to take notes, swear in people giving evidence, and support the proceedings.

The chief judge, Green, had the same foxy features as his son Elmer, Rosie observed from her wheelchair, parked unobtrusively in a back corner.

And Judge Green was in an extremely bad mood.

He glared from his stand above the lawyers and their clients below and bawled, "Sit down, Mr. Garcia, and wait till you are spoken to before you speak."

The California Land Claims court had been late assembling,

because, as the main claimant, the judge expected Bram Gordon to be there. He delayed getting under way for nearly an hour, while minions investigated if Gordon was delayed, if his arrival was imminent, or if he wasn't coming at all.

Dionisio Garcia stood red-faced, glaring up at the three men. His counsel, seated next to him, tugged nervously at Garcia's camel-colored leather jacket, desperately hinting it would be best to do what the judge said.

"I said 'sit down'," Green instructed again, his voice sharper and more irritable.

"We've heard quite enough from you for one day."

He glanced to the other side, where Ewan Campbell sat flanked by Fanny on one side and Alejandro on the other.

"My apologies, Marquésa, for this display."

He dipped his head to her in a sign of deference. The long white beard that hung a third of the way over his paisley waistcoat and sober black jacket seemed to bristle with a life of its own.

At his jaw it narrowed into two snow-white sideburns which ran up either side of his face and met at his thinning white hairline.

"Bad manners will not be tolerated in this court."

He glared at Dionisio, who finally took his lawyer's hint and sat down with a thump.

Apart from the claimants, the only other people in the dusty, timber-lined room were a couple of vagrants from the street, who were treating it as free theater, and a reporter from one of the business newsletters that followed the city's property stories.

The reporter had already questioned Rosie as to why she was

there—and she'd pointed to her wheelchair and indicated it was merely for idle entertainment while she recovered.

"Billy Sanders at your service," he said, thrusting out his hand. "Pleased to meet you."

"Do you get much out of these hearings you can use?" she asked.

"Depends," he said.

"On what?" she asked, fluttering her long lashes shamelessly.

"On what sort of mood Judge Green is in and whether Bram Gordon sees the deal through. He's a hard negotiator.

"Sometimes he lets them dangle until the very last minute. Oftentimes, they don't have a clue if he's going to go through with it or not.

"And if he renegs, the city doesn't get its debts paid and the judges don't get their sweet deal either, though I can never write about that. No proof."

He glanced to the bench to check if he was being observed, and then said quietly, "Judges can make a lot more money as lawyers presenting client's cases than they can on the bench, so it's generally accepted there'll be 'extra consideration' paid by successful plaintiffs."

"Really?" Rosie whispered. "I had no idea that's how it worked. You learn something new every day."

She put her finger to her lips to signal she didn't want to get caught talking in court and redirected her attention to the front bench.

Green was plainly put out by Gordon's failure to turn up or advise the court of his absence, because the original claim for the Los Putos ranch had been made in his name, and he'd never once failed to turn up for a hearing.

The paperwork for today's audience had been distributed to Ewan as well, as the court rules required. It was a relatively straightforward case. Bram Gordon was applying to settle outstanding rates on the parcel of land in return for being granted a lease in perpetuity, on the grounds that no living descendants remained and the unpaid rates were a drag on the common purse.

As he had done in other cases, Gordon made a cozy little arrangement with the judges to pay the rates, clear the debt, and be granted the use of the land in perpetuity in gratitude.

Expect that two thorns had already been raised to complicate the tidy little private deal.

First, Ewan had presented Fanny's papers, stating that Angel Castellanos was a 50 percent owner of the land and that his descendants were alive and laying claim to it themselves.

And then, just as Judge Green seemed to be about to enter into full discussions on that matter, Dionisio had stood uninvited and made a dramatic announcement.

"Your honor, if I may?"

Green's pursed lips and purple complexion indicated he may not. He made a noise like a gargle in the back of his throat, and the other judges rose higher in their chairs, on his alert, but Garcia ignored the warning signs.

"I wanted to advise the court: The original claimant, Mr. Bram Gordon, is so devastated by the death of his son that he has waived any interest in the property.

"He has given me permission to carry on with it as I have invested years of work in assisting him with the paperwork, and

Mr. Hasselthwaite will continue as my attorney.

"Mr. Gordon wants nothing further to do with it, but he is happy for me to remain, more or less as his de facto son."

The judges greeted with rising alarm the first two statements, Green being the most vocal. But when he got to the third statement about Bram nominating him his "de facto son," all hell broke loose.

Green leaned over his desk and scowled. "This is all most irregular, Mr. Hasselthwaite." He glared at Dionisio's lawyer, who so far had not said a word. Dionisio had taken over the reins and cut him off every time he attempted to speak.

"This court is adjourned until Mr. Gordon presents himself here and confirms in person that he has withdrawn from the claim."

He glanced over at Ewan.

"And meantime, you will be required to present copies of all relevant documents to Mr. Campbell before you leave today.

"Surely you appreciate we aren't going to accept your word at face value? It's all highly irregular, and Mr. Campbell must be given time to consider his options."

He glanced around, seemingly suddenly aware of Billy taking notes.

"We won't accept your word for Mr. Gordon's non-appearance. We need to see him here tomorrow or I'm dismissing the case outright and you'll have to apply for a new hearing."

He scanned the court, as if satisfying himself Gordon had not turned up in the last five minutes without announcing himself.

"Court adjourned till two p.m. tomorrow. And I'm warning you. If Mr. Gordon does not appear, I'll be dismissing this case and you will have to file a new claim on different grounds."

Fifty-three

"Mr. Gordon. Thank you for presenting yourself at court today."

Judge Green's voice had an acid bite to it, but his expression gave nothing away.

Bram Gordon stood and fixed his implacable stare on the judge, his sapphire blue eyes turning a steely gray.

"Judge, my sincere apologies for my non-attendance yesterday."

He slid a sideways glance to Dionisio, who sat on the other side of their attorney, Enoch Hasselthwaite.

"I had been led to believe by my fellow applicant, Mr. Garcia, that he and my attorney would be able to handle the matter and that my attendance was not required. However, I now understand that was misleading, for more than one reason."

His eyes rested on Hasselthwaite, who clasped his hands tightly in front of him, as if expecting his next comment to be a critical one.

"Your honor, I have not had an opportunity to brief Mr. Hasselthwaite on my position regarding some changes that were made in our submission yesterday. I seek permission to speak directly to you on this matter."

Judge Green's long white beard shivered, and the watery eyes behind the steel frames narrowed.

For a long minute, he gazed at the three men, the plaintiffs and their lawyer. Gordon dwarfed the other two.

Hasselthwaite seemed to cringe in his shadow, and Garcia, his face reddening, stared straight ahead.

"It's unorthodox, Mr. Gordon, but we've already had some unexpected submissions in this case, and in these land claims hearings I have the freedom to bend the rules, as you appreciate.

"In the interests of saving time and getting the matter expedited while the Marquésa is still in California, I agree." He glanced at Ewan, and added, "As long as her attorney has no objections."

Ewan shot to his feet. "No objections, your honor."

He sat down again just as quickly.

Bram Gordon commenced, his gaze roaming the bench as he spoke.

"I bought a share of Los Putos from Hernandez Valaquez in good faith. I didn't question his claim he was the rightful owner.

"I was unaware until recently that the Marquésa and her family were making a claim on this estate.

"I was also blindsided to discover that Mr. Garcia is about to make a claim on his own behalf as a descendant of Hernandez Valquez."

He glared at Garcia, who refused to meet his stare, sitting like a stone statue, eyes set forward.

"As you know, my son Alistair died in a confrontation in the home of Alejandro Castellanos. I believe Alistair was encouraged to unlawfully enter Mr. Castellanos' home by Mr. Garcia, and I hold him responsible for my son's death. I have told him as much."

He raised his steely blue eyes to Judge Green's expressionless face.

"In the circumstances, I withdraw from this claim in favor of the Castellanos family."

An electric silence echoed in the high-roofed chamber as Bram Gordon sank to his chair, his spine pressed hard against its back, upright in rigid dignity.

Judge Green's eyes widened, and he licked his lips, as if stalling for time before answering. Before he opened his mouth, Dionisio Garcia sprang to his feet, his mutton-chop hands beating the top of the desk.

"I protest!" he cried. "As the rightful heir to one of the original owners, I remain a lawful claimant, regardless of Mr. Gordon's wishes."

The Judge rose, his parted red lips displaying creamy pointed teeth.

"The court will adjourn for fifteen minutes," he barked.

He raised his hand and gestured to the two lawyers.

"I'll see you two for a conference in my chambers in five."

He glared at Garcia.

"And no, Mr. Garcia. That does not include you."

***

When Ewan re-appeared forty minutes later, his sandy hair hung lank over his tired eyes.

"Hasselthwaite is now acting solely for Dionisio Garcia. It's the only way he can see to get anything out of his work on the case, because Bram Gordon won't be putting in another cent.

"And he's persuaded the judge it's reasonable to continue with Garcia as a claimant even though his name was not on the original documents."

Alejandro gulped.

"That doesn't mean he's likely to award it to both of us? Fifty fifty? Lord forbid."

Ewan shook his head.

"No, I don't believe he'll do that. Hasselthwaite is asking for a ruling that will give a one hundred percent ownership to one party or the other.

"And he seems disturbingly confident it will be for his side. I've got an uncomfortable feeling we're in more surprises before this case is over. He's adjourned it till tomorrow, so we have time to prepare ourselves."

Fifty-four

"Remember, we arranged for Diana and Fergus to come to dinner? And you couldn't do it because of that dreadful Temptation Thompson woman?

"I think tonight would be the perfect time if she's free to come, don't you?"

Rosie trailed Fanny along the corridor to her Lick House suite, her fingers crossed behind her back as she pitched her latest idea.

They paused in the hallway while Juliana bent to insert the key and unlock it.

Rosie lowered her voice, aware of the possibility of being overheard by other hotel guests.

"From what you say, we're definitely going to need Diana's help for tomorrow. The evidence of faked documents she can present could be the thing we need to blow them out of the water."

Fanny tugged the corners of her emerald-green mohair stole more tightly around her shoulders and scanned Rosie's face with an interrogative glint.

"What exactly do you imagine she'd be able to tell us?"

Rosie was late to the hearing that morning and arrived after the judge adjourned to talk to the lawyers in his chambers.

But from the report she'd heard second-hand from Fanny on their way home, that deep down intuition that so often proved right, even if it did land her in hot water, was telling. If they were to win, Diana's story would be an essential part of the evidence they presented tomorrow.

And to arrange that, she needed Fanny's support. If she suggested it to Ewan and Alejandro, they'd dismiss her again as a fanciful woman. She was certain of it.

But if she had Fanny's backing, they couldn't ignore her.

Juliana turned the key, and they were silent as they wandered in, and Fanny gratefully collapsed into one of the big armchairs.

"Can you organize some tea, please, Juliana? I'm parched," she said as she fell back against the fat velour cushions.

Rosie tucked herself into the neighboring chair and hunched forward in a confidential huddle.

"I don't exactly know," she admitted. "That's why I think it would be great to talk to her."

She searched Fanny's face for clues as to the likely reception.

"If we ask her to do this, she'll be taking an enormous risk. She could lose her job, or worse. They could charge her with meddling with government records.

"I think we need to make it clear you will use all the resources at your disposal to protect her from repercussions."

Fanny's intelligent eyes probed hers.

"Even offer some sort of support. Not as a bribe, of course," she said hurriedly. "But to help her with her responsibilities.

"Pay for Fergus's school fees or something like that. She's doing it all alone, without the father's help."

"I see," said Fanny. "Remind me. What do we know already?"

Rosie took a deep breath and launched in.

"She's seen evidence of faked papers being presented. Things like ownership papers being doctored. In her job, she has access to all the records.

"If we knew what she should be looking for, she might be able to search them before the hearing tomorrow."

She hesitated.

"The man who spurned her, the father of her child, is the court registrar, Elmer Green."

Fanny's face registered alarm. "Green? The judge's son?"

Rosie nodded with a sick grin. "The same."

"Won't he be inclined to dismiss the notion if it's his son who is being accused of fraud?"

Rosie paused to think it through. "Perhaps she needn't accuse Elmer. She could give evidence of the discrepancies without pointing the finger at anyone in particular."

"I suppose..." Fanny frowned and sat quietly for what seemed like ages.

Rosie held her tongue.

"You're right, Rosie. As usual," Fanny finally said with a sly grin.

"See if you can get Diana and Fergus over for dinner tonight. Let's not waste any more time."

Fifty-five

Judge Green fingered the heavy parchment with the red waxed seal above Alta California Governor Pio Pico's flourishing signature: *Don Pío de Jesús Pico.*

In the early years, he was one of the richest and most influential politicians in the state.

He'd also approved thousands of acres in land claims to prominent Spanish families in the months before the US took control, the Valaquez's among them.

He pushed his glasses down his long nose and scrutinized Fanny over the gold rims. "I've no concerns that this is a false document," he said, flashing a nervous smile.

He traced lines of the wax seal with his index finger. "You see very few like this these days. I've been sitting on this bench for fifteen years, and I might have seen no more than two or three like this in all that time.

"But that doesn't mean it can't be questioned as to its authenticity. You appreciate, don't you, Marquésa, that Governor Pio Pico was notorious for approving thousands of last-minute land grants in Alta California.

"Even under Mexican law, many of those would not be

regarded as satisfactorily validated.”

Fanny dipped her head in wordless acquiescence.

“Most were never surveyed. The boundaries of many were so vague as to be unintelligible. And in many cases, the owners never occupied them. Perhaps never even knew themselves exactly what they were laying claim to.”

Ewan jumped up to intercede. “Judge, might I submit a further document? A well-drawn *discenio* dated !835, that outlines the area under discussion. As you’re aware, in the 1830s, surveyors were scarce and most of these properties weren’t surveyed.”

He stepped forward and passed another piece of ragged-edged yellow parchment into the judge’s hand.

Green eyed it for a long minute and turned his attention again to Fanny, who was seated next to Ewan, this morning wearing a gown of gold satin under a short purple velvet jacket edged in gold and tied at the throat with a gold ribbon.

“You do also appreciate, Marquésa, that we are now in 1872, nearly forty years after this grant was originally made. Why has it taken this long for you to remember it and reach out for it?”

”It’s unusual, your honor, and I understand your disquiet. I’d have to claim extenuating family circumstances. My husband was called into diplomatic service by the Spanish court soon after he and Hernandez got this grant, as I’m sure you know.

“Indeed, he was the Spanish ambassador to Mexico when the agreement between the US and Mexico over California’s change of ownership was made.

“Then he was called back to Spain, but he always hoped our

eldest son Rafael, who came to California in 1850, would be able to take up his share."

She flashed the judge a sad smile.

"Angel often spoke of the 'ranchero' with its lush grass and fertile river flats. It assumed a Garden of Eden status in his mind.

"But Rafael is one of the big griefs of our lives. We lost touch with him when he suffered a devastating family tragedy. His wife was killed, and two of his children went missing, apparently taken by wolves or the like.

"I've discovered since I arrived here that he died in depressing circumstances, never having received the many letters I wrote to him. His life was destroyed by that tragedy, and the letters I wrote him were stolen."

Fanny leaned back from the bench. She'd linked her hands and leaned on her elbows as she'd been talking, a mature Madonna touched by griefs too deep to name, but still transcendent in her beauty.

She rested her back against the spindly uprights of the Windsor chair and leveled the judge with a steady, penetrating gaze. She was challenging him, not seeking sympathy as she spoke next.

"Angel's dying wish was for me to find Rafael's children and make sure his share of this land was passed on to them. And I promised I would do all in my power to see that was accomplished."

The judge nodded in understanding. "Did your husband remain in touch with Don Valaquez after he returned to Spain? Did he receive any news about the land—whether the Don was farming it, for example?"

"I think the turbulence of politics for both of them in those days made it difficult. You know what it was like here in California with the hordes arriving for gold. In Madrid, Angel saw it as his role to protect a young queen. He and Hernandez lost touch soon after we returned to Madrid."

A bubble of silence seemed to hover above them as Fanny, every inch the aristocrat, regarded the judge and he gazed back.

Then it was rudely broken by the screech of chair legs on the tiled floor, and the opposition lawyer Hasselthwaite rose to interject.

"The lady's testimony is all very touching, I'm sure," he said with a snarky edge. "But what her husband may or may not have dreamed of for his son or grandson is immaterial to the proceedings."

Ewan jumped in like a dog not wanting to miss a scrap over a bone.

"Your honor, can we ascertain exactly whose interests Mr. Hasselthwaite represents here today? Yesterday it was Mr. Gordon's, but now are we to take it he's being paid by Mr. Garcia?

"Because yesterday Mr. Gordon said he was waiving his rights in favor of the Castellanos family?"

He glanced down and flashed a mischievous smile Fanny's way.

No harm in muddying the waters and getting his back up at the same time, it said.

It might even put him off his game.

Green peered down from his perch like an eagle surveying the ground for prey.

"I'll be the one to decide what is pertinent and what isn't,

Mr. Hasselthwaite," the judge said, with obvious dislike. "And it's a valid question. Let's clarify once again. Are you now retained to represent Mr. Garcia?"

Hasselthwaite's face flushed an angry beetroot color.

"I would have thought that was obvious, but apparently not to Mr. Campbell," he retorted.

A bad move to get up the judge's nose, thought Ewan with secret delight. *Whereas Fanny has just done a marvellous job of charming him with her gracious noblewoman act. It helps that she still looks rather gorgeous, too.*

Green quietly snorted like a mare choking on chaff and looked to Fanny.

"Just to complete your evidence, Marquésa, were you ever aware of Don Valaquez selling any of his share of the land? Did he ever notify the Marquess of such a move?"

Fanny's face registered a suitable alarm. "Oh my goodness. Never, your honor. I am certain if he had advised Angel of anything like that, he would never have asked me to come here to sort things out."

In the quiet moment that followed, Ewan reached out and surreptitiously patted Fanny's hand that sat closest to him on the legal desk.

Great performance, Marquésa. Our own Rosie Kelly couldn't have done better.

***

Hasselthwaite was still sullen and scowling fifteen minutes later when the judge resumed the hearing after a brief refreshment break.

He knows he's got ground to make up, Ewan thought. And long may it remain so.

But the course the evidence took in the next few minutes was far from what he'd expected.

The documents that he'd been provided after the first day by the opposing side included one purporting to be a sales agreement between Hernandez and Garcia, selling fifty percent of the ranch to an entity owned by Dionisio Garcia.

Ewan presumed they were going to argue that this was Angel's fifty percent, though how they could claim that without acknowledging his legal ownership, he wasn't sure.

Judge Green struck his desk with his gavel and announced, "The California Land Claims Court is once again in session."

He glanced at the stenographer who sat next to Elmer and was faithfully recording everything in a large notebook with a marbled-paper cover. He nodded imperceptibly, and the judge turned to Hasselthwaite.

"Mr. Hasselthwaite, can you please consult your records and give us your submission on this matter? And please, you do the talking. Keep your client silent."

"Thank you, Judge," said Hasselthwaite, his face reflecting a sense of mild relief.

I am at least getting my day in court, it said.

Hasselthwaite drew a handful of documents out of his briefcase and placed them on the desk before him.

"Your honor, I wish the record to show that we have written proof that Hernandez Valaquez accepted Dionisio Garcia as his illegitimate son soon after birth, and before his recent death, he signed documents recognizing him as his legitimate heir.

"I submit these documents for the court records, and request that you make two findings in this case.

"One: That Dionisio Garcia is the Hernandez Valaquez's only legal living heir.

"And two: That he is the legal owner of the claim referred to as the Ranchero Rio de Los Putos on Putah Creek, thirty miles from the confluence of the Sacramento and America Rivers, by right of being the sole living heir."

Ewan's blood turned to ice. He'd been half expecting to hear that Valaquez had sold Angel's share—or at least that they would claim that was what had happened.

But Garcia as Hernandez's sole legal heir?

I didn't see this one coming.

He jumped to his feet, bracing himself not to teeter, because his legs were tingling down to his toes.

"I object, your honor," he barked. "We've had no previous disclosure of this new information, and we've been given no time to check it for ourselves."

Judge Green speared him with eyes of disbelief.

"Objection granted," he opined. "Court will resume at nine a.m. tomorrow morning."

He glared around him, as if finding it impossible to decide whose behavior vexed him the most.

"And let's just I hope that will be the last of Los Putos," he said under his breath as he rose to his feet.

And then more loudly: "I'm not inclined to grant any more extensions on this matter, so I advise you to come well-prepared."

Fifty-six

"Guid efternuin." Good afternoon.

Bram Gordon leaned his six-foot-four-inch frame over the petite seated form of the Marquésa Fanny de Castellanos y Ordonez and took her pale white hand up in his cattleman's paws.

He gazed down at them, his hairy, sunburned mitts gently holding her slender fingers, and delicately kissed them, staring up into her face for a few seconds before laying her hand gently back down in her lap.

She's still a beautiful Scottish lass, this Spaniard, even though she's getting on in years, he thought.

The Caledonian greeting, and his gracious homage, caught Fanny by surprise, well versed though she was in the courtesies of the Spanish court. She gazed up at him with one dark brow raised in a wary question.

Then she shot him a quick smile and answered in broad Scots.

"Lang may yer lum reek!" Long may your chimney smoke.

She gestured to the armchair next to hers.

"Suidhibh sìos!" Sit down.

Fanny's eyes scanned his face, and she said in English with a broad Scot's accent, "What are you doing here?"

He gave a quick smile in response and replied in kind, "I've come to see you."

Fanny glanced up to Alejandro and Rosie, slumped at opposite ends of her Lick House dining suite.

Alejandro's hair hung over his washed-out face and weary half-closed eyes.

Rosie sat as far away from him as she could get, her hands clasped in a tense knot.

They were both staring in disbelief at Gordon, the unexpected visitor who'd been ushered in with Fanny's approval when he presented himself at the desk downstairs.

He knew from being a Lick House guest himself that the Marquésa was staying here, and after Dionisio Garcia's courtroom display over the last two days, he'd decided it was essential they meet.

He had nothing to lose and everything to gain.

The Marquésa straightened up in her chair, as if realizing she was the hostess here.

"Much as I'd like to continue conversing in the old tongue, Mr. Gordon, it's only right to introduce my son and a dear friend, and include them in our conversation."

She gestured to the two youngsters at the table.

"May I introduce Miss Rosie Kelly, and my grandson, Alejandro Castellanos?"

Bram cast a glittering eye over the young man's listless form.

About the same age as Alistair, but a lot more grounded.

He ignored the griping pain in his stomach and rose from his seat and bowed.

"Mr. Castellanos, one of my aims in calling here tonight is to apologize for the unwarranted invasion my son made of your home."

Alex's eyes widened, and he snorted derisively.

"A remarkably accurate description."

He gazed back at Gordon with hostile, narrowed gray eyes.

"If you were unlucky enough to be caught there, like I was, it felt more like a murderous ambush."

Gordon swallowed hard, his Adam's apple bobbing in the front of his throat.

"You're still angry about it," he said. "And justifiably."

The younger man's jaw tensed, and the pitch of his voice rose.

"I think you would be too if you had that policeman still dogging you, talking murder charges. I had no choice but to shoot. It was two against one, for starters."

Gordon spread his big hands out in front of him in a gesture of conciliation and nodded.

"Two against one. I appreciate that, Mr. Castellanos. Again, I say, I am sorry my son placed you in that situation, though I remind you, he paid for it with his life."

Alex flushed red, and his brow furrowed.

"It's a terrible thing to live with, to know you've killed a man," he murmured. "I wish on everything within me it hadn't happened like it did."

Bram's chest cramped, and he took a shallow breath.

"Please. I understand," he said, his voice husky. "My son is gone, and that's difficult, too. But I don't blame you."

An awkward silence hung between them.

Alex stared down at the carpet. The girl—Rosie, was it? She peeked anxiously from Alex to Bram.

Get on with this, Bram. Don't drag it out. It's torture for us all.

He tried to ignore his cramped chest and took an audible long breath.

He turned his gaze full back on Alex.

"I understand, Mr. Castellanos, if you want nothing to do with me. But I believe we have common interests. That's why I'm here."

He flicked his attention to Fanny, who was perched on the front of her chair, watching every moment with an eagle's gaze.

"Can I ask? The night of the attack, who was it with my son? Did you see the other man at all?"

Alex shook his head.

"The superintendent has probably told you already. I hid under the table when I heard them thumping down the hall.

"The one on my left fired a shot into the back wall when they arrived. As if to show they meant business. I jumped up long enough to get off one shot and bobbed back down again. I hardly knew where I was aiming. All I wanted was to scare them off."

His voice cracked. Recalling that night was a torment for him, Bram could see.

His eyes darted from the floor to Bram's face, dark and frightened.

"The second man cleared out in a heartbeat. I heard his footsteps banging down the hall while my ears were still ringing from my shot. He didn't hang around to survey the damage."

His strength drained, Gordon sat down with a thump.

"Just as I thought," he whispered to no one in particular.

His insides hollowed out, and the cramping knifed him in his chest.

He gasped for air.

"I never thought that Dion Garcia would turn out to be such a snake in the grass," he murmured, speaking under his breath to himself as much as anyone else.

"He set it up. He planned it. All the time he was acting like Alistair's best friend, he was planning to remove him. Playing at being my 'second son,' while he was planning to betray us."

He breathed out the words like exhaled smoke, his mind suddenly hazy.

His eyes glazed over as he looked up and saw everyone in the room staring at him in shock.

His attention coalesced in half a second, back to Lick House, and these people who now, hopefully, were his allies.

A quavering female voice floated to him in the stunned silence. The pretty young woman at the far end of the table, who hadn't uttered a word until now, was saying something.

He focused on her.

"He dropped something," she said. "The other man who was there that night. A piece of sequined braid from a jacket. I'm pretty sure it was from a Spanish jacket like Dionisio wears."

Her eyes faltered uncertainly to the Castellanos heir at the other end.

"One of Alejandro's friends found it the next morning, and they handed it to the police, I think? Didn't you, Alejandro?"

The young man sat up, suddenly alert.

"That's right. O'Halloran's got it."

"He's never mentioned it to me," said Gordon.

He leaned back in the chair, suddenly bone weary. His feet were lumps of wood, so heavy he wondered if he was capable of standing.

The Marquésa's eyes rested on him, and he had the uncomfortable feeling she could see right through him.

"You mentioned one of your aims was to apologize to Alejandro," she said in quiet, measured tones.

"What are your other reasons for coming here? There was more than one?"

She gazed at him with a tenderness which said she knew the pain of losing a son.

Her head dipped in a silent nod, as if she'd made an instant decision.

"But before we get to that, we're going to organize some hospitality. Forgive me for not doing it sooner."

She shot a look at her grandson.

"Alejandro, would you be a dear and organize refreshments with downstairs? Savories, cakes, tea, coffee and a touch of Scotch to help it down?"

Her grandson rose, he guessed glad to escape the tension in the room, and disappeared in a minute.

"It's not necessary," Bram muttered in a weak voice.

"Oh, but it most certainly is," said the Marquésa, the patrician in the Highlander asserting herself.

"We've still got a great deal still to say."

Fifty-seven

"Can you repeat that statement to the court, Mr. Hasselthwaite, so there is no doubt in our minds what your claim is based upon?"

Judge Green pushed his glasses down his nose and peered over them, his skeptical eyes glinting.

Green's neck prickled at the slew of challenges Garcia and his lawyer had presented in the first hour of the fourth and final hearing of Castellanos versus Gordon—Rancho Rio de Los Putos.

Police Superintendent O'Halloran had taken a seat at the back of the court, his rapt attention hovering as an unsettling presence over proceedings.

Why is he here?

His unannounced arrival set off alarm bells in Green's judicial mind. What had sparked his interest in a dusty case?

The claim is forty years old, for goodness' sake.

He'd heard whispers that Bram Gordon was also back, although he hadn't yet seen him.

The property king had withdrawn from the case two days ago, so Green was bemused as to why he was still loitering in the background.

Has he had a change of mind? And if he has, what's my attitude to that? Do I let him back in?

As he listened to Garcia's lawyer Hasselthwaite present his client's case, his eyes flickered to the flamboyant Mexican at the lawyer's right hand.

He overflowed with bulldog confidence, but as Hasselthwaite burbled on, Green's mind was elsewhere, ranging over previous cases.

He'd sat on this bench for a dozen years, and he had a good recall of most of them.

Is there any precedent for allowing a plaintiff who has withdrawn to be reinstated?

He'd allowed Hasselthwaite to present new evidence that had not been disclosed to the court ahead of time, so he concluded he should give the same latitude to Gordon.

Besides, the ranch owner was an influential player as well as a good friend of the court in past deals. He'd likely lodge an appeal if he didn't like how this hearing played out.

The judge emerged from these musings to find his court was silent, and all eyes were on him, waiting expectantly.

"My apologies, Counsel. I didn't hear that last statement as clearly as I'd like. Please repeat it."

Hasselthwaite's eyes narrowed.

"I asked permission for Mr. Garcia to be called to give evidence," he said.

Dionisio Garcia puffed himself up like a barnyard cock in a hen harem.

Green nodded acquiescence. "All right," he said with a note of resignation. "Call Mr. Garcia."

As Garcia rose to swear fealty, he glanced around the court with a glow that so resembled a rooster. Green suppressed a smile.

The man's crowing his triumph before I've pronounced judgement.

"I, Dionisio Garcia, lay claim to the Rancho Rio de Los Putos Spanish grant on the grounds that I am the only legitimate living descendant of the original claimant, Hernandez Valaquez, and I present documents in support of that assertion."

Garcia was reading from a paper prepared for him by his lawyer.

"One, a signed confirmation from Hernandez that I am his rightful heir.

"Second, a sales document which shows Angel Castellanos sold his share in Rancho Rio de Los Putos to Hernandez in 1852, thus making Don Hernandez the sole owner of the ten thousand acres under dispute."

He glanced up with a boastful smile.

"And finally, I submit the ownership papers, registered in 1859 by Don Valaquez, showing that he is the sole owner of Los Putos."

He sat down in a heady rush, as his lawyer rose, hands full of papers which he raised above his head like a newsboy announcing a new edition.

"Request permission to approach the bench and present the papers Mr. Garcia referred to, proving his case."

As he took his first step forward, Ewan Campbell charged up from his seat.

"I object, your honor. We've had no notification of this change of events. Mr. Gordon was the original claimant, and we've had no notice of a new heir.

"An alleged new heir," he added, with sardonic emphasis.

Green waved his hand in dismissal.

"We will allow this evidence as part of the proceedings, and I will give you my ruling on whether it is admissible or not at the end of the day."

I saw this one coming.

Campbell remained standing.

"I request a brief adjournment so we may view these new documents for ourselves," he said. "Under the circumstances…"

"You can take possession of them during the lunch adjournment," Green said. "They are, of course, not to leave these chambers."

Campbell sat down, mollified.

Green looked at Hasselthwaite. "Have you anything else to add, Mr. Hasselthwaite?"

"No, your honor."

"And have you any questions, Mr. Campbell?"

"I do, your honor. Could Mr. Garcia tell us when he first knew Don Hernandez was his father?"

Garcia rose, his assurance dimmed.

"I've always known the Don was my father. My mother told me that from my earliest days. It's no big deal in our world."

Campbell continued, unabashed.

"And how did it come about that after years of regarding you as a by blow, he accorded you full legitimacy?"

Garcia hesitated. His eyes darted around him, his sudden unease on display.

"When did he acknowledge me as his legal heir?"

Garcia raised his brows in a question mark and sighed, as if the entire process of cross-examination was tiresome.

Judge Green sensed he was buying time to formulate his answer, and he could see from the dubious curl of his lip that Campbell was convinced he was lying.

"He called me to his bedside when he was dying. He said now that his only other son was dead, he wanted me to inherit the ranch, because his wife and daughters had no use for it."

He gazed around him, suddenly enjoying being in the spotlight.

"He said he regretted not doing it earlier, and I had grown into a man he was proud to call his son."

Green swallowed hard. That was a last-minute, wishful addition to the script, he was certain.

"And how long after his son died did this meeting occur?"

Garcia shrugged, as if the date was of no particular interest to him.

"A few weeks? I don't remember the exact date."

"And when did you get the general to sign these documents? After all, he was close to death?"

"That same day I visited."

"So, you went armed with these documents for him to sign, swearing you were his legitimate heir, and you don't remember the exact date? Isn't that rather surprising?"

Garcia's face was turning red and his brow was dotted with perspiration.

"Not really. I've had a lot on my mind."

Ewan persisted. "You got Senor Valaquez to sign these documents within a few weeks of his son's death, when he himself was dying?"

"He wanted it settled before he died," said Garcia.

"And he was made heirless as a direct result of the sudden, violent death of his son, Emmanuel? Is that correct?"

Garcia's face reddened, but he stayed silent.

"Did you know Emmanuel Valaquez?"

Hasselthwaite jumped to his feet.

"Objection, your honor. Whether Mr. Garcia knew Emmanuel Valaquez is immaterial in these proceedings."

Green allowed a minute to fall, and then replied, "Objection overruled. As Emmanuel was the previous legitimate heir, I rule the questioning could be material."

Hasselthwaite scowled, and Campbell continued like a truffle dog in an oak forest.

"Have you ever been in Emmanuel Valaquez 's company? In the same room, for example? At the same card table, perhaps?"

Garcia's face darkened to thunder, and he shifted uneasily from one foot to the other.

"Emmanuel Valaquez? No. Why would I?"

"Surely, if you were a recognized son, even illegitimate, you went to the family gatherings. The annual branding celebrations, for example?"

Garcia stiffened. "I don't recall ever meeting Emmanuel," he said in a flat, defiant tone.

"And of course, you would remember, wouldn't you, Mr. Garcia? After all, as first son, he held a position you must have envied?"

Hasselthwaite bounced to his feet.

"Objection."

Ewan Campbell glanced up to the bench, and Green spotted a glint of satisfaction in his eye.

"No more questions, your honor."

We'll be hearing more about the trail he's laying here. I'd bet my judge's bench on it.

"Court is recessed for lunch." Green picked up the sheaf of Garcia documents without further examination and waved them in the direction of the Castellanos camp.

"Mr. Campbell. You're welcome to examine these in chambers over lunch."

Campbell hesitated and then asked, "Can the associated others"—he gestured vaguely to Fanny and Alejandro—"also be admitted to see them?"

"Anyone you think should see them, Mr. Campbell, but only in chambers. I want no stone unturned by the end of this marathon."

As he rose to leave, he peered to the back of the court, where O'Halloran was also levering himself upright, his eyes burning with unusual heat.

What's got his dander up?

Their eyes met, and Judge Jacob Green felt the sting from across the room.

Displeased is putting it mildly, he thought as he paused, caught in the intensity of the moment.

Our police chief has been caught napping, and he is not pleased.

But just who had incited his ire, he was yet to discover.

Fifty-eight

When the court resumed after lunch, word had got around town that something interesting was happening in the Land Claims Court, and the public area was crammed with expectant spectators.

The butcher, the baker, and the haberdasher had all scorned work for the entertainment. Jolly Joe was there from the bar across the street, along with a gaggle of street girls and sober matrons who held baskets of groceries over their arms.

Widow Brandy, who minded the liquor store for her husband Selwyn, had closed early, so she didn't miss out on the hottest gossip in town.

Along the bench from her sat the whiskery, rough-handed carpenter Emerson Pilbrow, well-known for the long tales about early California life he dispensed to anyone who would listen over a tavern pint in the evenings. Collecting more ammunition for his narrative, Ewan supposed, with the nervous jiggle in his gut.

Here's hoping I deliver something memorable enough he'll be recounting it for the next ten years.

The blistering sun beating on the adobe walls had turned

"

the courtroom so hot and stuffy that even the blowflies were bumbling and drowsy, but no one in the crowd was in danger of dropping off.

A roomful of feverish eyes gazed up to the three judges, with the registrar Elmer Green to their left. The atmosphere was charged with a tension that Ewan could taste—a strange coppery piquancy that set his nerves jangling whenever he licked his lips.

He picked up the glass on his desk and took a sip of water before resuming his questioning of Bram Gordon.

"So, Mr. Gordon, just repeat that statement, so there's no doubt in any minds about it."

"You say that never, in all your very close dealings with Dionisio Garcia, did he ever mention any relationship to the Valaquez family? Let alone share a detail like he was an illegitimate—or even better—legitimate son of the family patriarch?"

"That's correct, Mr. Campbell."

"And Dionisio was close to your son? His best friend? Tell the court about the conversation you had with Mr. Garcia following your son's death?"

"I asked him why he hadn't stopped Alistair from doing something as stupid as breaking into another man's house with a gun? I asked him what they were thinking?"

"And what did he say?"

Ewan could sense his audience leaning forward, holding their breaths, desperate to suck up every detail.

"He said it was better for me if Mr. Castellanos was out of the picture. And that he could step up and take Alistair's place as the person who would own and run Los Putos on my behalf.

"He said he regarded himself as 'practically family' anyway. We were all so close."

Behind him, a low murmuring rose from the townsfolk—a collective expressing of the thought "The cheek of it."

"And what was your reaction to that?"

"I was astounded. He seemed insensible to my feelings of grief and loss at Alistair's death. I got the impression he'd calculated and planned the attack on Alejandro Castellanos, though he'd made it sound like a drunken prank. And I remembered something else."

"What was that?"

"I remembered that when Emmanuel Valaquez died he'd been exultant. 'One more out of the way' was how he'd put it. I suddenly wondered if he'd had any involvement in Emmanuel's death."

"And did you ask him about it?"

"I did."

Any fidgeting, or gum chewing, any clacking of knitting needles or tapping of fingers against thighs, stopped. The court room was quieter than a grave.

"And what did he say?" Ewan flicked his gaze from Bram to the bench, where the justices watched slack-jawed.

"He shrugged and more or less said, so what? He was a blind monkey."

"A blind monkey? Did he use those actual words?"

Gordon's tan deepened under his blush, and he glanced nervously to the judge.

"He used swear words I can't repeat in the courtroom, Mr.

Campbell. But they meant the same thing, or worse. Emmanuel's death was no loss. He was a useless person, a piece of trash. And him dying made it easier for us to get ownership of Los Putos."

"What did you take from his attitude?"

"I was worried he might have taken things into his own hands and killed Emmanuel. I decided there and then I didn't want anything more to do with him."

Garcia jumped up, pumping his fist in the air.

"Lies," he yelled, his eyes wild and staring. "It's all lies."

The court erupted with a roar. Women were stamping, men whistling through their fingers.

Judge Green shot to his feet and slammed down his gavel.

"Silence!" he yelled, barely audible above the din.

"Be quiet at once, or I will empty the court."

The uproar gradually subsided to mutterings.

He glared at Garcia. "And you, Mr. Garcia, will remain seated and silent until called upon by either me or your lawyer."

The judge turned to Ewan.

"So, is that it, Mr. Campbell? I can't see how denigrating your opponent's character is necessarily going to help your case? Have you got any more surprises for us?"

"Yes, your honor, I would like to call Police Superintendent Seamus O'Halloran."

A moderate swelling of chatter in the public area was quickly quelled by another slamming of the gavel on the front bench.

"Silence! One more interruption and the court will be closed," Green roared, glaring out on the courtroom.

O'Halloran moved swiftly and confidently forward, the

crowd opening with murmurs to let him through.

Elmer Green swore him in and O'Halloran stood in the witness box facing Ewan's questions—and Garcia's chair.

"Superintendent O'Halloran, you are aware of the death referred to earlier? Alistair Gordon's death in the home of Alejandro Castellanos?"

"I am, Mr. Campbell. I am the lead investigator in that case."

"And were you aware that Mr. Garcia—according to Mr. Gordon's evidence—was the other person who accompanied young Mr. Gordon to the house?"

"I was not, Mr. Campbell. In fact, when I spoke to him, Mr. Garcia specifically denied being present. He claimed he was with his lady friend, Magdalena da Silva, the actress, and she backed him up. Said he'd spent the entire night with her."

"What evidence did you collect from the crime scene, Superintendent? Was there anything found that might link to the crime?"

O'Halloran hunched his shoulders forward and clasped his hands in front of him.

"There was very little evidence at the scene. A few signs of bullets in the back wall of the office, probably fired at Mr. Castellanos. He told us in his police interview he hid under the desk and someone fired over it, and the evidence confirmed that."

He licked his lips and flicked a nervous glance to the bench.

"Anything else?"

"As a matter of fact, there was. A piece of beaded fringe that looked like it came off a piece of clothing, like a skirt or jacket, was found on the floor right by where Mr. Castellanos said his attackers positioned themselves."

"Beaded fringe? Describe it more specifically."

"It's a piece of fringe about four inches long, brown in color, loaded with sequins."

His eyes flickered to Garcia, seated in front of him alongside his lawyer. "Similar in color to Mr. Garcia's jacket, there," he said, pointing.

Ewan caught the slight cringe of Garcia's body as the police super pointed at him. His eyes glowered mutinously.

"It was frayed along the edge. It's likely attached to a garment, and appeared to be torn away from a sleeve seam, or a side seam, perhaps?"

"I see. And where is this evidence at present, Chief O'Halloran?"

O'Halloran tapped his jacket pocket.

"I have it here with me, in my jacket. Safe in an envelope."

Ewan turned his attention to the judge.

"I ask your permission for Superintendent O'Halloran to present this evidence to the court."

Enoch Hasselthwaite was on his feet in a second.

"I object. How does this item have any relevance to the case in front of us?"

Green turned his eyes on Ewan.

"Well, Mr. Campbell? How is it relevant? You tell me."

"It relates to the integrity of the other main claimant, your honor. If Mr. Garcia is proven unreliable in the evidence he presents in this court, a lot of other aspects of this case are called into question.

"The flimsy nature of the supposed records he's presented as to his birth status, for example.

"I am going to bring further witnesses who will attest that none of the papers he has presented in court here today are lodged in the Land Court archives. Not one of them."

Garcia leapt to his feet and pointed at Elmer.

"That's his fault. He's the registrar. He was supposed to lodge them. I gave him copies to do that."

Elmer Green's face was ashen. He shook his head from side to side in denial, his mouth opening and closing like a frog's.

"I… I don't know anything about it," he croaked.

Garcia stepped out from around the table he was sitting at and sprang across the space toward Elmer.

Quick as a flash, O'Halloran slipped out of the witness box and blocked his way, his revolver drawn.

"Quieten down, Mr. Garcia."

Dionisio stopped in his tracks, snarling.

Repressed murmurs were floating up from the public area, but no one wanted to miss the rest of the show, so they weren't risking pushing the judge into closing the court.

Green glared from Elmer to Garcia, his mouth a disgusted slash in his red face.

He raised his voice yet again.

"You resume your seat, Mr. Garcia, and Superintendent, please holster the gun. We don't need guns in court."

A tense silence prevailed as they both obeyed the judge's instructions.

"Can I see that piece of evidence you referred to, Superintendent? The fringing?"

O'Halloran fished out an envelope from his inside pocket and placed it in front of the judge.

The judge opened it, drew out the fringing and draped it over his hand, examining it critically at close quarters.

With all eyes on him, he held it up to the light, and the sequins sparkled as they caught a stray shaft of sunlight that sliced into the room.

He scowled over the top of his wire frames, and beckoned to O'Halloran and Garcia.

"Approach the bench."

"Mr. Garcia, would you stand before me, please, with your arms raised?"

Dionisio glanced wildly at his lawyer and gabbled something unintelligible.

"Do as he says, Mr. Garcia," Hasselthwaite barked.

Garcia came forward and raised his arms.

The judge handed the fringing back to O'Halloran.

"Mr. O'Halloran. Take this and match it to Mr. Garcia's jacket, would you?"

Everyone stared as the police captain took the fringing between two fingers and draped it along the sleeve seam of the jacket. It became immediately obvious there was a gap on the sleeve where the fragment fitted perfectly.

"Superintendent O'Halloran, I believe you've located the other man who was present the night Alistair Gordon was shot."

He looked around him.

"I don't know where that leaves you with that case, but as far as I'm concerned, it convinces me I need to hear any further evidence you may have, Mr., Campbell, as to reliability of the evidence this witness has presented to the court."

<h1 style="text-align:center">Fifty-nine</h1>

"And then what happened?"

Diana's eyes were shining with excitement.

Judge Green had finished hearing evidence two hours ago, and they were back at Grandma's Kitchen café poring over the day's events.

Eilish was looking after Fergus while Rosie filled Diana in on every detail. They'd agreed that with Elmer and Dionisio there, it would be too risky for her to appear in person, but she'd given them critical information that Bram was able to present in court in her place.

It was just another routine weeknight at Grandma's.

The place hummed with tables filled with diners just like them. The whole town was agog at what had gone down in the Land Claims court earlier that day.

Diana ran her finger around the top of her glass of ice-cold homemade lemonade.

"Tell me. Who did Ewan—Mr. Campbell—call next?"

"He re-called Bram Gordon, and Bram gave evidence that he'd arranged for a search to be made of the court records and none of the documents Dionisio said had been filed were to be found."

Diana nodded with quiet satisfaction. "And my name wasn't mentioned?"

Rosie nodded, her eyes brimming with contentment.

"Not once. You don't need to have any worries about that. You gave us all the clues we needed to crack this thing, and Ewan found a way to present it in such a way it never got slotted back to you."

She squeezed Diana's wrist where it lay on the table.

"If Dionisio hadn't boasted to Violet, the party girl, about killing two men—one he didn't rate and his best friend—then Bram would probably never have come forward in the way he did on Alejandro's behalf.

"Meeting him at Fanny's that night, and telling him everything you knew about Elmer and Dionisio, it convinced him to dump Garcia for good.

"And what you told Ewan about Elmer's dealings in false records—that broke the thing wide open."

Diana's forehead creased.

"Do you think Elmer removed those records because he read the signs and was terrified of getting caught? Or maybe he never inserted them in the first place? Maybe he had a bad feeling about it all along?"

Rosie shook her head.

"I've no idea, and it doesn't really matter why he left Dino out to dry. Maybe he decided he was too much of a liability and he didn't want to go down with him. That was a wise move, but I'm kind of sorry he didn't get caught too."

Diane's mouth twisted.

"Oh, you know what the system is like. With a father who's

a judge, he probably won't ever get caught."

A blast of fresh air blew in from the street as a new customer stepped inside and paused to look looked around, the door swinging closed behind him. A diner looking for his friends who'd already arrived?

Rosie lifted her eyes, her attention momentarily distracted by the slight hush that had fallen over the place, as if the new arrival was someone people knew.

Her heart lifted in her chest as she watched a man who looked like he'd stepped off Savile Row cross to their table. It wasn't that he was overdressed for the casual diner.

His casually styled camel-colored suede jacket was suitable garb for the ranch, but the made-to-measure tailoring made it suitable for so much more.

The soft leather hugged broad shoulders for a man who wielded lassoes to catch runaway yearlings, or reined in fiery stallions. The newcomer crossed the restaurant floor with fluid ease and paused in front of them, giving a broad smile first at Rosie, and then Diana.

"Do you mind if I join you?"

Bram Gordon wants to join us?

Rosie's heart was in her mouth. "Ohhh. off course," she stuttered. She gestured to the spare chair at the four-seater table. "I was filling Diana in on the day's proceedings."

"Excellent," said Bram. "Just what I'd hoped."

He glanced around.

"Have you already ordered?"

"N- n- n-oo," she stammered.

"We weren't sure we were staying that long."

"Oh, of course you are," Bram said with another exultant smile. "And I am the one who's paying."

They both chorused their refusal to accept, but he was having none of it.

"You girls have been such a help. Between you, you supplied so much information, so many missing links. Things all the supposed professionals missed. Ewan Campbell's a fine lawyer, but he didn't have the underground sources you two did. I can't thank you enough."

He laughed appreciatively. "Of course, Dino never could resist a pretty girl in a frock. Just as well, too, from our point of view."

He glanced around and summoned a server to the table.

"A schooner of ale for me, and another drink for the ladies," he said.

"What will it be, girls? I seriously think it should be champagne. And we'll have a menu too please. Three menus, in fact."

As he toasted them with champagne and they filled themselves with hot chicken pie, he confided his views on what would happen next.

"Judge Green will certainly find in favor of the Castellanos family. It's clear Dionisio's 'evidence' is all a crock. Wishful thinking. He's reserving his decision for a day or two to appear suitably stern and considered."

He raised his ale handle to their flute glasses and clinked.

"It was all over for me when Alistair died, so I'm delighted to see it go this way."

"And what about Dionisio?" Rosie asked. "Will the

superintendent arrest him for breaking into Alejandro's house?"

"I'm not a betting man," Bram Gordon said, "but if I was, I'd wager Dino Garcia has already packed his bags and left town, taking his beautiful girlfriend with him. He won't be hanging around to find out."

"Well, at least O'Halloran will have to drop the idea of charging Alejandro with murder now, won't he?"

Rosie's brows furrowed, and her heart beat a little faster.

Am I offending him? Does he still want to avenge for his son's death?

Bram shook his head.

"I don't blame the Castellanos kid for what happened. Alistair was stupid to let himself be led into that. And if they'd killed Alejandro? It might have been Alistair, up for murder."

Rosie had such a big lump in her throat she couldn't swallow or speak. She had to fight back tears. To cover her distress, she gave a huffing, nervous laugh.

I've done what I wanted to. Made sure Alejandro didn't go down for murder. Now I can exit gracefully and let him get on with living a happy life.

Sixty

Rosie stood on the windy San Francisco Embarcadero dock, her battered suitcase by her side, and pulled up the collar of her thin winter coat around her neck.

The wind wasn't particularly cold. It was still late summer, after all. But the Bay could get damp and stormy, even on summer nights, and she'd never felt grayer inside.

Around her, a crowd of other passengers waited for the Oakland Ferry that would take them across San Francisco Bay. Most of them carried briefcases or shopping baskets, daily commuters returning to warm homes and families.

Only a few carried suitcases like she did, indicating they were bound for the Central Pacific Railroad base in Oakland, ready to board the train to Sacramento or even further afield, to places east of the Rocky Mountains.

She kept a sharp eye on the ferry steward, standing a few feet away in his navy blue jacket with gold braid edging, his silver whistle dangling on a cord around his neck.

A blast from that whistle would signal that the ferry was ready to board, and she couldn't afford to miss it.

Slipping out of Izzy and Seb's welcoming home unnoticed

was the hardest thing she'd ever done.

She left a note on Izzy's bed for her to find when she turned in, but if she missed the train, she'd nowhere else to go. There was no turning back for her now.

The hard pebble in her throat swelled to a stone that blocked her voice, and she coughed into her hankie, mopping her face as she did.

Silly girl, what have you to cry about?

Eilish is on the pathway to full health. The shadow of a murder charge no longer falls over Alejandro, and they'd got the shared joy of deciding what to do with the Los Putos ranch, with Judge Green ruling in favor of the Castellanos claim earlier today.

Everything I wanted, I've achieved.

Eilish is receiving the best medical care she's ever had, and Alex and Izzy are safe.

I just can't stand being around to watch something beautiful develop between them, Alejandro and my young sister. It's best for all of us that I leave.

I'll write to Eilish in a few days and explain the whole thing. But right now, I have to just get out of here.

The ferryman's hand went to his whistle. She'd taken her sling off, but her wrist was still weak and achy, so she picked up her suitcase with her left hand and strode to the gangplank.

This is the best solution for us all, she said to herself as she gamely stepped aboard.

She didn't stop to wipe her tears until she was lodged with her back upright against a railing, preparing her heart for her final farewells.

***

She had the collar of her marine-blue coat turned up, as if she was hiding in it, but he'd never have missed her brilliant copper hair. Alejandro imagined he could see Rosie's sparkling emerald eyes from the dockside too, but he knew that was just his lovesick imagination.

"Rosie! Rosie Kelly."

He called, and called again, and frantically waved, but in the crowd swamping the ferry deck to board, he knew it would be difficult for her to see or hear him.

His heart thumped in his chest. *If I let her get away from me now, will I ever find her again?*

In his head. a refrain sounded, over and over again.

Thank God or Providence or whoever the divine power is that Izzy went to have a late afternoon nap and found that note.

Followed by: *How could I have been so stupid?*

He jumped up and down again. He yelled and waved madly. Still, she didn't see him.

As the wind freshened, the crowds thinned. Most of the Oakland passengers were now safely aboard.

As if to confirm they'd made the right choice leaving San Francisco, thunder cracked overhead and seconds later, the heavens opened.

Icy rain pelted his head and shoulders, falling like a frozen veil which obscured even further the view from the ferry deck. Rosie's figure was enveloped in a wet curtain.

The ferry hooter sounded.

Alejandro needed no further prompt. He launched forward like a greyhound, dashing for the gangplank just as the deckhands were untying the restraining ropes.

"Last chance," one cried. "And that's it."

Even as Alex leaped for the deck, he felt the ramp shudder and rise beneath him.

Cold water streamed down his unprotected neck. His hair was sopping and flattened over his face. He slicked it back and stared around him.

The pole Rosie had leaned against was empty.

"You elusive wench," he muttered through chattering teeth. "You're not getting away that easily."

***

Alex prowled the ferry for fifteen minutes, his anxiety growing with every minute he failed to locate her. What if they docked on the other side before he'd talked to her?

If he let her escape into the wider reaches of the third biggest state in the Union, he might never find her again.

His heart expanded in his chest until he imagined it pressed against his lungs and impeded his breathing.

He was about to panic when he spotted her in the family lounge, talking to a young mother with two small children. She was nursing one tot in her lap while the mother fed the other.

He drank in the sight of her, reluctant to step forward and interrupt the conversation. Her face was paler, and more weary than usual, but her effervescent spirit shone through whenever she addressed the child, a boy of about two, who snuggled into her.

She tickled him in the ribs and he wriggled and laughed.

Then he stepped into her line of sight and studied her for her first, unguarded reaction.

He wasn't disappointed.

Her mouth dropped open, and her eyes widened in shock.

"What. What are you doing here?" she said breathlessly.

Was he imagining it, or was there a pink glow already creeping up her cheeks, overtaking the drained white out of her appearance?

He slipped onto the bench seat beside her.

"Looking for you, of course," he said.

"You don't think you're going to get away that easily, do you?"

She frowned, as if she couldn't believe what she was seeing and hearing.

Her eyes flicked to the young Mum, who'd halted, a teaspoon loaded with what looked like apple puree halfway to the older child's mouth, to stare.

"You know this dude? Do you want me to get rid of him?" she said under her breath to Rosie.

Rosie started, as if coming out of a trance.

Then she started laughing.

"Get rid of him? No no, Samantha, everything is fine. More than fine. Yes, I know him. And no, I don't want you to get rid of him. Not yet, anyway."

"You're all wet," she said, big, round green eyes searching his face.

He grinned. "Amazing powers of observation. You're not exactly dry yourself."

She patted the shoulders of her coat and smiled back.

"I suppose you're right. But I have dry clothes to change into. I presume you don't?"

"You're so right, but neither of us will need a change of clothes, because we're getting on this ferry when it turns around and going straight back home."

He scanned up and down her bedraggled figure with a frank, favorable assessment.

"Even in your rain-soaked state, you've never looked more beautiful," he said.

"What about Eilish?" she asked.

"What about her?" he replied, his granite eyes clearly puzzled. "She's a wonderful sister. That's all."

"I thought…" Rosie stopped, her brow creasing, her cheeks turning blush red.

"You thought what, my dear Rosie?"

The blush deepened.

"I thought you and she were… courting," she said, her face now flaming red.

"So you're not in love with her?"

"In love with Eilish?"

His chest contracted painfully.

"Whatever gave you that idea?"

Her eyes were tracing his face, from his frowning brow to his slack jaw.

"Ummmm. You… Just… seemed… to get on so well," she said haltingly. "Quite unlike you and I, always arguing."

"About that, Rosie. I've got a lot of making up to do. Please, give me another chance. I've been stupid. So stupid. Give me a chance to explain. To apologize."

She sat beside him, gazing up with those amazing gold-specked emerald eyes. The little Turk on her lap began to fidget.

His mother took him wordlessly off Rosie who still stared up at him, saying nothing in words but everything with her eyes.

He hardly dared breathe.

Then she put out her right hand, the delicate hand, the recently injured one, and gently tested his forearm.

'You are real, aren't you? I'm not dreaming?"

She turned to her new friend Samantha and laughed.

"Because I can tell you, this is a very different man from the Alejandro that I know."

She laughed up at him and blew him a cheeky kiss.

"This Alejandro? I rather like him."

She glanced back at Samantha, her eyes now sparkling with mischief.

"He's got a lot of explaining to do, that's for sure. But I think it's worth giving him a second chance, don't you?"

Alejandro put his arm around her shoulders and gently drew him to his side.

"I'm happy to start right away. Just as soon as we get you home and both of us get into dry clothes."

Epilogue

The Marquésa Fanny de Castellanos y Ordonez became a minor celebrity in San Francisco in the days following the Los Putos case, invited to balls and society lunches, approached to join the committees of prominent charities.

She was made an honorary member of the Society of California Pioneers because the committee members argued Angel was an original and they'd never recognized him.

But she turned down most of these invitations. She was happy to revel in her newly discovered family, fussing over Isabella's welfare, and relishing hours spent with George and Minette in simple pastimes.

Their favorites were the bedtime stories when she put on funny Scottish and Spanish accents. They loved her buying them gelato from street vendors selling the icy treats in all colors and flavors, from strawberry (Minette's favorite) to caramel for George.

And on sunny days, which were almost every day in San Francisco in August, they begged leftover loaves from Betty to take to the park for the pigeons and ducks.

She was dawdling in America, reluctant to leave until she'd

seen Isabella's child safely delivered, and hoping if she hung around long enough, she'd be a guest at a wedding before she returned to Scotland.

Rosie had been re-hired by the old Magdalena show and was working up a completely new entertainment to be launched soon.

She and Alejandro were inseparable, and Fanny was sure it was only a matter of time before they announced their engagement.

Meantime, Alejandro had concluded plans he'd already begun for Rosie's mother and the rest of her siblings to join them in San Francisco.

The Kelly tribe had arrived a week ago, and were settled in a big house downtown which would also serve as a preschool, if and when Eilish was ready to start her own facility.

Fanny was lunching at the Pioneer's Club with Carlos Alvarado, keenly aware of the last time she'd been here, on her first day in the city, and reflecting on how much had changed, when she felt a tap on her shoulder.

Across the table from her, Carlos raised his brows, his eyes twinkling in recognition.

"Superintendent, please join us," he said. "I'm sure the Marquésa won't mind…"

Seamus O'Halloran slipped into the empty seat beside her and dipped his police cap before setting it on the tabletop beside him.

"Marquésa… Mi'lady," he said, with obvious discomfort.

"I am sorry to interrupt, but it is rather urgent and your lady-in-waiting said I'd find you here."

Fanny reached out and patted the top of his hand that rested closest to her.

"Don't worry at all, Superintendent. Senor Alvarado and I are old friends. You've caught us reminiscing, that's all. Nothing critical to the world turning over…"

O'Halloran laughed and relaxed his posture, clearly relieved.

"I'll get straight to the point," he said, glancing at Carlos.

"I've arrested a person of interest who is in possession of personal papers of yours."

He paused for effect, as Fanny's heart thrummed harder.

"Not… you're not speaking of Temptation Thompson?"

"Indeed, I am," he said. "Now that Dionisio Garcia is wanted for the murder of Emmanuel Valaquez, she's under suspicion of collusion and harboring a wanted man.

"We believe she was hand in glove with Garcia for months before the court hearing," he said. "Even before he staged Emmanuel Valaquez's killing. They bribed one of Isabella's kitchen maids, which is how Garcia knew so much private information about the household.

"I've made it clear she'll get leniency if she returns the private material she stole from you, and she's agreed."

Fanny stared from Seamus to Carlos, as a giddy joy practically lifted her off her seat.

She clapped her hands and gave a dizzy laugh.

"If I try to stand right now, I think I'd topple straight over with light-headedness," she said through more laughter.

O'Halloran smiled. "I hope this makes up for the way I handled your grandson's break-in. Not my finest hour," he said, glancing at Carlos.

"I've retrieved quite a store of material she'd squirreled away, and it's in a safety locker at the station. It includes personal letters, a leather-bound diary and photographic journals."

He gazed into Fanny's eyes and she saw a sympathetic understanding there she'd never seen before.

"Send someone to collect them whenever it's convenient," he said.

He rose to go, and Fanny sensed a lightness in his gait, in the cast of his shoulders, that wasn't there when he'd arrived.

She jumped up to meet his eyes and put both hands out on his upper arms, to hold him at arm's length.

Unshed tears pushed at the back of her eyes, making them sparkle.

She leaned forward and lightly pecked O'Halloran on each cheek.

His complexion glowed a warm pink.

"Having my letters back, and some of Rafael's papers," she said breathlessly. "That more than makes up for any past mistakes."

As she watched O'Halloran's departing back, she let out a lingering sigh.

There you are, dear Angel. I hope you saw that.

And she could swear she heard an answering whisper as she turned back to Carlos.

Well done, my sweet wife.

THE END

WHAT'S NEXT?

I'm working on my next series, Sisters of Barclay Manor, set in Sydney, Australia in the late 1860s but with links back to characters in the Of Gold & Blood series.

Poppy Barclay, Nathan Russell's half-sister, and the oldest of three girls, faces ruin after her father's investment company collapses owing money to many of Sydney's wealthiest citizens. Her fiancé breaks off their engagement as a cabal of ruined investors seek revenge.

Download a Free Preview of Poppy's Dilemma, the first book in the new series

If you'd like to become a friend of Jenny's books and get the latest news of releases and free book offers, you'll get a FREE download of Sadie's Vow, the first book in the Home At Last series, as a thank for your support.

YOU CAN MAKE A DIFFERENCE

Reviews are the most powerful tools in my kit for getting my books noticed. Much as I'd love it, I don't have the budget of a big publisher to buy bill board ads and other national advertising.

But I have the promise of something more powerful–something publishers envy. And that's a committed and loyal bunch of readers. Honest reviews of my books help them gain the attention of others who might appreciate them, too.

Post Your Rosie's Rebellion Reviews Here:
For Amazon: https://geni.us/CdUm
For Goodreads:
https://www.goodreads.com/book/show/194820968-rosie-s-rebellion
For Bookbub: https://www.bookbub.com/books/rosie-s-rebellion-home-at-last-book-3-by-jenny-wheeler

ABOUT THE AUTHOR

Jenny Wheeler is the author the Home At Last Trilogy
Sadie's Vow #1 Susannah's Secret #2 Rosie's Rebellion #3

And of the Of Gold & Blood Old California mystery series:
Poisoned Legacy #1. Brother Betrayed #2. Double Jeopardy #3.
Tangled Destiny (Christmas novella and Prequel.) #4.
Unbridled Vengeance #5. Hope Redeemed, A Spanish Novella,
#6. Tainted Fortune #7 Captive Heart #8. Ancient Deception
#9 Dangerous Desires #10.
Book Bundles: Boxed Set/ Book Bundle Of Gold & Blood,
Books 1– 3.
Boxed Set Book Bundle #2 Poisoned Legacy and Tangled
Destiny Tainted Fortune
Book Bundle /Boxed Set #3 Book #5 Unbridled Vengeance
and #6 Hope Redeemed.
Book Bundle/ Boxed Set #4 Book #7 Tainted Fortune and #8
Captive Heart.
Three Holiday Novellas– Book Bundle/ Boxed set, Books #3,
#6, and #8.

WHERE TO FIND JENNY

Jenny's online home is at jennywheeler.biz or email Jennywheelj@gmail.com

You can connect with Jenny on:
Facebook: @JennyWheeler.Biz
Twitter: @Jenny_Biz
Instagram: @jennysbingereading
Pinterest www.pinterest.com/jennywheelbooks/
Goodreads:
www.goodreads.com/author/show/11371547.Jenny_Wheeler
Bookbub: www.bookbub.com/profile/jenny-wheeler